Also by Stephanie A. Cain

Sow the Wind
Fire Soul

<u>Storms in Amethir</u>
A Song of Storm and Shadow
Stormseer
The Weather War
Shroudling
Witchery's End (forthcoming)

<u>Storms in Amethir Holiday Novellas</u>
The Midwinter Royal

<u>Circle City Magic (urban fantasy)</u>
Shades of Circle City
Circle City Psychic

<u>With Other Authors</u>
Equus (Rhonda Parrish's Magical Menageries #5)
E is for Evil
F is for Fairy
G is for Ghost

If you would like to receive updates on new fiction, please join my monthly email newsletter list. I give newsletter subscribers first look at everything I do!

STORMS IN AMETHIR
BOOK 1

A Song of Storm and Shadow

STEPHANIE A. CAIN

*To my parents,
who have always believed in me*

CONTENTS

ranarr
the Blades
the Shield
kreyden district
marow
amethir
anderly
strid

part one
stormsinger

CHAPTER ONE

Following seas and a clear sunset. Arama Dzornaea closed her eyes and relished the feel of the wind in her face. It would be a short, easy sail from Maron Palace to Ranarr. She could do the run in under three days, with a good tailwind and skimming in close to The Blades. With Prince Vistaren on board, she had the dubious benefit of a stormwitch to provide those tailwinds, but there was no way she would risk the prince through The Blades. They would swing wide and take a leisurely week to make the trip.

Arama didn't think Prince Vistaren would mind the extra days; after all, they were going to Ranarr to meet his bride.

"Tighten up that topsail," she ordered, and watched her crew leap to obey. "Good. We'll be crossing the sandbar any minute. As soon as we're out, signal the lightkeepers."

Next to her, a man with short, spiky black hair gave a contented grunt. "It's been too long since I've been to sea. I'd thank his highness for this chance, if I didn't know he was so sick over the whole thing."

Arama glanced at him. "You're welcome on my ship any time you want, Lo."

He chuckled. "Aye, I know that. I suspect his majesty wouldn't care."

Arama turned her gaze back to the sea, smiling. "You might be surprised. King Rekel listens to me from time to time."

"He ought to. That last Strid vessel you took outfitted half the army."

She rolled her eyes at Lo's exaggeration, but there was no denying she was the king's top privateer. She'd received her letter of marque twelve years ago, after the *Bounder* went down off Swordfish Island, and she'd captured more ships than the next two privateers combined. She never had trouble filling out her crew of twenty, and though she was a half-Crelin of no particular rank, she had pull most aristocrats could only dream of.

"Are you expecting any trouble?" Lo scratched at the stubble on his chin, not looking at her. His light gray eyes were focused on the sea.

"Nothing from Strid or Tamnen, if that's what you mean," she replied. "And we've that stormwitch to protect us from bad weather." She couldn't quite keep the distaste out of her voice, so to hide it she shouted, "Get that signal flag up, and sharpish! We've crossed the bar and the lightkeepers need to send word to his majesty."

Lozarr hadn't missed it. "She's a good stormwitch, Arama," he said, his voice low. "I hand-picked her. She's prickly as the seven hells, but she's strong and resilient, and she knows her craft."

Arama cleared her throat. Lozarr saw her too clearly. It threw her off balance, though she had tried for years to settle into it. They'd met on the *Bounder*. He knew she hated stormwitches--and why. Sometimes his understanding about it made her want to shout and throw things. Other times--not often--that same understanding made her want to lean against his chest and let him wrap strong arms around her. Whenever that particularly disconcerting desire hit her, she went looking for a Strid ship to attack. Blowing things up always made her feel better.

It bothered her that Lo knew her well enough to understand all of that. He straightened and shrugged his shoulders. "Anyway. You'll meet her tomorrow. I'm going to check on Prince Vistaren and make sure everyone's settled. I'll see you in the morning." He leaned in to brush a prickly kiss against her cheek, and she permitted it only because he'd never tried anything more familiar.

"Dream well," she said, hoping her voice wasn't too flinty. She loved Lozarr. As much as she could love anyone, she loved him. She couldn't afford to drive him away. She wouldn't want to. She just couldn't afford to let him too close.

She didn't look as he climbed down the ladder from the quarterdeck. When he'd passed amidships, though, she turned and watched his broad, wool-clad shoulders as he went below deck for the night.

Arama Dzornaea, King Rekel's privateer, infamous Storm Petrel, couldn't afford the luxury of love, but she wasn't so far gone that she didn't lament the sacrifice.

"Will she like me, Lo?" Prince Vistaren had no illusions about himself. Despite his good Crelin genes and olive skin, he would only be called handsome by a particularly charitable observer. His face was too round, his frame too short. He was, to put a fine point on it, pudgy. Everything, in Vistaren's opinion, that a crown prince should not be.

Unfortunately for Amethir, he was the only prince they had.

"Of course she will. You're intelligent and affable, and you understand both the pressure and the privilege of duty." Lozarr Algot was a kind man. Not at all what a general ought to be like, Vistaren thought. Thank the gods for that.

And thank the gods Lo knew Vistaren well enough to realize he was fretting about Captain Dzornaea and not the princess at the end of their voyage. Vistaren was putting off fretting about Princess Azmei for as long as he possibly could.

"I've wanted to meet her since I was ten," Vistaren admitted. "I was studying the conflict between Tamnen and Strid, and read about the battle between the *Dawn Star* and the *Kerava*. Did you know her back then?"

Lo scraped a hand down his stubbled jaw, trying unsuccessfully to hide a smile. "I did. She was barely older than

you are now, and more full of herself than a he-cock on a--"
He broke off. "That is to say, she was...well. Arrogant."

There was a warmth in Lo's eyes that made Vistaren's heart jump. *That*, something whispered. *That* was what love looked like. Not a few stilted words exchanged on a page. Not a promise made for economic and political compromise. Not even lust. Vistaren might be young, but he understood lust. What he saw in Lo's eyes when he talked about Arama was the real thing.

"Deservedly so," Vistaren commented. "She was, what, twenty? And she took down the flagship of the Tamnese navy."

"She was twenty-two." Lozarr shook his head. "And I was twenty." He was smiling, but to Vistaren it looked sad. "We were so young."

"I ought to be offended at that."

Lo chuckled. "You're older at twenty than I was at twenty-five, lad. The shadow of the crown has aged you." He stood. "And taught you better manners than I've ever had. We ought to have been at breakfast five minutes ago, and Captain Arama runs a tight ship, my prince."

Vistaren jumped to his feet. "There goes my chance to make a good impression on her," he lamented. "How do I look?"

"Tidy." Vistaren twitched. He saw Lo fight a grin. After a moment, Lo added, "Elegant, but not arrogant, highness."

Vistaren gave a sharp nod and left the cabin. A man had to have standards, and for the past three years, he had decided elegant was his. Amethir wasn't the sort of nation that needed a sophisticated or flamboyant king. She was peopled with fisherfolk, shipbuilders, and stormwitches.

They sang songs and wrote plays, but they did not embrace high fashion as did the Strid, nor did they engage in convoluted political maneuverings as did the Tamnese. No, Vistaren was of Amethir, and he would be what she needed.

Even if that meant denying himself.

Chapter Two

Captain Dzornaea was everything Vistaren had hoped for--and nothing he had imagined. She was short and skinny, with skin the color of coffee with cream. Her eyes were blue, which spoke of Crelin blood, as did her blue-black hair. But her nose had the thin bridge and slope of a Sterr. She wore dark blue velvet breeches and a crisp, white blouse, with a fitted leather weskit over the blouse. A crimson sash held her sabre and pistol. Her dark brown jacket draped haphazardly over the back of her chair. Vistaren would have thought her formally dressed, except that her breeches ended several inches above her ankles, and her feet were bare.

"Prince Vistaren." Her voice was crisp but friendly as she bowed. "I hope you dreamt well."

Vistaren smiled. "I did indeed, Captain Dzornaea. And you?"

He didn't think he was imagining the flicker of a shadow in her gaze. "Well enough, highness." She gestured at the table.

Vistaren sat, which allowed the others to sit as well. He took a roll and a piece of meat, glancing at the captain. There were shadows under her eyes. Her hair, which was wavy and cropped jaw-length, looked tousled. For a brief instant, Vistaren allowed himself to imagine that she'd spent a passion-filled night with Lozarr. Then he remembered the lines of sorrow at either side of Lo's mouth and realized that couldn't have happened.

"Tell me about our journey," Vistaren said.

Arama smiled. "It's ill luck to say a voyage should be easy, highness." She sipped from a thick-walled mug. "I have made the run from Maron to Ranarr more times than I can count. If I skim in close to the Blades and have following seas, I can do it under three days. This trip, we'll swing well wide of the Blades and make the voyage in a week."

Vistaren nodded. "The *Dawn Star* is a fine vessel. I've read of your exploits, of course."

"I hope your highness does not expect battles at sea," Arama said. Her mouth was quirked up. Vistaren thought she was teasing him.

He made a show of mulling it over. "Not unless you feel it absolutely necessary, Captain," he said finally. "I understand it is a serious request to make of you."

She laughed. "Your father would have me keel-hauled if I involved you in a sea battle, Prince Vistaren." Her amusement warmed him. She thought he was funny. Then her expression sobered. "And I suspect your bride-to-be would object, as well."

It was like she'd doused him in cold water. "Indeed." He helped himself to several slices of bacon. He didn't want to think about Princess Azmei. "I have complete confidence in you, Captain Dzornaea, to see us safely to Ranarr."

She inclined her torso, which impressed Vistaren. He'd never realized one could bow effectively while seated. He dismissed the topic with a flick of his hand. "Tell me, Captain, how are the seas this morning? I have little sailing experience, so while I find the rocking of the ship exhilarating, I have no idea if we are in heavy seas or...well, whatever isn't heavy seas."

Arama laughed. "The sea is in a fine mood today, your highness. Having little sailing experience is no flaw, but we shall fill that lack before we reach Ranarr."

She launched into a lecture about the many moods of the sea. Vistaren felt his shoulders relaxing as Arama spoke, and soon he had all but forgotten he was sailing to meet his bride.

CHAPTER THREE

HE SINGS OUT OF *his loneliness.*

There is no answer. There has never been an answer.

He is aware of those who, like him, traverse the deeps and celebrate the cycle of dry and wet and storms. He is aware that he is not the only being of his kind. Yet he is alone.

There are other songs. He feels the songs against his skin, pulsing through him, resonating with the loneliness inside him. Those who are like him--like, yet unlike, somehow--sing too, but their songs are subtly different.

He tries to mimic them, but how can he perceive how his songs are received? He can only know how their songs feel on his skin, in his innermost being. He cannot imagine what his songs feel like to others.

Yet he sings on. Someone will answer him. Someday, somehow.

Someone will answer his loneliness.

# CHAPTER FOUR

"Captain Dzornaea." Kinnet smoothed her skirts and watched the back of the captain's head. When the captain turned to face her, Kinnet made herself smile.

"Stormwitch Ardelis." Kinnet appreciated how careful Arama was to keep her face turned toward her. General Algot must have informed her that Kinnet relied on reading lips. "Is there trouble?"

Kinnet inclined her torso, keeping her gaze on Arama's face. "I feel...echoes. I think echoes. I..." She drew her brows together. "I am not sure."

"Echoes of...power?" Arama asked. "Of a storm? Is there something building?"

Kinnet spread her hands and opened her mouth. After several seconds, she huffed out a breath and clenched her fists. "Echoes. My feet feel them. Through the floor."

"Deck," Arama corrected.

"Deck. They shake." Kinnet shook her head. "Vibrate."

Arama scrubbed a hand through short, blue-black hair. "What do you think it is?" she asked at last.

"I..." Kinnet let her gaze go unfocused as she searched again for any hint of recognition. "I don't know. I have never felt this before."

Arama swore. "What can you do?" She scraped her toes against a coil of rope. Kinnet wondered if they itched. What would it be like to go barefoot all the time, as Arama did?

Kinnet lifted one hand to curl around the large sea-glass pendant that hung at her throat. "I will try to sense what causes the disturbance."

"Good idea." Arama didn't hide the annoyance in her expression.

Kinnet flinched. She knew what the captain must be thinking. Any stormwitch who wore as much sea-glass as Kinnet did must be powerful. Sea-glass wasn't cheap by any measure, and a chunk as large as that pendant would have come dear. Arama must wonder why this wealthy stormwitch couldn't have intelligence that equaled her wealth? Well, Kinnet would show her. She was intelligent, as well as powerful. She had just never been given the opportunities so many others got.

Kinnet glared at her. "I must not be disturbed," she said. "And I will need a pitcher of water."

"Of course." Arama signaled one of her crew and gave the orders necessary. "Should I prepare to defend the ship?"

Kinnet's gaze turned inward. "No," she said at last. "This is something...not made by humans. I feel..." She trailed off, then clenched her teeth. Why should she try to explain how the power felt? Not even a ship's captain could understand the way stormwitchery called to you. "I will inform you when I have learned anything."

She swung around, her skirts swishing around her, and strode away, hips rolling with the pitch of the ship. She would show Arama Dzornaea. She would do whatever was necessary to protect Prince Vistaren. She would gain the prince's trust and admiration. And then Pralith Menever and all those buzzing toadies at the college would see that Kinnet Ardelis was more than a poor deaf girl who could channel lightning.

CHAPTER FIVE

T HE FIRST FULL DAY of their voyage was unremarkable. Vistaren talked to the sailors and attempted to stay out of Captain Dzornaea's way while studying the way Lo interacted with her. It wasn't as difficult as he'd expected. Arama was obviously fond of Lo, but she allowed no one to interfere with her duties. She would interrupt a conversation to stride across the deck and berate one of the crew members, or instruct the helmsman to change course. The first few times Vistaren saw that happen, he admired her dedication to duty.

After a while, he recognized it for what it was: an excuse to avoid whatever existed between her and Lo.

A captain's duties weren't as demanding as she made them look. Not on a diplomatic mission like this, at least.

He knew she had logs to keep and reports to write, but as far as the routines on deck, they seemed to run themselves. Vistaren watched the helmsman adjust course twice without Arama's intervention, and the first mate didn't hesitate to issue orders regarding the sails and lines without the captain's supervision.

Nevertheless, Vistaren wasn't certain of his conclusion until he saw Lozarr reach out and rest a hand atop Arama's on the railing. It was startling how quickly Arama went stiff and turned her face away from Lo's. She said something that made Lo's shoulders slump. Then she stalked off, snapping orders. Baffled, Vistaren watched Lo as the general watched her walk away from him.

How could Lo's high regard for her elude her so? She was gruff and somewhat unrefined, but not stupid. Lozarr Algot was a kind, well-bred man who obviously cared for her. Vistaren understood that Arama didn't crave rank or glory. She just enjoyed what she did. She was as one with her ship. She loved her country. She served her king. It was admirable and praise-worthy. Was it possible that she feared love?

It wasn't that Vistaren couldn't sympathize. He was going to meet his bride, after all. He wasn't sure if Azmei would even like him. Would she understand his proclivities or make allowances for them? He wanted to like the woman he married, but he was under no illusion that he would ever feel desire for her. It was simply one of those sacrifices that must be made in Amethir's name.

But surely such a sacrifice couldn't be expected of Arama. She had no rank to speak of, and therefore no duties that would prevent her marrying for love. She clearly cared for Lo, and Lo just as clearly cared for her. Why not allow herself such pleasure?

"My prince is obviously further away than his gaze would suggest."

Vistaren jumped. "Lo! Don't sneak up on a body like that!"

Even Lo's smirk was gentle. "I spoke your name twice. Is it my fault that you were inattentive?"

"Certainly." Vistaren shook himself. "You've been to Ranarr before, haven't you?'

"A few times, highness. It isn't so different from Maron."

"No, but the etiquette is very different. I have studied, but I would hate to offend anyone. Especially my bride," Vistaren added lamely.

Lo didn't look at him. "Your bride is from Tamnen. The customs there are rather different from Ranarr."

"Yes." Vistaren cleared his throat. "I require your counsel, Lo. Advise me on how to speak to Princess Azmei."

Lozarr was a tall man. He didn't look away from Arama as he ran a hand through his hair. "I have no experience on which to base any counsel about wooing a woman, Prince Vistaren."

Vistaren couldn't help himself. He snorted. "You damn well know more than I do, Lo. I've never wooed anyone who wanted to be told how pretty he was, or how soft his hands and perfumed his hair."

Lo arched an eyebrow. "Nor have I, Vistaren." He leaned against the railing and directed the full force of his gaze at his prince. "As you obviously understand quite well."

Vistaren's cheeks heated. That had been unkind. "My apologies."

Lo held his gaze for a moment longer, then nodded and looked away. "I am the last person to whom you should go for advice." His voice was low and rough. "I have never been wise about where I spend my affection."

Entirely ashamed of himself, Vistaren looked down. "She's worthy of it. But if she can't see--" He broke off as Lo barked a laugh.

"She sees well enough. Exactly what she wishes to see." Lo's voice was unwontedly bitter. "But I knew when I loved her that she had no basis for a love that didn't leave her. It isn't her fault."

Vistaren kept his breathing even. He felt stupid and young. Why had he thought he understood whatever was between Arama and Lozarr? He was twenty years old and only just unvirgined. What could he know of the complicated emotions that fed into that thing they called love?

Lo sighed. "I'm sorry, Ren. I'm not usually like this. I know she can't-- It just isn't..." He trailed off, shaking his head. "You're not like us. You can have something real. If you're honest with her, Princess Azmei will understand, and she'll find some way to be happy, just as you will." He rested a hand on Vistaren's shoulder. "It won't be perfect. Life itself is never perfect. But it'll be something."

Just two years ago, Vistaren would have been unable to breathe if Lo touched him like this. That had to mean he was growing up, didn't it? He wasn't throbbing with desire for a man who would never look twice at him. He was thinking instead of that man's happiness and how it tied to a woman Vistaren liked and admired. He was thinking of how he himself could find happiness with the woman his father and council had chosen for him.

No, it didn't help. Vistaren still felt selfish and inexperienced. He covered Lo's hand with his own. "Arama doesn't know what she's passing up."

Lo's laughter was sad. Vistaren didn't like it, but sad was better than bitter. "She does. But it's all right. Thank you for trying."

Vistaren looked out across the ocean. The water was impartial. Nonjudgmental. The sea would swallow peasant and king, general and privateer, without distinction. All that stood between them and impersonal death was one good storm. And storm season wasn't all that far away.

Vistaren's voyage had been planned carefully: he would leave Maron one full fortnight after the last rain of the rainy season. It would give the sailors shore leave without forcing him to travel during storm season. No one traveled during storm season if they could help it. Captains like Arama Dzornaea could outsail any storm the sea threw at her, especially with an experienced stormwitch like Kinnet Ardelis on board. But sailing during storm season was just tempting the gods to smite the proud. Best avoided.

Still. As Vistaren looked out across the swells, feeling the sea lift his long hair and tickle his cheeks, he wondered. What would it be like to see her in a fury? What would it feel like to ride the sea's wrath? He glanced around for Stormwitch Ardelis. Vistaren hadn't a smidge of stormwitchery. No member of the royal family did. But witchery, like love, was a power to be reckoned with.

Vistaren couldn't help but be curious.

Something was very wrong. At first Kinnet only had the odd echoes she could feel through the stormwitchery as proof. After speaking with Arama, though, she had retreated to the cabin provided for her. Using the sea-glass pendant as a focus, Kinnet had stretched forth her awareness, seeking whatever phenomenon might be causing those echoes.

She had found nothing.

That alone was a danger signal. Kinnet was more powerful than most stormwitches. She had spent the past five years in a silent rivalry with Pralith Menever, the king's stormwitch adviser, and she knew she was realistic in her self-assessment. If she could detect no cause for those echoes, it was because whoever caused those echoes didn't want her to detect him.

And yet...

She hadn't lied when she told Arama the echoes weren't caused by a human. She knew the power signatures of all the major stormwitches in Amethir, and no blossoming young stormwitch could be so powerful. If the echoes were the result of some human stormwitchery, she would be able to identify the power behind it. Since she wasn't, the only logical explanation was that the echoes were caused by some power that was not human but was somehow aware.

Who are you? she thought.

She had abandoned the sea-glass pendant in favor of a velvet pouch full of sand. It was a mixture. That alone would displease many of her colleagues. But Kinnet had learned in the past several years that sand was most useful when combined. The very nature of sand was to swirl and tumble under the surface, to sink beneath a wanderer's feet, to shift with the tides. Sand worked better as a focus when mixed.

She slipped her fingers through the sand, eyes closed, awareness extended to the edges of her ability. She could feel the *Dawn Star* both around her and cradled within her as her awareness floated with the sea. She could sense the wind above her and the currents inside her. She could feel no storms.

Yet she sensed some strange pulse, almost a pattern but not quite. She felt a call throb against her from without. A seeking of some kind, a summons. But it made no sense. Who would be calling her?

No, not her. Kinnet settled her awareness deeper in the ocean and let herself float. She wasn't the one called. But the echoes, they were echoes of a call. The results of a deep longing. Deep called to deep.

She thrust her fingers into the sand and curled the fingers of her other hand around her sea-glass pendant. *WHO?* she demanded.

For a long moment there was nothing, only the feeling of her inquiry stretching out in all directions away from her. She was slipping away, losing control of her power, diffusing in the salty waters of the sea. And then--

Companion! It was a faint cry. So faint she almost didn't hear it. But in the next instant, it came again, thundering so powerfully she felt it vibrate in her bones. *Companion!* There was shock and joy and a world of longing in that cry. It shook Kinnet to her depths.

"No!" she cried and pushed the pouch of sand away from her. She wasn't the answer to anyone's call. She was no one's companion. She was solitary, enough unto herself. She needed no companion, and no one needed her. That suited her well.

Companion—? The ponderous presence reached out for her, the joy turned to confusion and sorrow. Kinnet shoved it away. Whomever--whatever--sought a companion, it didn't seek her.

She rose from her kneeling position and dusted off her knees. She would rest and try again. Tugging her skirt straight, she glanced in the tiny, round mirror that hung on the wall over her bunk. Or perhaps she would wait until tomorrow.

The deck vibrated ever so slightly under her feet. Kinnet ignored it. The echoes undoubtedly had nothing to do with the prince. In a few days they would be in Ranarr and her duty to protect the prince would be discharged. She would worry about them after that.

CHAPTER SIX

HE SINGS FROM DESPERATION.

So many years has he journeyed alone. He has at times felt the presence of others like him, but they have never acknowledged him. He remembers from long ago, when he was a tiny youngling, that there were many like him. They passed their lives together, living in companionship and singing together.

Yet no one sings with him.

The years pass. He ages. He feels the wind on his skin, the water cool against him. He feels the ships pass near. He sings at the storms and thrashes in his solitude.

And then, a single call. One word out of the void.

WHO?

Joy suffuses him. He strains to answer, injecting that one word--Companion--with all the longing and loneliness and hope that is in him. But he is denied. He is pushed away.

Undiscouraged, he calls again, but again she denies him.

But he will not be ignored. He cannot be ignored. He follows the call, singing his journey to her.

His solitude has been shattered, and he will not allow it to build up again.

CHAPTER SEVEN

T HE DECK PITCHED AND Arama swore. "What is this? We're in the middle of the dry season!" she snapped. "Find the stormwitch--sharp!"

She didn't watch as her first mate scurried across the deck. Though there were no clouds overhead, the *Dawn Star* was pitching and rolling as if they were in the middle of a fierce blow. What did they have stormwitches for, if it wasn't to keep the seasons in order?

"Step lively there!" she called. "Get the sails trimmed!"

Prince Vistaren and General Lozarr were sitting on the foredeck, the prince leaning casually against the railing. They were having a lively chat, the prince waving a hand. Arama tried not to notice the easy smile on Lo's face. In frustration at her failure, she shouted. "Away from the rail in heavy seas!"

Vistaren and Lo both jumped and looked at her. Arama shoved away the guilt at how Lo bowed his head, the smile fading from his expression. She was trying to keep them safe, and they weren't helping. Taking ridiculous risks and ignoring common sense.

"Captain."

"What?" she snapped, then realized it was the stormwitch. Thank the gods Arama hadn't been looking straight at her. "Stormwitch Ardelis. Can you tell me what is happening with the ship?"

Kinnet squinted her eyes. Arama studied her. The woman looked frightened of something. That was odd. She would have been willing to bet Kinnet Ardelis didn't comprehend fear.

"Well?"

Kinnet folded her arms across her chest. It emphasized the low cut of her dress. "I have...felt...something."

"Oh, that's useful," Arama said before she could stop herself. "What sort of something? Is it dangerous? Is it nearby? What does it want?"

Kinnet flapped her hands. "Slow down."

Arama snorted but repeated herself more slowly. Kinnet shook her head as Arama blurted out the questions.

"I don't know if it is dangerous to us. It is..." She paused, searching for words. "Immense. But not malicious. Lonely, I think. If I had to pick a single word, I would say lonely."

Gods. Didn't Arama understand that. She sucked in a breath. "What does it want?"

Kinnet's answer was prompt. "To not be lonely."

Arama supposed she deserved that. She shook her head. "Whatever it wants, it won't find it here. Tell it to leave us alone."

Kinnet frowned. "I tried. I don't know if it listened."

"Damn. Well, we'll just have to make it listen." Arama looked up to where Vistaren and Lo were now standing on the quarterdeck. "Does it know about the prince?"

"I don't think so." Kinnet cocked her head to one side. "I don't believe it would care about the prince even if it did. It just wants a companion."

"I hope she isn't always this cranky," Vistaren said. He dusted off his trousers and looked across the ocean. As far as he could see, there was nothing but water and sky and clouds.

Lo's laugh was rueful. "Usually. But she doesn't mean anything by it."

Vistaren snorted. *Better you than me, he wanted to say,* but didn't. After all, who knew what Azmei would be like? And Vistaren was going to be married to her. He had no choice about it, no say in the matter at all. He would be tied to her forever, all in the interests of securing a lasting peace. At least Lo had a choice.

Beneath them the deck shuddered. Vistaren stumbled and widened his stance. "What the--"

"Hang on to something," Lo ordered. His voice was taut as a bowstring, all humor fled. "She was right. We're too close to the rail."

"Wait--" Vistaren's fingers were tight on the rope that served as a ship's rail. The sea just off the starboard bow was roiling and churning. "What is that?"

Lo came up next to him, one arm on either side of him and gripping the railing. Lo was shielding him with his body, holding him steady. A year ago it would have thrilled Vistaren. Now it just embarrassed him. No man, not even a prince, should be worth so much. "What is what?"

"There." Vistaren pointed. "See where the water's a lighter shade of--"

A vast shape broke the surface, lunging upward with such force the water exploded around it. Vistaren felt cold spray hit his face even as he reeled backwards. The ship bucked. Someone screamed. Someone else was chanting something. A prayer? It couldn't be witchery, could it? He didn't know witchery had words.

"Vistaren!" Lo's voice was frantic. Strong arms closed around him, then he was falling backwards, away from the railing. They were both falling. He thought Lo had thrown himself backwards as soon as he grabbed Vistaren. He relaxed, letting the general have his way. They landed amidships hard enough to bruise Vistaren's hips, but they hadn't gone overboard.

"What the blazing hells is that?" Arama roared. She sounded angry more than anything, and at that, some of Vistaren's fear faded. He tried to sit up, discovered Lo's arms were locked tight around him, and set about trying to work his way free.

"Are you all right?" he demanded.

Lo coughed and let go of him. He opened his mouth to speak, coughed again, and nodded. "Got the wind knocked out of me. You?"

"I'm fine. I had a nice cushiony landing." Vistaren gave him a half-grin and pushed to his knees, craning his neck. What had happened?

"It's a leviathan!" Lo breathed next to him.

Vistaren's head whipped around. "They're real?"

"Real enough. Arama told me she saw one once, from far off." Lo's voice was so hushed he was nearly whispering. "They're shy of boats. The stories say they travel in herds. Arama only saw one, though. She said it blew a stream of water as high as the mast into the air."

"Do they eat people?" Vistaren hoped his voice didn't quaver.

"I don't know. It looked like it was trying to eat us." Lo had rolled to his feet and was half-crouching, looking around them.

Kinnet Ardelis dashed across the deck to the railing. "Go'way!" she howled. Vistaren tried not to wince. He knew she couldn't hear herself, but how could she have no idea of just how loud she was? She'd shouted almost in his ear. "Go'way! Go'way!"

Something about her behavior struck him as odd. He couldn't say just then what it was, but he held out a hand to Lo. After a moment's hesitation, Lo pulled Vistaren to his feet. Vistaren grinned at him and followed Kinnet to the railing. He could see the lightning crackling around her fingertips, but she didn't look like she was afraid the leviathan was going to eat them.

He gripped her upper arm. When she looked at him, he mouthed, "What is it?"

Her gaze was fierce and hard. For too many heartbeats, those silver eyes pierced him. Then she said, "Lonely."

Vistaren's heart broke.

Leave me alone! I'm not what you think! Kinnet pushed the thoughts as hard as she could, fingers so tight around the sea-glass pendant that it cut into her.

Companion. The word ached with such loneliness that Kinnet felt tears slip from her eyes. How could such a magnificent creature be lonely? Why had it reached out to her?

I'm no one special. I can't be your companion. She wondered if it even understood. The leviathan had retreated beneath the surface, but she could feel it there. It brushed the ship, ever so delicately, and *Dawn Star* shuddered. Behind her, Arama was shouting. Prince Vistaren stood at the railing next to her, that general holding him in place like they might both fall down if he let go.

Help me.

Oh gods. How could she not? Kinnet squeezed her eyes shut and stretched one hand forth as if she could touch it. *How? You are so much greater.*

It didn't answer. She felt its presence, determination laced with confusion. It hummed through her ribs, making her feet tingle, but no words came through to her. Then something made her bones catch fire.

Kinnet jumped, letting out an involuntary shriek. What was that? Then she realized her hair was prickling, trying to stand on end. Lightning flashed above them in clouds that were gathering from thin air. What was happening? Another lick of fire ran through her bones.

Where was the leviathan? She leaned over the railing, peering into the sea. Rain lashed at her face, soaking her hair and making it stick to her cheeks. Lightning flared again. It made Kinnet realize how dark it had grown.

Companion! The word crashed into her just as fire licked through her again. The leviathan was singing! Kinnet looked up, her gaze surprising a dumbfounded expression on Prince Vistaren's face.

"What?" she demanded.

He shook his head, mouth open.

"What?"

"Ah--it's singing," he said.

"You hear it?"

"Don't y--oh. Yes. Sorry. I hear it. It's almost like it's singing up the storm." Vistaren rubbed the back of his head. "That is, you didn't call that, did you?"

"No!" Kinnet shoved her hair back from her face and hung over the railing. She could just see the leviathan through the frothy surface of the waves. *Stop*, she implored. She could tell at once that it couldn't hear her.

An arm seized her around her midsection. Kinnet flailed and the back of her hand struck something. The arm didn't let her go, so she hit again, harder this time. A hand seized her shoulder and wrenched her around.

"What are you doing?" Arama demanded. "Get below-decks!"

"I can talk to him," Kinnet insisted. "Let me go!"

"You're insane."

Kinnet found herself grinning. "Maybe I am."

"If you sink this ship, I'll have your guts for a harper to play on." Arama's eyes blazed, her lips thin and white. Kinnet shook her head. She pulled out of the captain's grasp and knelt against the railing, looking between the braided ropes at the sea below.

Please, talk to me.

Stubborn silence. She hadn't wanted to hear him before, so why should he speak to her now? Kinnet shoved aside her frustration and reached up to rip the sea-glass rings from her ears. She curled her fingers around them, thrusting her will through them.

I am not your companion. But we can find one. There are others, aren't there? Other leviathan? She couldn't tell if she was still crying. The rain was cold and it needled into her cheeks. *I feel your song.*

It was singing up the storm. Kinnet gasped. Leviathans had once been called stormsingers. There were bits of lore in the college that suggested the stormsingers had taught the first stormwitches, back when humans had first conquered Amethir. Maybe there was truth to those legends.

She extended her awareness, touching the storm, skimming the very surface of the power. *Stormsinger, welcome,* she thought. *May I join your song?*

CHAPTER EIGHT

*H*E FEELS HER, THIS *human stormwitch that answers his call. Now that he is close, he can tell she is not his kind. He can tell she is small, weak--though not as weak as many--and landbound.*

But she speaks to him.

She hears him.

He sings for her, sings all his loneliness and rage and sorrow. He sings his aching for companionship, his urge to raise younglings of his own, his wish to teach the storm-songs to others. He sings his disappointment and grief that no one has answered his calls until now. He sings his confusion that the others of his kind ignore him so profoundly.

To his shock, she sings with him.

He feels her song against his skin, in the brush of the water against him and the push of the air pressure over him. He throws himself into the air and crashes back to the waves, seeing the lightning flicker over him and laughing to himself at the spike of delight he feels from her. He shows himself to her and feels her awe and--yes, even love.

And when he thinks he is at the end of his surprise, she changes his song.

And everything else changes with it.

CHAPTER NINE

SOMETHING WAS OFF. KINNET could feel the wrongness of his song, the jarring parts that jostled each other. She didn't know what it was that made it so. She wondered what it sounded like to the others. She opened her mouth and pushed vibrations from her throat, not knowing and not caring what the prince or his general or the captain would think of her. She abandoned her dignity and matched the stormsinger's song, and when she had the grasp of what was wrong with it, she fixed it.

It was sheer arrogance to think she could sing better than this great leviathan, this master singer. It was madness to believe she could correct his mistake.

But when she changed the song, she felt an instant answer. Not in the storm, for there was no reprieve. If anything, the lightning flashed more furiously than before. And not in the sea, for the waves tossed them, sending the *Dawn Star* rolling one way and then the other.

But there was an answer.

Tears streamed down Kinnet's face, mingling with the rain, and she shook with the power of the answer. *They will come,* she told the stormsinger. *They hear us.*

"Reef those damned sails!" Arama howled. She'd had to help Lo drag the prince back from the foredeck to amidships, and she was perilously close to tying the prince to the mast. What was he thinking, leaning over the railing like that in the face of a leviathan? And that gods-be-damned stormwitch, taunting the monster and trying to get them sunk.

"It won't hurt us," Vistaren was saying. "It isn't here for that."

"And what makes you think that, your highness? Have you suddenly learned you have the witchery?" She tried to keep the bite from her voice, but she couldn't. Her bare toes were freezing; her clothes stuck to her. She was terrified. Arama hated being terrified.

"Kinnet told me," he said.

To Arama's shock, Lo let go of Vistaren's shoulders. "What are you doing?" she screeched. She heard the hysteria in her voice and despised herself. How could she be so weak in the face of danger? Even danger brought on them by an arrogant stormwitch who had more power than she had sense?

Lo shook his head and moved away. Arama began to turn and face him, then recoiled as a line slashed her in the face. She felt the end of it lay open her cheek. Blood gushed hot down her face.

"Get below!" she snapped at Vistaren. She slapped a hand against her cheek and lunged for the line as it whipped through the air. "Please, Prince Vistaren! Get to safety!"

Her fingers closed on the line and she threw her weight backwards, securing the line. The prince nodded and lurched his way the dozen steps to the cabin. Arama closed her eyes for a moment, breathing a prayer of thanks to the sea god.

That was when Kinnet Ardelis began to sing. It was the strangest damn sound Arama had ever heard in her life. A primal noise, wailing and howling in the higher pitches, then dropping to a moaning croon. It blended with the keening groans that rose from the sea underneath them. Lightning crackled overheard. Thunder crashed with the force of a slap.

And they came.

The sea erupted around them as more leviathans broke the surface, driving up more than an oar-length into the air before crashing back down. Kinnet's voice throbbed with exultation. Arama realized there were tears on her face, mixing with the blood on her left cheek. Hands closed around her shoulders.

"She brought the others." Lo's lips brushed her ear. There was a surprising joy in his voice.

"What?"

"She said he was lonely. It was how Vistaren knew he wouldn't hurt us." Lo tugged her back, ever so gently. "Your cheek is bleeding."

Arama let herself be pulled back against his chest. It was as broad and strong as she had always imagined it would be. Her throat tightened. She couldn't allow this. She couldn't enjoy this. But--

"The line caught it," she managed. "I'm all right."

"Feel that?" He staggered once as the bow of the ship dove into the next trough. The wave they climbed next wasn't as steep, though, and the trough that followed wasn't as deep. "The sea is calming."

Arama swallowed. Her heart was racing. She closed her eyes and let her head sink back until it touched Lo's shoulder. "The leviathan was singing up the storm, wasn't he?"

"Him or Kinnet, or maybe both of them. You need to lie down. You're losing a lot of blood." Lo's voice was kind. Lo's voice was, she thought, always kind. But at the moment she appreciated that kindness. He wasn't saying anything about her uncontrolled terror from before.

"Surgeon'll...look at it..." she murmured. She was exhausted from the fear energy leaving her. She allowed him to guide her inside. "Tell the mate--"

"I'll tell him," Lo interrupted. "He knows what to do. Let's get that cut stitched."

"Not until the sea calms down more." Arama closed her eyes. "Could put out an eye otherwise."

The pleasant sound of Lo's chuckle lingered on the air as he went back out.

Chapter Ten

"HE JUST WANTED A companion." Vistaren had been repeating some variation of those words at least once an hour since the seas calmed and the leviathan swam off with his new-found companions. He couldn't get beyond it. Sitting in his cabin with mere days between him and his future bride, he found himself even more frightened than he had been before. "All that because he was lonely."

"Loneliness is powerful, my prince." Lozarr's gray eyes hadn't lost any of their sadness, but the lines around his mouth had relaxed a bit. Vistaren thought Arama was still holding him at arm's length, but he'd seen the trust she'd placed in Lo when he'd carried her into the cabin. It might be enough for Lo.

Vistaren didn't think that would be enough for him.

"So much pain because no one understood him." Would that happen to him? Would his marriage steal any hope of happiness and companionship from him? Would he be driven to wander, crying his loneliness to the deeps--

"Someone did understand him," Lo said. He rested a hand briefly on Vistaren's shoulder. "Kinnet understood him."

"She wasn't what he needed, though."

Lo arched an eyebrow. "Are you so sure of that? She met his need. She answered his song. She found him his companion."

Vistaren made a face. "All right, I see what you're getting at."

"Do you?" Lo straddled a chair and leaned his arms on the back, meeting Vistaren's eyes. "I've seen you watching us. Arama and me. It's not always like this, Ren. And your situation is night and day away from ours, anyway. You don't have a choice about a political marriage, all right. But you do have a choice about whether you'll make it easy on her, or hard. You have a choice about whether you'll be happy or not. And you may feel no passion for her, but there are other kinds of love. You act like this is a situation that's entirely black and white, but it isn't."

"You know that isn't me, though, Lo." Vistaren looked at the planks between his feet. He couldn't keep holding that gaze. Lo had to have known about the mad passion Vistaren had felt for him last year. He had to have noticed that it wasn't the court daughters who caught Vistaren's eye.

"I know. I didn't say it was fair. I know the sacrifice you're being asked to make. But it's one of the things I've always admired about you, Ren. You've always done what you think is right for Amethir." Lo squeezed his shoulder. "I know you will again."

"But what's best for Amethir?" Vistaren burst out. "For them to have a king who loves men? Or for them to have a king who denies everything he's ever felt to give them an heir of the body?"

Lo's gaze was sad as he smiled. "I'm not the one who can answer that."

Arama's fingers crept up her cheek again. With an effort, she jerked her hand back down at her side and clenched her fist. The surgeon had done a good job sewing her cheek. It probably wouldn't scar. Not that scars mattered, but she wanted to avoid infection.

The duty was done. She'd brought the prince and his honor guard safely through to Ranarr. On balance, Arama thought the trip might have been safer if they'd skimmed in close to the Blades. She'd never seen leviathan anywhere near the Blades. But done was done, and she couldn't deny that Kinnet Ardelis had been stormwitch enough to get them through safe.

The stormwitch in question approached, her bag slung over one shoulder. She thought highly of herself, there was no denying that. It was clear in the tilt of her chin and the way she carried her shoulders. But she didn't think herself above carrying her own bag, so there was that.

"Stormwitch Ardelis." Arama wasn't sure what to say. *I'm glad you're off my ship? Someone ought to warn* the next captain you sail with? She fought a smile at the thought of Kinnet Ardelis with a parchment warning tied around her neck.

"Captain Dzornaea. Thank you for allowing me to sail with you. And..." She paused, her gray eyes flickering. "Thank you for not throwing me in the brig after what I did."

Arama tilted her head. "What, learning how to communicate with one of the leviathan? Discovering the stormsingers were--are--real?"

Kinnet smiled. It was a true smile, and the first Arama'd seen from her. "Nearly sinking your ship," she said. "However unintentionally."

"Eh. Throwing you in the brig would have been too much trouble, since you didn't sink us." Arama waved a hand. She was still watching Kinnet make her graceful way down the gangplank when warm fingers curled around hers.

Lo. She felt her throat squeeze, but she didn't pull her fingers away.

"You're the finest captain I've ever sailed with," he said. "Thank you for keeping the prince safe."

Arama cocked an eyebrow at him. "Try to keep him that way. He hasn't exactly chosen an easy path." She wasn't just talking about Vistaren.

Lo must have picked up on it. He smiled, though the old sadness was still in his eyes. "I'm not sure how much of it was a choice," he murmured. He leaned in and pressed a kiss to her cheek, whiskers scraping pleasantly against her skin. "Take care of yourself, Arama."

"I will."

She watched him walk away. He was tall and handsome and capable, and he cared too much for her. Maybe someday she would be able to accept that. But not today.

"After all," she muttered, "taking care of myself is what I'm good at."

CHAPTER ELEVEN

*H*E IS NO LONGER *alone.*

The stormsinger pushes his mighty way through the sea, companion by his side. Sometimes they are joined by others of their kind. Sometimes they swim alone. When they sing together, his companion begins the song. He cannot sing alone--Kinnet Ardelis showed him that.

The best songs were never meant to be sung alone.

part two
tannen

Chapter Twelve

"Come, one last match," Azmei pleaded, looking up at her brother. "Think of how long it might be before we ever see each other again."

She had waylaid him after breakfast, knowing he had responsibilities--but she had responsibilities too, after all. Besides, she was leaving in a fortnight, perhaps forever, and Razem was travelling east to take command at the front. They might never see each other again.

Razem's stern expression melted. "You know exactly how impossible it is to resist you when you look at someone like that, don't you?" He scowled at her trousers and plain shirt, the sword and dagger hanging from her belt. "You planned this."

"Of course I did." Azmei was unrepentant. "We haven't tested our blades against each other in ages, and this might be our last chance, at least until after I'm an old, married matron. I want to see if I've grown better than you in the past year."

"Small chance of that, shortling," he teased, and ruffled her hair. "Come along, then, let's find an empty ring."

Azmei felt like skipping as they made their way to the training yards. Once upon a time, she and Razem had fought practice matches every few weeks. She had always longed to beat her brother, but it never happened. She had just reached the point where she could wear him down and score a touch on him when Razem began training with the professional warriors of their army. After that, he didn't have much time for Azmei's recreational swordplay. Princes were expected to prove their valor in warfare, and the bloody conflict over the Kreyden District would give him that opportunity. It had been at least a year since Razem had seen Azmei fight.

They stretched and limbered up. In anticipation of the match, Azmei had worn her hair braided back from her face. Grinning at him, she drew her sword in her right hand and her dagger in her left.

"Very well, let's see if you're any better than you were last time." Razem's sword was longer, and he had the reach of her, but Azmei had always been quicker than he. It was perhaps the only advantage in being so small. She was able to dart in, feinting, and then skip out of his way before he could touch on her.

What began as a laughing, lighthearted bout quickly turned into a more serious match as Razem discovered how much Azmei had practiced recently. She'd gone at her exercises more strenuously since learning she would be going on a sea voyage. Most of the danger would be averted simply because the Storm Petrel--Amethir's most notorious privateer--would be escorting the Amethirian prince to meet Azmei, and therefore not preying on Tamnese ships. But there was always the chance a Strid ship would decide the *Victorious* looked like easy prey. Azmei would not be the sort of princess who relied on others to protect her.

"You've been practicing, little sister," Razem said. He wasn't out of breath yet, but his voice no longer had the easygoing tone.

"And observing the training classes as often as possible," she agreed. She danced in, feinting with her sword while thrusting with her dagger. Razem deflected it neatly and turned it into a counterstrike. Azmei swore under her breath, and Razem laughed at her.

"Less bragging, shortling," he advised. "Let your actions speak for you."

They fell to it in earnest then. She could tell Razem was feeling her out for any weaknesses or slow maneuvers. She couldn't quite match him stroke for stroke, but her footwork came with less effort than his. Probably all the dancing practice she'd been forced to do lately.

Their blade hilts locked. Azmei shoved her hip against Razem's, trying to knock him off balance. He hooked a foot around her ankle and jerked. Azmei tumbled, swearing.

"You always try that trick, and you always fail." Razem backed up, lowering his blade, but Azmei rolled to her feet, lunging at him. He managed to parry--but only just.

"That's a new trick," she crowed, falling into the guard position again. Razem grunted and came at her again.

"You'll probably pester the Storm Petrel for fencing lessons, won't you?" he muttered. "My sister, surrounded by stormwitches and pirates. It's sickening."

"It's practical," she countered, blocking his dagger with her own. She didn't have too many tricks with her blades--she just practiced the ones she had until they were polished. Most of them didn't work on Razem, since he was used to her fighting style, but the new one should have worked.

"Father sold you to the Amethirian prince!" Razem's swings had more force to them. Azmei felt the shock of countering them all the way to her shoulders.

"He maneuvered me into a position to be useful to you," she snapped. "And you'd do better to be grateful for it! Have you forgotten about Dinnsan?"

She ducked under Razem's next swing. She came up under his blade, hitting at his stomach with the pommel of her dagger. He twisted to avoid it and stumbled several steps. He spat into the dirt of the ring. "Honorless dogs."

Dinnsan had been the final blow to an already-crumbling defense of the western Kreyden District. The Strid legion had burned the entire town after breaching the wall. Razem and Azmei's cousin had been killed in the defense. His death was what made her agree to the peace treaty. Six months later, Razem was still furious about Dinnsan. While Azmei had lapsed into grief, her anger flaring occasionally, Razem's hatred burned strong.

Azmei sighed and lowered her blade. "I shouldn't have brought it up," she mumbled.

Razem's blade rang against hers. It caught her by surprise. Her sword went flying and landed in the dirt. Azmei glared at her brother.

He sheathed his blades. "Never let down your guard. The moment your enemy seems weakest might be the moment he's arranged to disarm you."

Azmei wanted to stick her tongue out at him, as she had when they were just learning how to hold a sword. She sighed instead and went to pick up her weapon. She checked it for nicks and wiped the dirt from the blade using her shirt tail.

"I shall keep practicing," she said. "The next time we meet, I'll beat you."

He didn't laugh. "I believe you might. I must practice more diligently in anticipation."

Azmei looked around and saw a servant standing by with a jug of water and drying cloths. Their match had drawn more attention than she'd intended. She and Razem both washed their hands and faces, then drank gratefully.

Before they parted, Azmei to return to the onerous task of packing whatever she might need for her new life in Amethir and Razem to attend whatever meetings or councils he had skipped to humor her, she put a hand on his arm. "Thank you, big brother," she said, and went on tiptoes to kiss his cheek.

His gaze softened. "I am glad I could oblige, little sister."

"Be careful," she implored. "After Venra--" She broke off, nose prickling. Venra had been their favorite cousin. But Razem understood what she didn't say.

He bent to kiss her forehead. "You be careful too, Az. I'm not the only one going into danger."

...And I look forward to meeting you in person, my esteemed friend. Until our appointment in Ranarr I remain,
   Yours most cordially,
   Azmei Reera Corrone

Azmei signed her letter with a flourish and glowered, dissatisfied, at it. She had used the finest parchment and a beautiful violet ink, as befit a princess writing to her betrothed. And her handwriting was tidy, if too careful. It was the reason for her letter that left much to be desired.

But she'd sworn, after Venra's death, that she would do anything in her power to end the war. Then again, six months ago, she hadn't realized it would cost her freedom. Now she was planning to marry a boy she'd never met, living halfway around the world.

Azmei huffed impatiently and stood, touching a chime that resonated through her apartments. Her handmaid Guira came from the sleeping chamber, a folded blanket in her hands.

"See that this makes it on the *Dancer* before she leaves harbor, please," Azmei said.

Guira's smile was sympathetic. "Another letter to Prince Vistaren?" She set aside the blanket and took the letter.

"Probably the last I'll be able to send before we leave to actually meet him," Azmei said. She caught the doleful note in her voice and despised herself for it. She was a princess of Tamnen. She had been raised to be stalwart and proud. She spoke three languages and read four. She danced well, even if her embroidery was appalling. And she could marry the Crown Prince of Amethir if her kingdom needed it.

There was no place in her life for self-pity.

"He seems a kind and intelligent man, my lady." Guira didn't look up as she folded the letter and sealed it with violet wax. "I am looking forward to seeing him in person."

"I don't care if he's an ogre who can't string a sentence together, if this marriage ends the war with Strid," Azmei lied.

Guira laughed as she was supposed to, which made Azmei feel better. "I am certain he isn't an ogre. Even Amethirians with their stormwitchery must have standards."

Azmei shivered despite herself. She didn't know much about stormwitchery, but it both intrigued and frightened her. Amethir, it was said, never saw snow. There was no winter at all in Amethir--just dry, wet, and storm season. Life would be very different in her husband's country.

Outside her apartments a bell rang three times. Guira jumped. "Oh! I'd better hurry. The *Dancer* leaves on the evening tide." She dipped a perfunctory curtsy and hurried out.

Azmei didn't want to be left alone with her thoughts. She knew she had much to be grateful for. She could have been given to a Strid prince, for example. It might be a better hope for peace, but her father had said the older Strid prince's offer had been insulting, and the younger prince was a boy of eleven. A good king did what was best for his kingdom, but Marsede was a good father as well, and had chosen a path more likely to make his daughter happy.

"So stop complaining," she told herself, and went to find the book of Amethirian hero tales she had begun reading yesterday.

Chapter Thirteen

"Hurry, you fool," Orya Perslyn muttered at her cousin. "If you make us late, I'll have your right hand to match your foot. This is why you'll *always* be left in the shop!"

"I'm sorry, my lady, so sorry. I will go faster." Wenda had been born with a twisted foot. Orya knew it was unkind to tweak her about it, but she was too used to demonstrating her superiority over the others.

Orya took a deep breath. "Just--You know how important this is. For the patriarch to summon us--"

"I know, Orya. I'll do better. I'm honored he chose me to accompany you." Wenda picked up her pace, though it was obvious from how her limp deepened that it hurt her.

Of course she was honored. She should be. Orya was among the brightest of her age group, and she had never--*never*--failed to complete a contract since her second one. A failed contract was deducted from your tally, and Orya carried a double tally as it was.

The click of her shoes echoed as she ran up the marble steps. When she reached the top, though, she forced herself to wait. If she arrived without Wenda, the patriarch might doubt her ability to work with others. He might send someone else, despite the importance of this contract. Orya couldn't risk losing it. She stilled her fingers on the polished wooden banister and waited.

She had trained all her life for this mission. Though she hadn't known the particulars until two months ago, she had been raised in an atmosphere of competition and ambition. The patriarch provided for the family, but each member must haul their weight. Contracts didn't fulfill themselves after all, and her family's reach was far enough that it took many, many daughters, sons, aunts, and cousins to do the patriarch's will.

So Orya had learned her trade even as she learned her place in the family. Each family member was expected to provide a tally of one hundred contracts, not counting their years of apprenticeship, after reaching the age of majority. Orya was in her eighth year, and the patriarch himself had promised if she clinched this contract, he would declare her first tally complete. She wanted to be the youngest to complete her tally. She had to be.

Princess Azmei's proposed betrothal to the Amethirian Prince had been unexpected, but Orya's was an adaptable philosophy. The wedding would provide an entirely new market for them in Amethir. Traveling with the princess would give the impression Orya was Azmei's favored and lend her cachet upon arrival in the neutral Ranarr.

And she needed Wenda to help her sell that. She glanced over her shoulder and saw her cousin struggling with the next-to-last step. Holding in an impatient sigh, Orya turned and held out a hand.

"At least we'll have good quarters on the ship," she said, ignoring the look of surprise on Wenda's face as she gripped hands with her. "You shouldn't have to deal with any ladders. And we'll hire a chair for you when we get to Ranarr."

The way Wenda's face lit up twinged at Orya's conscience. There was precious little kindness in their family. Orya's branch of the trade didn't allow for it, but she needed to remember that Wenda was not her adversary.

"Come," Orya said, her voice sharp again. "The patriarch is waiting."

The patriarch wasn't as old as the title implied, though he had at least five decades behind him. He was tall and needle-thin. His hair was pure white and cropped close to his head; his beard was similarly short. Dressed in white and gray, he looked hard. His wit and his tongue cut like a new pair of shears.

He was drumming his fingertips against the window as Orya and Wenda went to their knees before him. His gaze was fixed on something beyond the glass. Orya knew it was meant to convey how insignificant she was. It was also unnecessary. He had conveyed her position very clearly to her already.

"You are late." His voice was thin and cold. Orya tried to remember a single moment in her life when it had warmed, but failed. Her only recollections were of his wielding that voice like a whip to tease out the slightest failure or imperfection.

"I am very sorry, patriarch," she replied. There was no point in excuses. They would only make her look pathetic and foolish. You did not make excuses; you accepted the consequences of your failure and did better next time.

CRACK! She jumped at the sound of his palm slapping the stone windowsill. "You are sorry." His voice was soft. Orya stayed still only by sheer will as he paced towards them.

"It was my fault, patriarch," Wenda said. Orya pressed her tongue against her front teeth, biting back words. Stupid Wenda, answering him back! She would earn herself a beating she was ill-equipped to take.

But to Orya's surprise, the patriarch's expression softened. "Yes, I expect it was, Wenda," he said, cupping her chin in his hand. It almost looked like a caress. Wenda tilted her head to accept the affection, then recoiled as he slapped her.

"I have reasons for selecting you, of all people, to accompany Orya," he hissed. "Do not mistake those reasons for need. If you hinder Orya's execution of her assignment in any way, I will terminate your contract with the family."

Wenda pressed her lips together, her eyes cast down at the floor as her cheek reddened. Orya's estimation of her went up. A lesser cousin would have babbled excuses or apologies, hoping for mercy. Wenda had more strength than Orya had credited.

"As for you," the patriarch said, swinging around to look at Orya. "You are arrogant, brash, over-confident, and too eager to please. Your desperation reeks of weakness. Your emotions betray your foolishness." He sighed. "Yet I have reasons for selecting you, of all people, to carry out this mission." He went to one knee in front of her, steely gray eyes meeting hers. They were like sharpened mirrors; Orya felt them slice through her pretenses.

"If you fail, you will not be punished." His lips were thin. They curled ever-so-slightly at the edges. He saw her fear and hatred. He reveled in them. "You will merely be sent back to apprenticeship to relearn your duties."

Patriarchs came and went, but this man had been patriarch for fifteen years, since his father's untimely death. Orya had known life under another patriarch, but she remembered it only in scraps and patches: being lifted to someone's shoulders, having a blanket tucked tenderly under her chin, thin hands resting on the top of her head. She hated this patriarch even more for his mockery of such things.

"Of course, grandfather," she said. "Your will shall be carried out."

CHAPTER FOURTEEN

T HE BALLROOM WAS FULL of Tamnen's nobility come to bid Azmei farewell. Her ship sailed in a week, but the leave-taking celebration had to take place on an auspicious day, so the augurs had said.

Azmei didn't think the evening terribly auspicious, herself. She'd broken one of the ribbons holding her dancing slippers on, and she was fretting over the way she'd translated that last hero tale. She just knew she'd missed a nuance in the language where Rona was weeping on the neck of dying Fann. It had seemed a fine project when she'd begun, translating the nationalistic epic of her husband-to-be's country into the language of her homeland. But there were fine tricks of the Amethirian language she obviously hadn't mastered, since she kept wavering between thinking Rona and Fann were merely broth-ers-in-arms or suspecting a closer bond.

She would have to ask Vistaren, she decided. She had wanted to present the work as a betrothal gift to him, but it wouldn't be a very good gift if she'd gotten that wrong.

"Wake up," Razem hissed beside her. "Lady Talt is head-ed this way with her daughters. You have to protect me from them. One of them treads on my toes whenever we dance, and at this rate I'm going to end up crippled."

Azmei rolled her eyes up at her older brother. "Very soon now, brother mine, you'll have to learn to fight your own battles." She meant it as a joke, but her gut twisted as she said it.

Razem's dark brows pulled together, his jaw clenching. "Don't remind me." He lifted his head to look beyond her. Azmei studied him, fixing him in her memory. His brown skin, the strong line of his jaw, the shoulder-length, straight, black hair that was currently held in check by a gold fillet. Their training had gone different directions over the past several years, but for all that, she and her brother were close. She believed he would be a good king, even greater than their father, and she wouldn't be here to see it happen.

Razem's tawny gaze darted back to her face. "Ah, gods, you look melancholy, sister." He took one of her hands in both of his, holding tightly. "I hate this."

Somehow his distress gave her courage. Azmei squeezed his hand and smiled up at him. "As do I. But we will bear it. We are royals of Tamnen."

Razem leaned in to kiss her forehead. "As always, your bravery puts mine to shame," he murmured. "Very well, I shall go deal with Lady Talt and her abusive daughters myself." He left the dais and strode to where the approaching noblewoman watched him eagerly.

"The princess seems distracted tonight."

She looked up to see a pretty woman about her own age smiling at her from a deep curtsy.

"Caught out, I'm afraid," Azmei admitted with a rueful smile. She didn't recognize the woman, but her dress was of fine silk from their southern regions.

"Orya Perslyn," the woman said. "Of the Meekin branch of the Perslyn family."

Of course. A textile family of some means. That explained the silk. Azmei smiled and nodded in greeting.

"I am honored to be sailing on your highness' ship to Ranarr, and I was eager to meet you before we sailed." At Azmei's arched eyebrow, Orya looked sheepish. "I've never been to Ranarr before. I thought having a friend on the ship would help."

A friend? Orya's brazen attitude amused Azmei. She gestured for Orya to walk with her.

"And what takes you to Ranarr?" she asked. "You already know why I am going."

Orya's laugh was crystalline, like the dancing of bells. "I am to negotiate a contract on behalf of my family to supply silk for two Tamnese dress shops in Ranarr." She leaned in, too familiar and irresistibly charming. "Hopefully I can finalize the contract in time for a royal wedding."

Azmei couldn't swallow a laugh at that. "If things aren't going well, tell me, and I'll delay the wedding," she promised.

Orya proved clever and easy to talk to. Over the next hour of the ball, Azmei spent more time talking to her new friend than she did dancing. It was just as well, with that hastily mended slipper ribbon, but eventually Azmei caught the exasperated glances her father and Guira were both directing at her. She took her leave of Orya and danced with the sons of a dozen noblemen and another dozen important noblemen themselves. By the time the ball ended, Azmei had lost track of her new friend's whereabouts entirely.

Nevertheless, she felt decidedly less anxious about the voyage that awaited a few days hence.

Azmei slept late the morning after the leave-taking ball. She was vaguely aware of Guira trying to wake her at one point, but Azmei was dreaming about a red horse with eyes that seemed to see into her heart. She mumbled at Guira and slipped back into her dream, where she and the red horse ran across the desert to the edge of the ocean and beyond.

When she truly woke, Azmei had a headache. She stared at the gauzy curtains hanging around her bed, wondering why she should even bother getting out of bed today. She hadn't finished packing, but that could wait. And there was her translation of Rona and Fann for Prince Vistaren, but she would have plenty of time to work on that on the ship.

What was the point anyway? Vistaren probably wouldn't care about reading things in her language. What was the point of anything? She sighed and rolled over, burying her face in the down comforter. *I'll sleep all day,* she thought, *and perhaps I'll dream about the red horse again and forget any of this is real.*

The longer she lay there, the more aware she was of the throbbing in her head. Having nothing to distract her from the pain, she focused on it until it seemed magnified tenfold from when she first woke.

Some indeterminate length later, the curtains were jerked open. "What are you doing still abed?" Guira demanded. "Up! You have your final appointment with the bookbinders this afternoon, and then you have to decide which dresses we are taking with us."

Azmei groaned and burrowed further under the covers.

"If you leave it up to me, I shall dress you in pink from head to toe."

That made Azmei sit up, which actually made her head feel better. "You wouldn't dare."

Guira's smile was wicked. She and Azmei both knew she very much would dare. It was one of Guira's lifelong sorrows that Azmei refused to wear pink. The fact that several pink dresses existed said a lot about the level of Guira's determination.

Azmei huffed and threw the covers back, swinging her legs over the edge. "Very well. I want breakfast and nalatooth tea. My head is aching."

"Right away, m'lady," Guira said, with just enough edge to her voice that Azmei realized she was being petulant.

"Straighten up," Azmei muttered to herself. "You needn't take it out on Guira. She's no happier about this than you are." She sighed and turned her attention to getting dressed.

The nalatooth tea did help, and breakfast helped even more. By the time Azmei's carriage was ready to carry her and Guira to the market district, her headache had faded almost entirely. Not quite enough, she discovered as the carriage jolted on a loose cobblestone. But she clenched her teeth and bore it. It would be worth it. The bookbinder was providing a fine, leather-bound tome, into which Azmei could copy her translation. She could have sent Guira to pick up the order, of course, but as this was her betrothal gift to Prince Vistaren, Azmei wanted to be able to say she had done it all herself.

As the carriage rolled into the market district, Azmei leaned against the window, gazing past the mounted guards accompanying them to take in the familiar sights. She would miss her occasional excursions to the shops. She had one particular ink dealer who was her favorite, and she was certain no Amethirian shop could compete with Sumina Books and Bindings.

"Princess Azmei! Your Highness is gracious to visit us in person yet again!" Sumina herself hurried forward, a wide smile on her craggy face. She had run the bookshop for as long as Azmei could remember, and always knew just what books the princess would enjoy. It was possible, Azmei conceded, that Sumina had helped shape her interests, as well.

"Goodness, Sumina, you know this shop is one of my favorite places in the city," she said aloud. As Sumina curtsied, Azmei reached out and caught her hands. "Honored bookseller, I would thank you one last time for your service over the years." Sumina's eyes widened as Azmei drew her upright and kissed her on each cheek. "May you always prosper as you advertise that you are the royal bookseller to both Tamnen and Amethir."

Sumina's mouth dropped open, but she stared, speechless, at Azmei.

Azmei laughed. "Dear Sumina. You have always pleased me, and I am bearing your workmanship as a betrothal gift to Prince Vistaren. Did you think I would fail to extend you the honor?"

"I hadn't dared hope," Sumina, replied at last. She blinked several times and shook her head. "I thank you." She squeezed Azmei's hands. "Let me show you the volumes I have for the prince. I prepared four for your examination."

As Azmei followed Sumina back to the counter, she breathed in deeply, trying to seal the scent of dust, vanilla, and leather into her memory. What would she do without Sumina? Amethir would have booksellers aplenty, but it would not have the woman who knew that Azmei preferred adventure tales to romances.

"Here we are." Sumina placed on the counter a bundle wrapped in soft fabric. As she unfolded the cloth, Azmei's eyes were drawn to a brilliant red tome. Sumina had done lovely work dyeing all four leather covers, but the navy, green, and brown were so drab. Red was the color of passion--appropriate for the epic stories as well as for a betrothal gift.

"This one." Azmei stroked the soft leather. "Of course. This one."

After she had paid for the book, she visited the shop next door, where she purchased several packets of fine paper and two extra bottles of ink. She didn't want to run out on her way to Ranarr. It would be embarrassing if she had to switch colors halfway through Prince Vistaren's book.

Guira insisted they go to Azmei's favorite dressmaker after the stationers, but the dressmaker's shop was closed, a hastily-lettered sign in the front stating the dressmaker was ill. Azmei turned to head back to the carriage, but Guira's hand closed about her wrist. "There's another just up the street," she said. "I know you don't care for her, but I need to buy ribbons, and you ought to have a better hat for onboard the ship."

Azmei heaved a sigh but followed obediently. She should have bought that slender volume of fantastic tales she'd seen in passing at Sumina's. It would at least give her something to look at while Guira chatted with the dressmaker about fabric and cut and texture and whatnot.

This dressmaker was a short, square-jawed woman who kept rubbing her hands together. Every time she glanced at Azmei, she half-bobbed a curtsy, as if she were afraid of giving offense. Azmei frowned at her, at which the woman blenched and looked back at Guira. Guira began listing out everything she needed while the woman trotted from one side of the shop to the other, gathering everything in a pile on the counter.

Azmei tried to keep her boredom from showing as Guira and the dressmaker debated the merits of velvet. Finally it was decided that, while velvet was certainly too hot for Ranarr, it might be all right in Amethir, so Guira only bought a small amount. Every time the woman glanced at her, she rubbed her hands together and then rubbed her fingers against her lips. The dressmaker began pressing another blend on Guira, but Azmei was finished waiting.

"Enough," she said. "If I take too many dresses with me, it will be a waste. I will undoubtedly have new fashions to purchase in Amethir. Guira, have her tally the sale. We are done." Guira flashed her an annoyed look that smoothed away as she turned to face the dressmaker.

Not waiting to see what the final cost would be, Azmei went to stand at the door of the shop. One of her guards met her glance, and she smiled at him.

"I positively loathe buying new dresses," she murmured. "Go down and make the carriage driver ready. I'll walk back, but it wouldn't do for me to catch him napping."

The guard grinned. "Of course, your highness," he said, and started down the street. Azmei turned to look back into the shop. Guira had finished her purchase.

"Come," Azmei said. "I have much to do back at the palace." She waited until they were outside to add, "I know you're annoyed with me, Guira, but I couldn't watch that woman twitch any longer. She looked as if someone were poking her with hot needles."

"Mm. She was behaving rather oddly, wasn't she?" Guira frowned. "I've dealt with her before. She's never been so nervous in the past. Then again, you aren't usually with me."

As they came abreast of the closed dressmaker's shop, Azmei said, "Next time you see Innah, tell her I was sorry I couldn't say farewell. I hope she isn't terribly ill." Innah was, like all dressmakers, too fond of pink, but at least she was polite about Azmei's hatred of the color.

Whatever Guira had planned to say was lost as the door of the shop burst outward. It slammed into one of Azmei's guards, sending him reeling. Two armed men leapt through the door into the street. One of them slashed his sword, and another of Azmei's guards fell, cursing.

"Ware!" shouted Azmei's third guard as the second armed man charged. "Ware! Protect the princess!"

Azmei had no weapons, nor anything to protect her except the thick tome in her arms. She had insisted on carrying it herself. She was glad of that now. She raised the book in front of her. It might not stop a sword, but it might break the force of a blow.

Fortunately she didn't have to try it. The guard she had sent to the carriage came at a run, followed by two more who had been guarding the carriage, while the guard who had shouted jumped between Azmei and the attackers. The guard who had been knocked down by the door had clambered to his feet and joined the fray as well.

"No wedding! No peace!" shouted one of the attackers. Azmei didn't see what he did to the guard, but suddenly the guard who had shouted was on the ground, clutching at his groin. There was no one between Azmei and the shouting attacker. Blood slid down his sword as he advanced on her.

"Damn you!" she shouted at the attacker, and threw the book at him. He had to duck, and it slowed him enough for the last of her guards to reach them. He was behind the man, who was too focused on reaching Azmei to notice him. His sword sliced cleanly through the attacker's neck, severing head from shoulders.

Guira had thrown herself between Azmei and the attacker. Azmei jerked Guira backwards as the attacker's headless body twitched and fell to the ground.

The first attacker had been subdued while Azmei was occupied with the second. He knelt in the blood-spattered dirt, staring defiantly at the princess. A crowd was beginning to gather. Azmei looked around, fearing the worst for Innah. "Check the dressmaker's shop," she ordered. Then a thought occurred to her. "The shop we were in!" she snapped. "Find that woman. See if she knew something."

The guards who had come from the carriage took control of the prisoner while the others went to check the shop.

"Why did you do this?" Azmei demanded, stepping closer to the prisoner. He couldn't be much older than she. "Why would you raise a hand against your princess?"

He glared at her without speaking. One of the guards shook him. It made him wince, but he still didn't speak.

"Do you care nothing for the thousands who have died in this war with Strid?" she persisted. "Have you so little love for your countrymen that you would condemn thousands more to die needlessly? Why would you have no peace? Why would you have no wedding?"

"No peace except through victory," the man said. He spit at her feet. Azmei stepped forward and slapped him.

"My cousin died in Dinnsan, dog," she hissed. "I will have peace to honor his memory, rather than a hollow victory."

As soon as she was close, the man twisted, kicking the guard that held him. The guard didn't let go entirely, but his grip loosened enough that the attacker could lunge for Azmei. She recoiled. As quick as lightning, another guard slashed out with his sword. The prisoner fell into the dirt, bleeding. The attackers had been armed, but not armored. The guard's stroke had opened a bloody slash across the man's back.

Azmei stumbled backwards until strong hands steadied her. "Here, my lady," murmured the guard she had spoken to earlier. "Allow me to aid you."

She hoped it was the weakness in her knees that made her snap, "What is taking the others so long?" She hated leaning on him, but she wasn't sure her legs would hold her yet. A practice fight with her brother was one thing. An actual battle, however small and short, was not at all what she had imagined.

The guards reappeared from the dress shop. The dressmaker walked, wrists bound, between them. Her jaw was reddening, her eyes downcast.

"We must get you back to the palace," murmured the guard.

"Wait, where is Guira? Guira!" Azmei turned, staring around, until she saw her handmaid kneeling beside the wounded guard. She had pressed the bolt of velvet cloth against his wound to stanch the blood. Warmth flooded through Azmei. She straightened.

"Thank you," she murmured, glancing at her guard, and went to stand over Guira. "Will he be all right?"

"It is a bad cut, my lady, but listen." Guira didn't look up as she spoke. Azmei did as she bade and realized the alarm bells were ringing through the city. Pounding hoofbeats were approaching at a gallop. "They will get him to a healer and he will live." One of the guards took Guira's place.

Azmei knelt beside him. "Guardsman, I thank you," she said, laying a hand on his shoulder. He was sweating, his lips pulled away from gritted teeth. "What is your name?"

He was breathing hard. "Sennal, your highness."

Azmei kissed her fingertips and touched them to his forehead. "Guardsman Sennal, you saved my life. You and your family will never want in this life."

He grimaced at her, but she decided it was actually a smile twisted by pain. "You honor me, Princess Azmei."

"No, *you* honor *me*." She stood and swept the rest of her guard with a look. She sensed them straightening as her gaze touched each of them. "You all honor me. I do not disregard the heavy price you pay to protect me. I thank you all."

The hoofbeats were very close. When she looked up, she realized it wasn't the city guard, or even the palace guard. It was her brother, riding at the head of a column of soldiers. When he saw her, he shouted.

"Azmei! Protect the princess!"

Azmei forced a smile for the wounded guard and went to stand inside the circle of guards until her brother arrived. Her handmaid joined her inside the circle. "My lady, I am so sorry," she breathed. "If it had not been for me, we wouldn't have been at the dress shop."

"Nonsense. This is not your fault. I fear for Innah, though. We must be sure she is well."

"It was my suggestion to visit the dressmaker--"

Azmei cut her off. "And it was a reasonable suggestion. No, Guira, I will not allow you to blame yourself. I am unhurt. Sennal will recover."

"He may never walk straight again," Guira murmured.

Azmei swallowed. "A risk he understood when he became a royal guard," she said. "And we shall provide for him. Come, I do not blame you. You must not blame yourself."

Guira was smiling tremulously when a man's voice said, "Your highness?"

Azmei turned. It was the guard she had sent to the carriage. "My lady, you threw this at the attacker," he murmured, holding it out. "I fear it is somewhat worse for wear."

"Oh." Azmei stared down at the book. The wrapping had torn and several of the pages were bent at the corner. Worst of all, the entire front cover was bloody. "I--Thank you, guardsman." She took the book from him. It suddenly seemed much heavier than it had. She stared down at the scarlet cover. She couldn't tell how much of the color was from dye and how much from blood.

"Go back to Sumina's," she told Guira. "I can't give this one to Prince Vistaren." Her hands were shaking. She wiped the cover, smearing red across her fingers, but the blood had soaked into the leather; wiping it did nothing to clean it.

"Which of the three colors would you like?" Guira, Gods bless her, had recovered from her self-recrimination. Azmei had need of her, and Guira would answer.

"I don't care!" Azmei snapped. Her eyes stung. "Wait, no. The blue. Buy the blue. Amethirians love the sea, don't they? He'll like that."

Guira curtsied and hurried off, two soldiers following close behind.

CHAPTER FIFTEEN

"THEY TRIED TO KILL her!" Razem shouted. "Father, you cannot send her away! What might happen to her when she is out of Tamnen?"

"I am standing right here," Azmei pointed out. "Do you care what I want?"

Razem turned on her. "Shut up!"

King Marsede pressed his fingertips together. He was a calm man, slow to wrath. "And if I keep her here? Would you have us anger the Amethirians as well as the Strid? We cannot afford another enemy."

"The dressmaker won't talk," Razem said. He wheeled and paced away. "Did you know that? She remains silent in the face of everything I threaten her with."

"I will not allow her to be tortured," Marsede said. "She will be punished. Perhaps she will pay with her life. But I will not have her tortured beforehand. That is what makes us different from the Strid."

Razem halted. Azmei saw a dark flush creep up his neck. "I--I wasn't suggesting torture," he muttered.

Marsede sighed. "Razem, I understand your anger. I, too, am angry. And I am afraid." He stood and went to stand in front of his son. Azmei had never realized how much alike they looked. "I am afraid of losing my daughter, who is precious to me."

"Do you truly believe the Amethirians can protect her?"

"Have we done so well ourselves?" Marsede's smile was rueful. "We knew there would be those opposed to the idea of peace. There is so much hatred. There have been too many years of war. An entire generation has grown up without their parents." The king bowed his head.

Azmei knew he had won the argument when Razem's hands came up to grip their father's arms. But Marsede didn't stop speaking.

"I would have peace. I cannot give the Kreyden District away, for we all know the Strid would kill everyone of Tamnese descent if we surrendered the district. The Strid care only for the mines and other resources. But I cannot continue this war. It will beggar our nation and embitter another generation. I cannot leave that as my legacy."

Azmei went to put her hand on her father's shoulder. "Enough, Father," she said, keeping her voice soft. "I am marrying Prince Vistaren of my own free will. Of course none of us wish it. I don't wish to be parted from you and Razem. But I am Princess of Tamnen, and my duty is clear." She glanced sharply at her brother. "Razem is done arguing."

Razem glared back at her, but Marsede, head still bowed, didn't see it. "Of course I am," Razem said, matching Azmei's tone. "I'm sorry, Father."

Azmei allowed the silence to continue for several heartbeats while she tried to think of something to say. When inspiration refused to speak, she said, "Come, Father, Razem. I believe tonight is the perfect night to open my bottle of birth wine. We can celebrate twice over my being alive."

"I packed it with the other volume of Tamnese history," Guira said, an edge to her voice.

Azmei yanked a dress out of the trunk and tossed it aside. "It isn't in there. I looked."

"I had to take out the rose silk to fit the Tamnese history in. Why you're taking so many books, I don't know. You have more books than you can read on such a short voyage." Guira scooped up the dress and smoothed out the fabric. "Reading so much will make you seasick," she added darkly.

"I need both volumes! I won't have my children growing up in a foreign country with no knowledge of my country's history." Azmei could hear the tears in her voice and took a deep breath. *This isn't you,* she told herself.

"It's a bit early to think about that." Guira slipped the dress back into the trunk. "And I am certain even Amethirian booksellers have Tamnese history books."

Azmei drew in another deep breath through her nose. "Don't tease. I just need my books, Guira, not someone else's." She went back to the first trunk and tugged out another dress. There was the book in question. *The Birth of Tam and the Founding of Tamnen City*. Nestled next to it was *From the God-Wars to the Great Slumber*.

Behind her, Guira sighed. "I shall begin repacking."

"What about the love poems of Hafana?"

Guira expelled a heavier sigh. "I believe they are hiding under your pillow, where you pretend not to like them. Do you wish me to pack that volume, as well?"

Azmei growled wordlessly at her and stomped off to her bed.

By the time Azmei's father and brother accompanied her and Guira (along with a dozen of their most elite bodyguards) to the *Victorious*, she was heartily sick of packing and looking forward to a fortnight of monotony at sea.

Not that Azmei expected to be bored. She had dozens of books she would probably not have time for in a small chest along with her writing kit and jewelry. Her plan was to spend as much time as possible completing work on her betrothal gift for Prince Vistaren.

She and her father had a silent parting. They had already said what needed to be said. Anyway, Azmei wasn't sure she could force anything out past the lump in her throat. She flung her arms around her father, who held her tightly and sighed against her hair. When she pulled away, her cheeks were wet, and she saw the glitter in his own eyes.

Razem was more violent in his farewell. He lingered until the captain was shouting for any last passengers to hurry their sorry selves up and quit making the princess wait. Razem didn't speak, but huffed and fumed like a volcano. Finally he seized her in a tight hug.

"Remember, little sister, if you don't like him, you needn't marry him. And if he treats you ill, I shall kill him for it."

She let out a breathless laugh. "After all the trouble Father and the Ranarri Diplomats went to securing the treaty, he will have to be fundamentally flawed indeed for me to reject him." She pulled away and gripped his elbows, staring up into his face. "Nay, Razem. You have always protected me. Now it is time to allow me to protect you."

"But to do it by selling you--" He cut himself off, turning his head and staring out to sea. "I love you, Az. You had better write to me often."

"I shall. I promise." She gripped his forearm. "And you--be careful. Don't go to Kreyden trying to win the war while I'm busy trying to stop it entirely."

"I won't stand idly by while Anderlin of Strid murders our people and ravages our land, Azmei." His voice was hard.

"Nor do I ask you to." She straightened, lifting her chin to stare up at him. "But I ask you to remember that you have an obligation to live for our kingdom. And for me." She gave him a crooked smile. "As a wedding gift, promise me."

Razem gave a curt nod. "I'll be careful. And I won't start any fights. I give you my word."

Without so much as a backwards glance, Razem strode away, his boots loud even through the clamor on deck. Everyone paused minutely in their work to watch him pass.

Azmei watched the sailors cast off, trying to pinpoint how she felt. Not brittle, exactly, but as if she were a minstrel's puppet strung but loosely together. "But though my duties pull those strings, I will choose how I dance," she muttered. She straightened her back and folded her arms about herself, cupping her elbows in the opposite hands.

Perhaps Vistaren would understand her better than she feared. Hadn't he responded to her first letter with as much courtesy and curiosity as she could have hoped for? And subsequent letters had shown his keen grasp of the conflict between Tamnen and Strid. He had frankly acknowledged how little they knew each other and how, left to their own choices, they would likely choose others to wed. He seemed an honest, yet kind, man. She hoped he turned out to be the man he seemed.

Azmei listened to the captain calling orders and the ragged chorus of the sailors repeating each order as they obeyed. The harbor side slipped past, and Azmei was seized by a sudden need to memorize each detail of the city she loved. What if this was the last time she saw the city before her wedding? If she and Vistaren ratified the marriage agreement, they could be married at any time, and it could be years before she returned here...and when she did, it would be home no longer.

Blinking at the stinging of her eyes, Azmei gazed at the harbor front markets, the warehouses, the sanctuary spires that rose above all other buildings. No matter what came, Azmei must remember for whom, for what, she did this.

part three
the victorious

Chapter Sixteen

Princess Azmei obviously loved her brother. Orya had observed them together at the departure ball, and she had noted then how Azmei talked about Razem. There was a bond between them, and it was one of the things that intrigued Orya. Orya's relationship with her own brother was very different. She loved him, yes, but it was as much out of obligation as true affection.

There were other qualities, like the willingness Azmei displayed to do her duty to her family, or the princess' self-deprecating manner. In another person--in someone of the Perslyn family, for instance--it would seem only disingenuous, but with Azmei, it was genuine. That ought to make Orya hate her, but she was drawn to her instead.

It was an odd feeling, being fascinated by and jealous of someone all at once. Orya sighed.

Wenda looked up from her sewing. "Cousin, is anything amiss?" Her broad face wrinkled in concern.

Orya forced a smile. "No, not really. I tire of my book, though. Set aside your sewing, Wenda. We can play cards and open a bottle of wine."

Wenda's brows furrowed for a long moment, but eventually she smiled. "Very well. I shall have time to work tomorrow." Her lips curved. "Or yet tonight, should you bore of beating me." She secured her needle in the cloth and folded her work carefully. "I am not very good at Queens or Ship's Trade, and I know those are the games you favor."

"Nonsense. I am sure you only say that so I'll be shocked at how much money you win from me." Orya tossed her book aside. She stood and went to retrieve the bottle of wine, annoyed that Wenda's crippled foot made her so unsuitable a servant.

You don't get angry at Yarro for being different, she reminded herself, returning to thoughts of her brother. Everyone else, it seemed, did, but how could Orya? She had almost raised him after their mother's suspicious death. And though it was rare that he could stand so much human contact as to snuggle with her, the fact remained, she was the only one he permitted such familiarity. And she alone had ever been on the receiving end of his smile.

But Yarro was able-bodied and willing. He just saw the world and interacted with it differently. In another family, he might have been lauded as an augur. He certainly had some of the odd behaviors the augurs displayed; he often seemed to stare inward, and he sometimes made declarations with such authority Orya believed him, even if it was something he should know nothing about. And then there were the trances...

Orya ran her knife through the wax and uncorked the bottle, pouring each of them a generous glass. It wasn't an expensive wine, but it was good nonetheless; had Wenda ever tasted anything like it? It was occurring to Orya that she knew little of how the girl had lived her life. Their areas of training were so far removed from one another as to be two separate trades. Perhaps it was time for Orya to correct that lack in her knowledge.

She smiled as she carried the glasses back to the sitting area. Wenda was already shuffling the cards, her fingers nimble. *Shame on you,* Orya thought. *You let yourself believe that crippled foot meant all of her was deficient.* She should have known better than to make such an error. A merchant could never underestimate those around her, or she might lose the upper hand in her dealings. Observation had been an important aspect of her training, and she had neglected to apply it to those closest her.

"What shall it be, cousin?" Wenda asked. "Ship's Trade?" Her fingers paused, sliding unconsciously along the curved corners of the cards.

"Queens, I think," Orya said. It was less competitive, and she wished to observe her cousin as they talked over their cards.

Wenda nodded and dealt them each four cards to act as a queen and three knights. She placed the rest of the deck face down on the table.

Orya inspected her cards. A moon warrioress, two cups, and a shield. It was a decent hand, but nothing remarkable. "Tell me, cousin, what was it like, growing up in the Kreyden?" She pursed her lips and, reluctantly, set aside the shield. It would be held in reserve, rather than sacrificed outright, but only if she drew a lower card of the same suit.

Wenda fumbled and one of her cards fluttered to the tabletop. Orya forced herself not to glance at it. She was not above cheating at cards when it mattered, but this game did not. She selected her new card and studied it as if Wenda's response were inconsequential.

"How--I--I did not know the patriarch had told you that," Wenda said. She sipped her wine and dabbed a napkin at her lower lip. "Parts of the Kreyden are still very beautiful. There are fertile fields of gold, with green hills above." She didn't have to say she missed it; longing laced through every word.

The patriarch hadn't told Orya anything about Wenda--it was the way she pronounced words like *cousin* and *work*--but she didn't bother correcting her cousin. It wouldn't hurt for Wenda to believe the patriarch trusted Orya more than he did her. It couldn't be further from the truth--he expected his granddaughter to outstrip all the others, and even when she did, he was displeased. But cruelty had been directed at Orya many times because she was seen as the darling of their instructors. Subtle bruises and sly pinches had driven that knowledge deep when she was a child.

"I have never seen the disputed lands." Orya watched as Wenda set aside a card and drew, grimaced, and discarded a low-ranked crown. She blinked; Wenda's hand must be far superior to hers if she was discarding crowns. "I was never allowed to leave Meekin until my apprenticeship was finished. Hateful city, with its canals and fountains."

Wenda laughed, her shoulders relaxing. "And I wouldn't know, because I've only seen Meekin in passing. We took a canal boat to the capital when I came to join you."

Orya set aside another card and drew again. "I hate canal boats. They're so slow. And the insects! Give me the open sea any day. But do the waves not trouble you?"

Wenda shrugged. "Not much. I am used to pitching about unsteadily, after all." Her lips twitched as she waved at her foot, but she didn't actually smile until Orya laughed. Wenda and Yarro were nothing alike, really, despite the fact they were both different from normal. Orya rarely had actual conversations with Yarro the way she was having with Wenda. But something about Wenda reminded Orya of her youngest brother. It was almost comforting.

Someone knocked on the door. Wenda jumped, but Orya merely folded her cards into a stack and went to answer the knock.

Princess Azmei's handmaid was at the door.

"Lady Orya?" The woman was tall and bony, with graying dark hair. Orya didn't like handmaids with sharp eyes. "The princess invites you to dine in her cabin with her this evening."

Orya curtsied deeply. "I would be honored. When shall I attend her highness?"

The woman sniffed. What was her name again? Orya knew she had been with the princess more than a decade, but couldn't remember her name. Geesa? Garia? Something like that.

"At the next bell, if you please," the woman said.

Guira, that was it. Orya smiled and saw the woman relax a bit. "Thank you, Guira," she said, and that softened the woman a bit more. Good. It never hurt to have the servants on your side, even if inwardly you couldn't care less for a mouse's fart than for them. And Orya was never one to turn away an advantage.

Guira left and Orya closed the door, turning away from it. "I am afraid our game is being cut short," she informed her cousin. "I am to dine with the princess."

It was almost embarrassing the way Wenda's eyes lit up. "Oh, how lovely for you, Orya! You will have such fun! And to have won the princess' approval! My trademistress was right when she said I would learn a great deal from you."

Orya shrugged. "Come and help me dress, if you want," she said carelessly, "and we can keep talking."

Chapter Seventeen

Azmei chewed the end of her pen, frowning. Rona was kissing Fann's forehead. She absolutely knew there were no other ways to translate that word. A kiss on the forehead could be a blessing, so it could be that her brothers-in-arms approach to the interpretation was safe. But then again, it could be a *kiss*. She growled and shoved the book away from her.

It wasn't as if it bothered her to think Rona and Fann might have been lovers. Well, in one respect it did, because Rona was married to Aevver, daughter of the sea king, and that was a nasty thing to do if you were already in love with your best friend. But the notion that two of Amethir's heroes may have been same-lovers didn't bother her. It was uncommon in Tamnen, to be sure, and the priests preferred it be done in secret, or at least kept private, but it wasn't actually taboo. And in Ranarr and Amethir, she knew, it was openly accepted. Even celebrated among some ethnicities.

But if she didn't know for sure that Rona and Fann were lovers, how could she translate it properly?

"You are chewing your thumbnail again," said Guira's voice from behind her. "You dwell too much on your anxiety."

"I want his present to be right."

"It will be." Guira gathered the books, papers, and pens and swept them all into a tidy stack without even glancing at them. "Your dinner guest will be arriving in fifteen minutes. Please allow me to wash the ink from your fingers."

Azmei rolled her eyes but extended her fingers to be scrubbed with the perfumed solution that always removed even the most stubborn ink stains from her fingers. Azmei always meant to ask about the solution, but she wasn't the one who cared about ink stains. Left to herself, she would probably never bother getting all the ink off, because she knew she would just get more on her.

"Orya Perslyn will be dressed prettily," Guira said. "Let's find something nicer for you to wear. Perhaps that brown silk tunic and the split skirt that goes with it?"

Azmei wanted to roll her eyes again, but she suppressed the urge as she followed Guira to the built-in wardrobe where her finest clothes were hanging. She was actually fond of the brown silk tunic, partly because brown set off her skin tone and eyes nicely, and partly because she'd actually managed to insist on split skirts instead of full, heavy, traditional skirts. A long-sleeved ivory silk blouse went under the tunic, and brown sandals finished off the outfit nicely. Of all the clothes she had brought with her on the trip, this was her favorite outfit, and the one she planned to wear (no matter what Guira said) when she met Vistaren.

"Captain Destar isn't upset that we are dining privately tonight, is he?" Azmei asked.

"He seemed relieved, actually." Guira's thin lips pursed. "The ship is very fine, but its captain is rather rough around the edges yet."

"Oh, it doesn't matter, anyway. There aren't enough passengers to bother with a fancy dinner, and I expect Orya and I can dine with Destar tomorrow without its having to be a fine affair. It's silly to make too much of a fuss."

"You are a princess of Tamnen." The corners of Guira's mouth turned down, but there was a telltale glimmer in her eyes. She had served Azmei far too long to expect her to change into the perfect lady at this stage.

Guira had been Azmei's mother's maid until Izbel's death twelve years ago. Azmei had been eight years old. A week after Izbel's funeral, Guira had rolled up the sleeves of her mourning gown and marched into the nursery. With eyes red-rimmed from crying, she had informed the princess that it was high time she had a maid, and who better than Guira for the job? Azmei had looked at the tall, gaunt woman, so different from her plump, beautiful mother, and burst into tears. Guira had gathered her in strong arms and within half an hour she had won Azmei's devotion.

"I am a very practical princess," Azmei informed her now. "And I see no reason to put people out simply because I outrank them."

"Practical." Guira snorted. "What you are is a prince in a princess' body. But as I have indulged you all these years, I suppose it is too late to persuade you to become a proper princess." She slanted an affectionate look at Azmei. "Practical will have to do."

Orya arrived punctually for dinner, which probably endeared her to Guira forever. Azmei, whose habitual tardiness caused Guira endless shame (at least to hear her tell it), sighed when she caught the gleam in her maid's eye.

"Princess, your invitation honors me," Orya said, curtsying.

Azmei wondered if Vistaren got as tired as she did of all the ridiculous protocol. Or maybe he was the sort of prince who enjoyed it. She inclined her head to a proper angle and waved for Orya to sit.

"I hope you find your accommodation satisfactory," she said, doing Orya the honor of pouring wine for them both.

"Oh, yes! I've never traveled on such a ship before. It's glorious fun. Though I'm certain I overheard someone calling the Captain 'my lord'." Orya tilted her head in charming confusion. Azmei wondered if Orya were only pretending to like her because of her position; the gesture seemed too calculated.

Azmei shrugged. "Of course Destar is a lord. I'm a princess of Tamnen." Then she smiled, knowing it would spoil her appearance of careless superiority. "Our ship is under the command of Destar Thorne, Lord-Captain of Tamnen's navy. He is the head of my guard."

She expected Orya to feign awe, but the other girl impressed her. She smiled and nodded. "I did wonder when I heard that. After all, this treaty is so important, and if anything went wrong... well." She folded her hands in her lap.

"Nothing will happen that Destar cannot handle," Azmei said. She lifted her goblet to wet her lips. The wine was sweet and comforting. It tasted like oak leaves and lush Tamnen soil and snowmelt.

"Tell me about your family," she suggested.

Orya took the change of topic in stride. As Guira ladled a cold soup into the bowls, she sipped her wine and smiled. "I am the middle of four, all boys save me. My youngest brother isn't even prenticed yet. They're mostly awful, but he isn't. I rarely get to see him, though."

Azmei loved Razem, but for the past decade, he had been occupied with learning to become a king, while Azmei learned how best she could serve him. She had often wished for a little brother to tease and teach and cuddle--one who would follow her around as she wished to follow Razem. "I envy you." She smiled. "And Meekin? What is it like?"

Orya shook her head, tipping it slightly. "It is a trade town, mostly clean with little crime. My favorite place in the town is a store that caters to musicians at the bardic school. I like looking at their instruments, but I've never learned to play."

"Are there a lot of people?"

Orya finished her soup. "Not so many, except in the spring when the first trade caravan gets through. When they arrive, there's always a fair."

"It sounds lovely." Azmei took a piece of flatbread and contemplated the savory spread before choosing spicy instead. "I should have liked to see it."

"Oh, you should! The main park has such a fountain--" Orya broke off, blushing. "I beg your highness' pardon. I forgot myself."

Azmei's lips tugged up despite herself. "You forgot you were talking to a woman who has been effectively banished from her kingdom?" She shook her head. "Never mind. I forget myself sometimes, for a moment or two."

"Your Highness, if I--"

"Enough," Azmei interrupted. "I am not so easily offended as all that. Never mind. Tell me about your shop in Meekin, and your trade."

Guira snorted and laid out two plates of grilled fish. "Perhaps Lady Orya will condescend to teach you an appreciation for fine cloth on this voyage," she remarked, and withdrew.

Orya stared after her. "You allow her to speak to you that way?"

"She practically raised me after my mother died," Azmei said. "I should be insulted if Guira were not familiar with me, after all these years. I take it very ill if people slight her." It was meant as a warning, and she saw that Orya realized it.

The other girl bit her lip and reached for her wine glass. "I believe the trade families must have very different customs than the nobility. My mother would never brook insolence from a servant--even a trusted one." She smiled across the table at Azmei. "If I am to teach you about cloth, it seems I have much to learn from you, as well."

Relieved that she would not have to be cross with her new friend, Azmei inclined her head in agreement and took advantage of the moment to ask about the trade agreement Orya hoped to reach with the Ranarri.

That carried them into dessert--rich fried pies stuffed with steaming fruit filling.

After dinner, Orya and Azmei played several hands of cards, until Azmei began hiding yawns. The third time she lifted her cards to her face in an attempt at delicacy, Orya begged her pardon and explained she was feeling fatigued from the excitement of embarkation. Azmei agreed the sea air was quite stimulating, which naturally led to early bedtimes.

As she was undressing for bed, she found herself wishing she had made an effort to learn more about Orya Perslyn before they left Tamnen. She was a pleasing person, but it was difficult to determine whether her personality was one carefully crafted to please, or if she were naturally akin to Azmei.

"Do you like her?" she asked Guira as her maid brushed out her hair.

Guira deliberated for several strokes of the brush. "I cannot yet say. She seems pleasant, but confined quarters often lead people to assume familiarity that would not otherwise be proper. Perhaps that is why she has me wrong-footed."

"Or perhaps it isn't."

"It isn't my place to say," Guira demurred.

"Well, observe her. If you make up your mind about her, let me know."

"Of course, my lady."

Azmei huffed a laugh and kissed Guira on the cheek. "Good night, my dear."

Guira's hand ghosted up to stroke Azmei's hair. "Sweet dreams, my princess."

CHAPTER EIGHTEEN

Azmei did not lie awake long that night. The rolling of the ship was unfamiliar, but somehow comforting. Her bunk was wide and luxurious, built right into the wall. She had been given the richly appointed stern cabin; the *Victorious* was the royal family's ship, and her bunk boasted a thick feather mattress and a dozen pillows. A white, silk curtain hung around it, giving her the feeling she was wrapped in a cloud. Sinking in downy softness, rocked by gentle swells, Azmei slipped easily into sleep.

The next morning she met with Destar Thorne. She liked the Lord-Captain's gruff, no-nonsense manner. He observed all the proper courtesies, but in a way that made her feel it was all merely part of his job, rather than obsequious fawning.

The captain's cabin was not as luxurious as Azmei's, but she found it more inviting. Maps--no, she corrected herself; at sea they were called charts--were tacked to the wood paneled walls, and a large, heavy desk took center stage. Destar was a clever man, perhaps even a genius; he had won two major sea battles against the Strid before he was twenty. The war had been more heated back then, and the Navy had accepted volunteers as young as fourteen, though that particular practice had since been abolished.

Enclosed cabinets along the walls held, she knew, leather-bound tomes and ledgers. She knew some of those tomes well, though most of them had been left behind in Destar's office in the palace. Destar had spent hours coaching the young princess through strategy lessons and military economics; he had made the subjects appealing by creating detailed scenarios for her to puzzle out. Iron brackets over the window held crossed sabers and a brace of pistols.

As soon as she arrived for their meeting, they went over the security arrangements for at least the dozenth time. Azmei had pored over diagrams of the *Victorious* so she would know all its hiding places in the event of an attack. If she were honest, she would like to be useful in an emergency, rather than playing the role of baggage to be stowed in a hiding place until the thieves were gone.

"There are those who don't wish for peace. Some of them will do anything to see that we reach no agreement that might eventually lead to a treaty between Tamnen and Strid." Destar tapped his fingers against his leg, gazing off at a corner of the cabin.

"This is only a tiny step in that direction," Azmei protested. "Amethir's empire is strong, but they already take Strid ships when they can. And the Strid started attacking Amethirian vessels once the peace talks convened in Ranarr. They won't stop attacking Tamnese troops, marriage to Amethir or no marriage."

"Aye, but when Razem's sister is queen of the greatest nation in the eastern world, he will have more bargaining power than your father has." Destar rubbed his chin. "Princess, you know there are those, even close to your father, who would prefer to stay at odds with Strid. Some of the marcher lords like the raiding. They can seize commodities and treasures they would not have access to, were we friends with our neighbors."

Azmei sighed. "It's a stupid reason for people to go on killing each other."

"I said nothing about intelligence or honor," Destar said. "War rarely involves either." He sighed. "I may be good at fighting, but I cannot pretend to enjoy it much."

"There is no denying your skills are useful." She swallowed what she was going to say next. No amount of wishing would stop the killing in the Kreyden District.

When Destar was satisfied of both her comprehension and her cooperation, he allowed the discussion to be steered the direction she wished.

"Do you know anything about Vistaren?" she asked.

"Only what most folk know, my lady. He is a tidy man with elegant taste and no apparent love of warfare." Azmei darted a look at the captain, but his bluff, honest face held neither hatred nor dislike. He held a piece of seaglass, stroking a thumb over its smooth, opaque surface.

Azmei knew the Amethirian stormwitches used seaglass in their witchery. Many people knew, because of the trade it created. In Tamnen the trade was prohibited because of the potential for mayhem, if not outright sabotage--a single stormwitch with seaglass from Tamnese ports might wield little power, but several of them working in concert might destroy a port town with almost no warning. The prohibitions led to a brisk black market, which her father attempted to stamp out whenever possible. Yet another difficulty, Azmei thought, that might fade if her marriage was successful.

"Have you ever met him?" Azmei asked, returning her thoughts to her husband-to-be.

"No, my lady. He was not present for the peace delegation last year. He had agreed previously to entertain the notion of a marriage alliance, and with the king insisting on being present himself, I suspect the Amethirian Council felt it prudent to have the heir on home soil."

"Or the queen," Azmei murmured. "Perhaps she wanted to keep her only son safe if her husband was risking himself. Vistaren *is* the only heir, isn't he?"

Destar nodded. They were silent for several breaths. "My lady is good and noble to agree to this."

Azmei shrugged. "I knew I would have to marry someone someday. It might as well be for a good reason. And it has always been my desire to serve my brother somehow. Perhaps, with this treaty, he will be able to finally defeat the Strid, or at least reclaim the Kreyden District." She didn't admit that she hoped they would at least like each other. She could at least protect that much of her dignity.

Destar grunted. "May the Great Mother hear your words and wake from her slumber," he murmured. It was an automatic turn of phrase; no one expected any of the gods to pay attention to humans these days. But Azmei occasionally found herself wishing that the Great Mother *would* wake from her slumber. Perhaps what this world needed was a good shaking.

"Indeed," she murmured. She stood up. Destar's chair scraped as he stood half a beat later. Azmei smiled. "I will let you return to your duties. Thank you for your time, Captain Destar."

Destar bowed and she left.

Orya leaned on the ship's rail and watched the City-State of Ranarr grow larger with every roll of the ship. She had enjoyed the sea voyage, and the past two weeks had acquired a timeless feel to them, lulling her into complacency. Half believing the voyage would never end, she had allowed herself to relax into friendship with Princess Azmei.

She should be flogged for allowing herself to care about the princess. It was one thing to like her; after all, a lot of folk were likable. But caring about the princess as a human, as a friend, was going too far. In trade, there was no room for friendship. Orya meant to profit from the princess' wedding, and if the princess chose not to ratify the treaty, the necessary leverage would vanish.

There was no room for failure. If she failed, she might as well not return home. Orya had been the best and brightest of her age group in the family. Returning empty-handed to Tamnen was unthinkable. Once she fulfilled her own tally, she could begin working against Yarro's tally. Her brother would never have to join the trade he was so ill-suited to.

She took a deep breath and held it for a few moments before releasing it. She had always been ambitious and proud, and in the past, it had made her hasty. This assignment would be the biggest test of her patience yet. She must not fail either the test or the assignment.

"The White Stone is beautiful, is she not?" said a gruff voice. Orya glanced over as Captain Destar Thorne joined her at the rail. "I've made this trip dozens of times, yet I still catch my breath every time I see her towering out of the bay."

"The White Stone? Is that what they call Ranarr?" Orya knew better, but she was unsure of Thorne. She didn't know how to speak to him. He seemed to be a respected servant of the princess, but it was possible too that he was a trusted friend or advisor. She didn't want to say the wrong thing and offend him.

"Not the city," he said, "the island, the stone itself. It's limestone straight through, but the miracle of the White Stone is that she has fresh water. That's the only thing allowed the city-state to get as powerful as it has. No one could lay siege to that island, with its water supply unreachable by the sea. Of course, the water has trynen in it, which is what gives the Ranarri that funny chalk-colored skin. But I'd say it's a fair bargain."

Orya looked over at him. "What about starving them out?" She wondered if Thorne viewed everything through the eyes of a military engagement. Then again, he did have an appreciation for beauty, so perhaps not.

He scratched his ear. "I suppose they could do, but there is some crop production there, and it would be hard to cut them off from fish. Folk say there are sea caves underneath the stone."

Orya looked back at the white limestone monolith towering several hundred feet in the air. It seemed almost to loom above them, dwarfing the *Victorious* along with several other ships approaching and leaving Ranarri Bay. "I wonder anyone dared to live on the island, if it has sea caves. Are they not afraid of it crumbling into the sea?"

"Don't know. But it's been there hundreds of years, so I don't guess it's likely to." His expression was open, unveiled. She still was unsure if he were merely humoring her or if he were enjoying their conversation.

"And the crops? How do they grow anything up there?"

"There's a layer of soil in some places. Not many, but enough. They don't rely on the crops, anyway. A lot of it's herbs that go well with fish." He snorted. "They eat a damn lot of fish."

Orya laughed.

They were silent for a few minutes, watching the approaching shore. Just as Orya was thinking about excusing herself to her cabin, Thorne sighed. "I know you and the princess have become friendly on this voyage," he said.

She turned to stare at him, but he wasn't looking at her. He was still leaning on the rail, staring at the rock island. Orya let out a faint noise of acknowledgement.

"I'm grateful. Our princess is a brave woman who loves her country, but she has looked melancholy of late. It cannot be easy, crossing an ocean to marry a stranger."

Orya slid her eyes away. "I imagine so."

"She does it out of duty to her people and her family. Yet I would see her happy as well."

"True happiness lies in serving your family," Orya said. "She will see that in time." Orya had.

"Aye..." Thorne said slowly. "It may be as you say."

They did not speak again until he excused himself to supervise the navigation into Ranarr Bay.

part four
ranarr

Chapter Nineteen

Azmei would have preferred a quiet arrival upon Ranarr. Her legs wobbled as she stepped off the *Victorious*, and she fought the impulse to see if anyone had noticed. The university appeared to have sent a welcoming committee. The various gray-skinned men and women seemed pleased to receive a wayward Tamnese princess, but several of them had the expressionless faces of Diplomats. She wondered if any of these had brokered the peace treaty that brought her here.

She got through the formal greetings and introductions and delivered her father's compliments to the Ranarri. By the time everyone was finished being pleasant at one another, her legs felt steadier.

At home, the privileged and wealthy rode in horse-drawn carriages. Here, with so many levels of the city built along the steep contours of the White Stone, everyone used chairs with carrying harnesses. The harnesses allowed one person to be carried by a team of four people up the many broad steps and sweeping ramps leading from the harbor to the university. Their guards walked before and after each chair.

All the buildings they passed seemed to be built of white limestone. Was it harvested from the White Stone herself? Some of the houses were painted, but most were left unadorned. Azmei couldn't remember if plain dress was favored by all Ranarri, or merely the Diplomats. She had never met any other sort of Ranarri-born person, and though she had read about the city-state, she had forgotten.

"Princess, would you care for a tepid tea? It is a great refresher." One of the servants had come alongside her, holding a cup high enough that Azmei, at shoulder height, could reach it.

She didn't want tepid tea. "Thank you," she said, accepting the cup. She sipped once, proud not to have spilled it. It had an odd aftertaste; after another sip, she identified it as anise.

"May I offer you anything else?" the man asked. "Seedcakes or fish rolls?"

"Thank you, no." Azmei hoped it wasn't rude to refuse, but the thought of eating during the chair ride—though a surprisingly smooth one—seemed too difficult.

The man bowed and took his leave. Azmei was left to enjoy the rest of the ride listening to the murmured conversations of the city itself.

When they arrived at the university, Azmei and Guira were shown to their quarters, and finally Azmei could relax her shoulders and breathe deeply again. It was ridiculous for her to feel so anxious in the company of the Diplomats—of all the people she would encounter over the next several weeks, the Diplomats were most likely to respect her, since she was sacrificing her personal freedom for peace.

"Did you know the Ranarri worship a god who loves peace?" Azmei asked, tugging off one shoe and looking over at her handmaid, who was unpacking their trunks.

"I believe everyone knows that, my lady," said the unflappable Guira. "Are you considering converting? I am not certain the Amethirians revere the peace god quite so highly."

"Mmm. I suppose not. Too bad. I'd rather fancied the thought I might be a living sacrifice to the peace god."

Guira snorted. "You shouldn't mock the gods. Even the ones you don't worship yourself." She hung a dress carefully in the wardrobe. "It is a wondrous thought, though, that peace might be such a holy thing. I fear our people would be poor postulants of such a god."

Azmei hummed. How would one even worship such a god? Sit in silence until the god blessed you? But of course not. Clearly the Ranarri Diplomats worshiped by making peace whenever possible, just as they had managed to find an accord between Tamnen and Amethir. The Diplomats traveled wherever they wished, revered or at least respected by all they met. They never showed emotions, according to all the stories, and they were gifted in reaching compromises. That must be how they worshiped—by living out the peace of their god.

"My lady is very quiet. Have I offended you?"

Azmei looked up. Guira had paused in her unpacking and was studying her, dress draped forgotten over one arm. Azmei forced a laugh.

"Of course not. I'm only tired. I love the sea, but all that salt air wears one out. Will you fetch me a light lunch to eat here? And fetch a bit of gossip while you're about it. Something to distract me."

Guira went obediently off while Azmei wandered the suite of rooms, enjoying the feel of cool stone under her bare toes. When Guira returned with a spread of cheese, breads, fish, and fruit, Azmei settled down for a meal.

"The *Dawn Star* has not yet arrived from Amethir," Guira informed her. "It is expected any day now, carrying Prince Vistaren and captained by none other than the Storm Petrel herself."

Azmei tried to suppress a childish thrill of excitement, though they had all but known. "Dzornaea? Do you think I will be able to meet her?"

Guira's silence drew out for longer than necessary. "My lady, if you find the prince acceptable, Captain Dzornaea's ship will carry us to your new home."

The bread in Azmei's mouth suddenly felt like ash. Of course. How foolish. She swallowed that mouthful and took another bite. She didn't trust her voice.

To be fair, Azmei had never heard anyone claim the Ra-narri Diplomats knew how to throw a good party. That reticence did not, she felt, excuse the fact that her welcome banquet had consisted of an extra invocation to the god of peace before each meal. Oh, there had been dancing, but it had been a display of measurement and distance, couples circling each other at arm's length without touching or making eye contact. The Ranarri, Azmei had decided, were an extraordinarily dull lot.

"I don't know much about parties, but I'm bored," she whispered to Orya, who was seated on her right. On her left was a Diplomat. He was handsome enough despite his chalk-gray skin, but he had merely lifted one eyebrow in greeting and offered a series of platitudes designed to set her at ease. Instead, they were setting her teeth on edge.

Orya giggled and lifted her fan to cover the emotion on her face. At least the girl knew something about Ranarri manners; around the Diplomats, men and women alike used elaborate fans for modesty. Showing emotion in conversation, while not actually indecent, caused a great deal of discomfort for all involved.

"Ooh, look," Orya said, leaning in and aiming her fan at the terrace. "There's a ship coming in to harbor."

The Diplomat on Azmei's other side had keen hearing. He lifted both eyebrows. "That is not just any ship. It is the *Dawn Star*, bearing Prince Vistaren's contingent."

Azmei's stomach flipped unpleasantly. Her husband-to-be was on that ship. She stood. "Pray excuse me," she said, smoothing her skirt down. Orya jumped up and followed her away from the table to the terrace wall.

"Highness?" she murmured. "Are you well?"

"Of course!" Azmei kept her gaze on the ship. "I wanted to look at the ship. She looks fast, doesn't she?"

"I don't know a lot about ships," Orya reminded her.

"Oh, of course." Azmei fluttered her fan, tracing the silhouette of the *Dawn Star*'s mast and sails. From this high up, there was no discerning among the figures, but Azmei could imagine the captain shouting orders.

"When will you meet the prince?" Orya murmured. "Have you chosen the dress you will wear?"

Azmei laughed. It was good to be reminded of Orya's interest in the matter. "We meet formally the day after tomorrow, and yes, I have my dress ready." She and Guira had argued about the dress, but eventually Azmei had acquiesced to Guira's wishes. She would wear a fancy green silk with golden laces. The brown silk tunic was simply not formal enough. "If the meeting goes well and we desire to move forward, we will set up a series of meetings, as I understand it. At that point, I will go dress shopping. It may be there will be a sudden demand for Tamnese silk."

Orya smiled. "I foresee that I shall be busy the next two days, my lady."

The *Dawn Star* had all her sails reefed and was approaching the dock, where hands stood by ready to receive mooring lines. Feeling abruptly better, Azmei returned to the party.

CHAPTER TWENTY

VISTAREN STUMBLED AS HE stepped from the deck of the *Dawn Star* to the gangway. He swore mentally and took two more quick steps to catch himself. Lozarr had warned him that after a week at sea he might be unsteady on land. It was just his luck that he had tripped and made a fool of himself as he arrived at Ranarr.

At least there wasn't much of a crowd on the docks.

They had arrived at the same time as one other ship, but had docked too far for the disembarkation of each ship to interfere with the other. There was a small group of people approaching them, still some distance away.

Vistaren couldn't help grinning at Lozarr despite the churning of his stomach. He'd never been anywhere but

Amethir, and finally he was able to see some of the rest of the world.

Lozarr grinned back at him, though Vistaren could tell his heart wasn't in it. Arama was remaining behind to "settle the crew," which was probably the main reason for Lo's demeanor.

Behind them, Stormwitch Kinnet followed, her bag hitched up over one shoulder. Vistaren knew she had more luggage than that, as he did himself, but he admired that she was willing to carry her own bag. Perhaps it was filled with valuable seaglass for her witchery.

"That's one of the Diplomats coming to greet us," Lozarr said, pulling Vistaren's attention back to the front.

"How can you tell?" Lo's eyesight was obviously keener than his. Vistaren peered at the group approaching—two men, one in Amethirian regalia, and one wearing robes of muted colors, though in the deepening dusk, Vistaren couldn't tell what color they actually were. Behind them were several chair-bearers.

"The robes. That cut and color indicate a Master Diplomat, which is appropriate for greeting a visitor of your rank." Lo's voice was pitched low.

"That fellow next to him is our ambassador, isn't he? Renat?" Vistaren matched Lo's volume.

"I think so. I've never met him in person."

Vistaren continued down the gangplank, relieved when he had his feet on solid ground again—or at least, as solid as a dock could be. He watched the other party approach.

The man in regalia swept a deep bow as soon as he reached them. "Your Royal Highness, it is an honor. Welcome to Ranarr."

"Ambassador Renat, I am pleased to meet you," Vistaren said. He gestured for the man to straighten.

Renat was a tall man with dark hair worn in multiple braids. His olive complexion, indicating Crelin heritage, had clearly been affected by the time he'd spent here. Over the course of several years, he had consumed enough of the trynen-laced water of Ranarr to lend him some of the chalky gray overtone to his skin. His gaze was direct and his smile friendly, but there was a tension in his broad shoulders.

"I hope your journey was a good one," he said.

Vistaren drew in a breath, uncertain of the best response. It had certainly been a memorable and instructive one, but he didn't think it wise to go into all the details here. "It was very educational, Lord Ambassador," he said after a moment, and heard Lo's faint snort behind him.

The ambassador's eyebrows rose, and it seemed to Vistaren that he had almost glanced over his shoulder before catching himself. "Had you never been to sea before, highness?"

"Only near the coastline," Vistaren said. He smiled at Renat. "It is very different, traversing the deeps and seeing all the sea's moods."

Footsteps behind him told him Kinnet was approaching. Vistaren stepped to one side, giving the ambassador room to greet the others.

"Greetings, General Algot," the man said. He bowed again to Kinnet. "Greetings, Stormwitch..."

He trailed off, obviously expecting Kinnet to supply her name. For an awkward moment there was only the sound of waves slapping against the docks and laughter as the other ship disgorged its crew. Then Vistaren realized Kinnet hadn't seen Renat's face as he spoke.

"This is Stormwitch Kinnet Ardelis," he informed the man quickly. "Please rise and speak clearly to her face. She cannot hear you."

Renat straightened quickly, a flush darkening his cheeks despite his trynen exposure. "My deepest apologies, Stormwitch Ardelis. Welcome to Ranarr."

Vistaren was pleased that the man did as he was instructed without raising his voice or over-emphasizing his words. Either the man had met deaf people in the past or he was simply well-trained. Either way, Vistaren's estimation of the ambassador went up.

"Thank you, Ambassador Renat," Kinnet said. Her atonal voice was a little loud, but well modulated.

"Have you been to Ranarr before?" Renat asked her. He darted a quick glance over his shoulder, and Vistaren's curiosity increased.

"I am aware of the strictures in place here," she told him. Her expression gave no hint as to how she felt about those strictures. Vistaren made a mental note to ask her about them later.

"Ah, good, good." Renat beamed at her. "We wouldn't want to have any misunderstandings as we negotiate the prince's nuptials."

Vistaren tried to ignore the sudden lurch of his stomach.

He was spared having to think of a response when the Diplomat stepped forward. He, too, bore the physical traits of a Crelin Amethirian, except that his skin was a pure chalky gray color. Now that he was closer, Vistaren could see his robes were of a rich brown.

"Allow me also to welcome Your Highness to our nation. Ranarr is pleased to host you and your companions." His voice was almost as strange to Vistaren's ear as Kinnet's. There was little tonal variation in his speech. It leached any emotion from the words.

Vistaren merely nodded.

"I am Master Diplomat Revalis Ingan," the Diplomat continued. "You may perhaps recognize the name because of my brother—"

"Balahar, yes!" Vistaren interrupted, and then felt himself blush at having interrupted the man. But there was nothing for it. He pushed on, forcing himself to smile. "I see the resemblance now that you say it."

"It is kind of Your Highness to say so. I fear our complexions are very different from one another now. He is my elder, and I have been in Ranarr for many years."

"He sent a letter with me," Lozarr said from Vistaren's side.

Ambassador Renat had been glancing around them, his gaze following each person that came anywhere near them. He straightened and gestured to the chair-bearers behind him. "Perhaps we should save some of this until we are at the University," he suggested. At his gesture, the men stepped forward.

"It is a long climb to the University from the docks," Renat went on, "and many new arrivals have been at sea too long for it to be a comfortable one. I arranged for chairs to make the last bit of your journey easier."

Vistaren glanced at Lozarr and found the general looking back at him. There was an odd look in Lo's gray eyes, so Vistaren merely smiled at the ambassador.

"Certainly. I am looking forward to a meal, a bath, and a bed."

The chairs were very smooth, though Vistaren couldn't help feeling sorry for the men who were forced to carry him. He knew he was overfond of his food, and although he enjoyed riding and fencing, his physique was a product of his eating habits. It was probably a good thing chair-carriers weren't in fashion in Amethir. Though the climb from the docks to Maron Palace was nowhere near as steep as this one.

Vistaren had very nearly dozed off when the chair came to a stop. He jolted fully awake and straightened in his chair. They had been carried to the main entrance of the University, which served as the seat of the Ranarri Diplomats and was, as such, the center of power in Ranarr.

It took very little time for them to be settled in comfortable quarters. Renat promised to return in the morning for a full orientation and to go over Vistaren's schedule while they were in Ranarr. Revalis informed them that Princess Azmei and her contingent had already arrived, which set Vistaren's stomach churning again.

And then Vistaren, Lozarr, and Kinnet were alone, with only Vistaren's complement of guards and the servants they had brought to get them settled in.

"What do you suppose that was about?" Vistaren said once the door had closed firmly behind Renat and Revalis.

"I've no idea, but I intend to find out," Lozarr replied.

"Perhaps stormwitches here felt our encounter with Singer Qiaru," Kinnet said thoughtfully.

"Would that be allowed under the strictures he mentioned?" Lozarr asked.

"For that matter," Vistaren put in, "what *are* the strictures he mentioned?"

Kinnet shrugged. "No major witcheries are allowed here, if they will affect the weather. No storm-calling, no storm-laying or diverting, nothing like that. Smaller witcheries, and passive ones, such as surfing a storm to follow its progress, or workings to cool or heat an immediate area—sleeping quarters, for example—are acceptable."

"Thank you for knowing that, Kinnet," Vistaren said. "I hadn't given it any consideration, beyond knowing that it's impolite to do major workings in another sovereign nation's territory."

She smiled faintly. "It is part of my duty to know such things, highness."

"And it's part of *my* duty to know what has our ambassador so anxious," Lozarr said. "I shall excuse myself to see about that."

"Certainly," Vistaren said. "But don't stay out too late. We've all earned a good night's rest."

Lozarr spent the better part of an hour talking to the soldiers under his command. He had to send two of them out for civilian clothes, because they hadn't all brought anything that would fit in at a tavern. He hoped he was wasting his time, but it was better to take precautions and feel foolish later than to be caught unawares by something he could have averted.

He didn't know Ambassador Renat, of course, but the king had entrusted the man with finalizing Vistaren's treaty betrothal to Princess Azmei. A heedless or less savvy man wouldn't be given such weighty responsibilities. Renat had at least a decade in the diplomacy game, some of it in Long Coast cities, but at least four of those years here in Ranarr. If Renat was anxious about something, Lozarr wanted to know what it was.

By the time he'd set things in motion, his stomach was grumbling about how long it had been since he'd eaten. He should have taken time for some of the refreshments in Vistaren's apartments, but he didn't want to settle down for the night before Arama came up.

Provided she did come up. He sighed and scrubbed a hand through his hair. It wouldn't surprise him if she stayed with the *Dawn Star* overnight. She didn't show vulnerability easily, but the voyage from Maron had shaken her. There were too many things that had been out of her control, and if there was one thing Arama Dzornaea hated, it was things being out of her control.

First she had been forced to have a stormwitch on her ship—something Arama hadn't allowed since the *Bounder* went down with her first captain and foster father aboard. Then they'd detected that strange thing Kinnet had called a witchery echo, which had turned out to be Stormsinger Qiaru seeking others of his kind. All of that on top of being responsible for the life of Amethir's only prince had been a lot to ask, even of the infamous Storm Petrel.

No, it wouldn't be out of character at all if she chose to sleep in her safe cabin on her ship.

Which was why he was surprised, when he finally headed toward the room assigned to him, to see Arama trudging up the hallway in his direction.

"There you are," he said, forcing false cheer into his voice. "Get the crew all sorted?"

She jerked her head up and then immediately relaxed again, giving him a faint, sheepish smile. "I'll have them keep watch, though all ought to be secure. I know we're as safe in Ranarr as we would be in our own slip at home, but it's good practice for them."

Lozarr didn't answer right away. He was eyeing the short row of stitches on her left cheek. The surgeon had done a neat job. It probably wouldn't even scar, though one more scar to a soldier or a sailor was no big thing.

Arama stopped walking. "What?"

He jerked himself back to attention and shook his head. "I'm probably just being overly paranoid."

"Not likely." She put her hands on her hips, planting her feet wide. It was a stance he was used to seeing, and it usually came just before she issued an order or reprimanded a young midshipman. "Tell me."

Lozarr shrugged. "Ambassador Renat struck me as a bit twitchy. And not just me. Vistaren noticed it."

She grunted. "He's a sharp lad." Then she paused, shook her head, and said, "A sharp man. He's full grown, for all he seems young to me."

"He's inexperienced still," Lo said, feeling an upswelling of affection for his prince. "But he has good training and good instincts."

"He must, if he caught on to a twitchy ambassador. Renat's been doing this for a while. He wouldn't have obvious tells." Arama tilted her head. "And I'm sure you're not just sitting about brooding over it without taking any action."

Lo grinned. "I've a few of my soldiers dressed in plain clothes. They'll hit some of the nearby taverns in pairs, see if they can hear anything that catches their interest."

"It might have nothing to do with the prince."

"That doesn't ease my mind as much as you might think," Lo said ruefully. "That stormsinger didn't have anything to do with Vistaren either, but he could have wrecked us all the same."

"Point." Arama yawned and stretched. She blinked a couple of times, scratching her side. "Well, whatever it is, you'll uncover it. No sense borrowing a storm in dry season."

"Mmm." Lo studied her for a moment. "Want a hot drink before bed?"

She raised an eyebrow. "If by hot drink you mean spiced rum and citrus, aye. But if you're going to offer me hot tea and milk, I think I'll pass."

He laughed and tilted his head toward his door in invitation. "Ranarri take their tea tepid, remember?"

Arama shuddered. "Don't remind me."

As soon as they were inside, she tugged off her boots. Lo hid a smile as he turned to the cabinet, where earlier he had noted several bottles of spirits, along with tea leaves and a few syrups. He was glad he'd thought earlier to ask one of the Ranarri attendants to bring an assortment of food. It was a sight better than offering trail rations, though he knew Arama wouldn't have complained.

His room was comfortable without being so small they had to sit on the bed together. There was a table and two chairs, the food and drink cabinet, a low sofa, and a narrow bed. As he cased his gaze over it, the bed called out to him. He was exhausted, but he was unwilling to pass up a chance to spend more time in Arama's company.

She settled on the sofa and stretched with a satisfied sigh. "As much as I love the sea, I don't mind having a few days when I don't have to be on watch or in command," she admitted.

Lo gave her a look of mock astonishment as he lit a burner to heat water. "Arama Dzornaea not wanting to be in command?" he said.

"Hush, you," she said, glaring in a half-hearted manner. "This was not exactly a routine run from Maron City to Ranarr."

"At least no one was firing cannons at us." Lo opened two bottles, sniffing at them, before he located the citrus spirit Ranarris distilled. It mixed well with spiced rum and honey, and it was a lovely drink to have before bed.

"Truth."

She picked a handful of nuts and dates out of a bowl on the table. For a time there was silence, except for the hissing of the burner and the snap of Arama cracking nut shells. Once he'd fixed them each a drink, Lo settled next to her on the sofa, careful to leave her plenty of space.

"Not that I'm complaining about this fare," Arama said through a mouthful of food, "but I've been looking forward to good Ranarri food all week. The tea's not much, but their food... I aim to eat my own weight in heartfruit and seedcakes while we're here."

"And the fish rolls," Lo agreed. "Especially those ones with grape leaves."

"Mm, why don't we do that in Amethir?" Arama agreed. She took another handful of nuts. "You've been to

Ranarr a couple of times, haven't you? Anything you're looking forward to?"

"The market," he said promptly. "Especially the spice market."

"You and your plants," she said, grinning at him.

"Not just the plants," he said, his cheeks heating. "I like the smells of the spice market, too."

"No, it's nice, actually." Arama took a long sip of her drink and leaned back. "Here you are, consummate warrior and commander, and you've a soft spot for pretty flowers."

Was she making fun of him? He'd always been interested in plants. His grandmother had been good at growing and making herbal remedies, which was perhaps how his interest had started. He supposed it wasn't quite as manly as the hunting and fisticuffs many officers passed their time with.

Arama flapped a hand at him. "No, I mean it. Some of these military folk I've met, they're single minded. Determined to kill folk for their work and for their pleasure. It's boring as week old salt fish. You, though, you do more than spend your every waking hour focused on how to be more deadly." She took another sip of her drink and gave him a lazy smile.

Lo eyed her, not sure what to think. She'd seen him sketching over the years, making note of new plants he saw, especially if they had any medicinal properties. He didn't make a secret of his botanical interests, but he'd never realized she'd given it much thought.

"So what's your favorite flower, then?" Arama asked. She drained her cup and poured another, then held it out to top off Lo's.

"Not a flower, actually," he said. "Well, it *does* flower, but not in a showy way. The flowers are clusters of tiny blossoms in purple and green, and they don't have a pleasant smell. But the dragonheart vine is a fascinating plant."

He paused, but she nodded for him to go on.

"It grows in places like the Sandswamp, warm and wet locations, though it can be cultivated in a hothouse, if it's kept humid enough. I know one fellow back in Maron City who arranged to have a stormwitch tend his every few days. She can alter the humidity in his hothouse."

"Huh." Arama drained her cup again, and Lo wondered suddenly if she'd had enough to eat for the amount of rum she was putting away. He held out the bowl of nuts, but she picked out two dates and waved it away. "So why's it your favorite?"

With a mental shrug, Lo took a sip of his own drink. "It's a creeping vine, and in the right conditions it grows so quickly it's almost like a serpent rather than a plant. The smell of the flower attracts insects, and the leaves of the vine curl around them, trapping them."

"It eats them?"

"It does." Lo grinned at her delight. "In fact, the vine constricts small mammals if they get close enough. Mice and so on."

"Bloody vicious." Arama grinned back at him.

Lo shrugged. "Just about anything has defenses."

"That's different from luring things in and killing them," she pointed out. She poured her cup half full and tossed it back. She set her cup down and snuggled back into the sofa, tipping her head back and watching him from half-closed eyes.

"Look at roses and their thorns, though," Lo said, wondering if she was planning to settle in for the night.

She yawned. "Not much for roses, m'self. These dragonheart vines sound more my style."

That statement didn't surprise him in the least. "We really ought to get some sleep. We'll have a full day tomorrow, like as not."

"M'good here." She yawned again and tilted sideways just a little.

"You might not be later," he muttered, but the only reply he got was a faint snore.

Well. He certainly hadn't intended to lure her into his room to seduce her, but he also hadn't expected her to fall asleep on him. He wondered suddenly if the healer had given her any painkillers before turning her loose. If her easetea and rum were interacting, that would explain why she'd faded on him so quickly.

With a rueful smirk, Lo shifted a little further out of Arama's space. He turned off the spirit burner, dragged a blanket off the bed to cover them both, and closed his eyes.

CHAPTER TWENTY-ONE

GENERAL LOZARR ALGOT WOKE to the sound of his door closing. He tensed and sat up, reaching for the dagger he kept under his pillow—but the room was empty. The scent of gunpowder, coffee, and salt still lingered in the air, though, and he recognized Arama's scent. They'd sat up late talking, and Lo had obviously dozed off.

The pale light of dawn was peeking in his window—had Arama fallen asleep in the chair? With a groan, he rubbed his hand over his face and then forced himself to sit up. He was awake, so he might as well start his day.

Once he'd consumed enough coffee to keep his eyelids open and the throbbing of his head at bay, Lo went looking for his charge Prince Vistaren. He found him in a little courtyard full of peaceflowers. Vistaren held a practice blade in one hand and was going through the forms carefully. He wasn't a bad swordsman, but he had no particular love of the sword—or any type of violence. He loved horses, though, and it was during long rides across the countryside of Amethir that Lo and Vistaren had first bonded.

"Your highness," Lo said, bowing.

"Rot," Vistaren said, dropping his sword. He turned and scowled at Lozarr. "You startled me."

Lo raised his eyebrows. "The university at Ranarr is likely the safest place in the world, your highness," he said, keeping his tone bland.

"Oh, don't 'your-highness' me," Vistaren said. "I wasn't enjoying myself, anyway. I'm off form, and I know it. I can hardly walk in a straight line after all those days at sea."

Lo grinned. "Then I have just the remedy. I thought you'd like to see the market."

"Would I!" Vistaren perked up. "I want to try all the food and scour through the booksellers. And I want to buy rugs for my apartments back home," he added, as if in afterthought.

The apartments he might soon be sharing, Lo thought, provided the meeting with Princess Azmei of Tamnen went well tomorrow.

"Perhaps you'll find another little gift or two for the princess," he suggested.

When Vistaren's face fell, Lo regretted it. He opened his mouth to rework the suggestion into something less terrifying, but Vistaren visibly squared his shoulders.

"You're right, I should. I know Arama said the letter-writing set was a good gift, but..."

Lo shrugged. "Inoffensive, at least, since you've been corresponding with the princess. It is a bit on the, er, bland side, though."

"Boring," Vistaren said, and sighed. "Just as she'll probably find me boring. But on the other hand, better she know it from the beginning."

"You do yourself a discredit," Lo chided. "You're a fine young man, and you will be a great king. I have every confidence in you," he added, lowering his voice. "And I'm certain that Princess Azmei will like you at least as much as I do."

It wouldn't be enough, of course. Vistaren had never actually told Lozarr that he loved men and not women, but he had never actually hidden it, either. Lo had seen Vistaren's admiring glances at the brawny young men in the king's guard. He had also seen Vistaren's eyes shining a little too brightly when he looked at Lozarr from time to time.

Thankfully, that seemed to have passed. Lo didn't mind it, but he hated having to hurt the prince, and Lo hadn't been designed to look on men as he did on women.

"Thank you, my friend," Vistaren said. His hand gripped Lo's briefly before he pulled away. "Let me wash off this sweat and we'll go to the market. Bring Arama. My father ordered me to go nowhere without at least two guards."

The Ranarri market was actually a series of markets built in stair steps down the steep contours of the White Stone. The university market was closest to the top, positioned for the convenience of the diplomats and scholars who governed Ranarr.

Lozarr, who'd always had a keen interest in plants, enjoyed the exotic flowers and herbs, though he spent more time watching for any possible threats than he did shopping. Vistaren was clearly having a good time poking through the various texts and maps. Arama mostly looked bored, but then, as the king's most notorious privateer, she had traveled more of the world than either of them.

When Lo found a stall selling things carved from the bones of seadragons, he knew he had to buy something for Arama. There was a fine selection of knives in amongst the combs and pens and hand mirrors. A dagger made of seadragon bone would make a fine set with the siren's tooth he'd given her for Longnight more than a decade earlier. The sea dragon bone was lighter than tea but darker than alabaster, and the hilt was wrapped with dyed turquoise leather.

Lo bargained the merchant down to an acceptable price and tucked the knife into his jacket. He had switched to summer weight cloth, but his shirt was still damp with sweat. He was inland bred, and Ranarr's island humidity didn't agree with him.

When he caught up with Vistaren and Arama, she was bargaining with a fish roll merchant. Vistaren caught Lo's gaze and rolled his eyes.

"I got us some seed cakes and fruit and wine, but the captain said I shouldn't drink anything too heady without having meat in my belly."

Lo snorted. "You mean she got the wine and you insisted we needed real food to go with it."

Vistaren shrugged, his face innocent, and Lo knew he'd hit on the truth. Vistaren seemed to have developed a healthy case of hero-worship for the infamous Storm Petrel. Not that Lo could blame him, he thought ruefully as he watched her argue with the merchant.

Arama was strong and a bit short-tempered, but she was one of the bravest people Lo had ever known. She loved the sea and scorned the use of stormwitches on her ship, which in Lo's mind made her a better sailor than those who paid stormwitches to channel the wind for them. He found himself grinning as she turned and came triumphantly back to them. It also didn't hurt that she fenced better than Lo and knew more bawdy songs than he did.

They found a seating area screened from the rest of the market by a large, limestone planter containing date palms and some sort of flowering shrub. A small fountain burbled in the center of the area, providing a pleasant counterpoint to the shouting in the market.

For a time they sat in silence, sharing their food. The fish rolls turned out to be spicier than Lo had expected, with a pleasant bite to them. The wine Arama picked provided the perfect counter to the rolls, and the seed cakes were aromatic and sweet.

As they were finishing their meal, a tall, burly man with the rich brown skin and gray eyes of Sterr ethnicity approached them. Lo guessed the bulge at one hip was a purse rather than a weapon, but in case he was wrong, he interposed himself between the man and Vistaren. The man moved his hands both away from his sides.

"I can see you're an Amethirian by birth," Lo said. "Who are you, and what do you want?"

The man glanced at Lo, his eyes widening tentatively, and then he looked back at the prince. His bow was a little rough, but courteous enough. "Prince Vistaren," he said. His voice crackled like a fire, but he spoke quietly. "Your subjects living in Ranarr have been eagerly anticipating your visit. I would beg a moment of your time."

"What would you ask of your prince?" Vistaren said. His voice sounded cordial.

Lo darted a glance at Arama to see if she was watching the man. She'd shifted her stance, ready to intercept the man if he attacked. Lo turned enough so he could see Vistaren's face as well as the stranger's.

"My name is Yadian Shemma, your highness, and I'm the—well, you might call me the elder of the Amethirians who live on this rock. And we have issues to air with you."

"Issues?" Vistaren's tone had cooled. "And have your issues been brought before our esteemed father?"

The man ducked his head. "Your highness, we've had no chance to air these grievances to the king. The Amethirian ambassador sits in the university and won't meet with us. Says he's got more important things to worry about."

Vistaren arched an eyebrow. "He is attempting to broker a marriage treaty, after all," he said, but there was humor creeping into his tone.

That made Shemma flinch. He bowed more deeply—and also a bit more clumsily—and said, "Many apologies, your highness. I meant no disrespect. But we've been waiting a long time, and when we heard you was coming here to meet the Tamnese princess..."

"You saw an opportunity," Vistaren murmured. "Well." He was silent for a time, gazing at the man's face.

Lo knew Vistaren doubted himself at times; he'd been too young to fight in the war that had been the making of Lo's military career. Vistaren was a keen judge of character, though, and Lo had confidence in his young friend.

After a long moment, Vistaren sighed. "Well," he said again, "Ambassador Renat might be busy arranging my marriage, but I find myself with a bit of time on my hands. I am willing to hear your grievances. You understand, I will not undermine the ambassador's authority here. That is not the purpose of my visit to Ranarr."

"Of course, your highness. Thank you." Shemma bowed again.

"Have you listed your grievances in writing?" Vistaren asked.

"We have, your highness. We've sent several letters to the ambassador, as I said—"

Vistaren waved a hand. "We will hear nothing against our ambassador, Shemma. Give us your documents."

Shemma reached into his tunic slowly, his gaze on Lozarr now instead of Vistaren. He wasn't stupid, Lo thought; if Lo suspected him of reaching for a weapon, the man would be dead in a heartbeat. When Shemma drew out a packet of papers, Lo nodded.

"Your highness, may my people and I call on you at the university?"

"No," Vistaren said, his voice thoughtful. "No, I should like to see the Amethirian quarter. We will call on you, Shemma. Two days from now." He glanced at Arama.

"There's a fine tavern called the Chatty Raven, highness," she volunteered. "I've had many a merry meal there."

"Very well. We will call upon you at the Chatty Raven in two days," Vistaren said.

"Thank you, your highness."

Lo stepped closer to the man. "Now be off," he ordered. "You've taken enough of the prince's time this day."

Shemma met his gaze, and Lo could see the man's resentment, but Lo's visit to Ranarr had just gotten much more complicated thanks to this man. He would have to place a watch on the Chatty Raven and take steps to ensure it was a secure location. Shemma bobbed another bow and left.

"That wasn't necessary," Vistaren murmured, though there was no censure in his voice.

"He presumed a great deal," Lo replied, his voice just as quiet. "I will not see you treated with less respect than you deserve."

"Than my rank deserves, you mean." Vistaren bit into a fish roll, his brows drawn together.

"I meant what I said," Lo corrected. He folded his arms, staring at Vistaren until the prince sighed, hunched his shoulders, and nodded.

"You'll come with me, won't you, Lo?" he said. "When I meet with Shemma and the, well, whoever has these grievances?"

Lo let his expression soften. "You think I would let you go without me? Your father gave me one task on this trip—to ensure you return safely to your country. I'm not going to let some fellow with 'grievances' jeopardize that."

Vistaren nodded and finished his fish roll. When Lozarr looked up, Arama was watching him, her brows raised and her lips pursed. When he caught her gaze, she looked away.

"We should get back to the university soon," she said gruffly. "The security is better there, should anyone else have grievances to air."

Chapter Twenty-Two

A ZMEI HAD INTENDED TO spend the day after her arrival in Ranarr reading the slender volume of Amethirian history she had packed. It had seemed at the time like a good compromise between resting all day, as Guira wished, and exploring the city, as Azmei preferred.

As usual, her plans bore little resemblance to reality.

Despite her late bedtime the night before, Azmei found herself wide awake and staring at the canopy of her bed when the sky was only the gray of pre-dawn. She tried to go back to sleep, but the bed no longer seemed as comfortable as it had. She shifted and sighed and finally sat up.

She could hear Guira's delicate snore from the outer bed chamber. Good. There was no reason for them both to be wakeful. Azmei took extra care to be quiet as she climbed out of bed.

She hadn't chosen any particular outfit for today, but she already knew she was too restless to sit at a desk all day. She eased open her wardrobe and decided to console herself with the brown silk tunic and split skirt. She supposed it would be irresponsible for her to go exploring alone, but she could at least find herself some breakfast. The university was probably the safest place in the world. While there might be danger away from the university grounds, Azmei felt certain that, within the confines of the walls, she was secure.

The tall, stone passages were all but empty as she made her way from her rooms to the dining area. She smiled at a short woman with blue-black hair who was slipping out of a room. The woman started when she saw Azmei, then gave her a smile with a wry, rueful quality to it. She turned the opposite direction without speaking, and Azmei continued on in search of breakfast. She could smell spiced coffee.

When Azmei appeared in the door to the dining room, a servant was quick to ask what she could bring Azmei. A few minutes later, Azmei was settled in front of a steaming bowl of oat porridge, grapes, and coffee. She looked through a window to a small courtyard as the sun rose. Birds were flitting back and forth, singing and chattering with one another. One flew in to land on Azmei's cup. It pecked idly at the thin clay, ran its beak through its olive and brown plumage, and flew away again. Azmei laughed. This was a type of bird she'd never seen at home. At first the thought excited her. Then she remembered the plaintive sound of doves that usually woke her. A wave of homesickness hit her. What if everything in Amethir was completely unfamiliar to her?

She sipped her coffee. *You know better*, she reminded herself. *They have plenty of things we have. Horses and hoshni flowers and chocolate. Just because there will be no snow doesn't mean there will be nothing to love in Amethir.*

"There you are." Guira spoke with some asperity. Her handmaid sat across from her. "You shouldn't rise and leave the rooms without me, princess."

"I couldn't sleep, and I was hungry." Azmei took a bite of porridge.

"Then you should have wakened me." Guira poured herself a cup of coffee.

"I was glad to see you rest. Besides, I wanted to think."

Guira's eyebrows shot up. "And you can't think because I'm distracting you, is that it?"

Azmei suppressed a twinge of guilt. "That isn't what I meant. I just wanted to be alone for a time."

Guira lowered her gaze to her own coffee cup, her knuckles whitening as she gripped it. "Perhaps I should have told you sooner how difficult this is for me," she murmured. "You cannot think I like having you marry this prince you have never met. I follow you to Amethir because I know of no other way to live than in your service. But I would just as soon serve a happy princess given liberty to pursue her own interests. I would just as soon serve a princess who doesn't feel cast off by her kingdom." She sighed. "I would just as soon serve a princess who was never forced to grow up."

Azmei stared at her. "Guira--"

Guira looked up at her, her lips curving ever-so-slightly. "I think of you as I would my own daughter," she said, closing a hand on Azmei's. "I wish I could protect you from this fate and allow you to read books and explore cities to your heart's content." She squeezed Azmei's hand. "But this is what it is to be a princess."

Azmei swallowed against a sudden lump in her throat. "I know you love me, Guira. And I love you." She squeezed Guira's hand back and sighed. "Very well. You're right. I must grow up. I must cease feeling sorry for myself and look forward to whatever comes next."

To her astonishment, a slow, sly smile curled across Guira's mouth. "Well...perhaps you needn't grow up until tomorrow." She leaned in. "Why don't we explore Ranarr's markets and temples today? I hear the university market has a very fine selection of parchment and pens."

Orya slipped into a narrow alley without a backwards glance. She had already ascertained no one was following her. Obviously Thorne thought her no more than a silly merchant noble, which was exactly what Orya had wished him to think.

The flagstone-paved alley was steep, with buildings so tall and close together they let very little sunlight in. That suited Orya perfectly. With her brown skin, she was un-mistakably *not* a native Ranarri, and while people of all nations were welcome here, it was entirely possible she could be recognized as one of those who came with the Tamnese princess. She was relying on that recognition to help her with her legitimate trade negotiations; her errand in this alley, however, required anonymity.

After all, no one wanted to be identified as the person who had assassinated a royal.

A mangy, skeletal cat scuttled across the alley in front of her, almost making her trip. Orya swore under her breath as she caught her balance. Someone snickered. Orya looked up to see a broad-shouldered woman, arms folded across her chest, leaning in the doorway of a shop. The mangy cat was twining around her ankles.

"Pardon me," Orya said, smoothing her face into an appealing expression. "I am looking for dyer's supplies."

The woman grunted. "You're in the right place." She unfolded her arms to display hands dyed a deep blue. "Step on inside."

Further down the street, a tall, thin man ducked into a door. Something about the movement seemed furtive, which caught Orya's attention. She noted the dark gray cloak swathing him from head to ankle, then dismissed it. There were herb and ink sellers along this tiny street as well as dyers.

Orya followed the woman into the shop. "I have a list," she said. "My craft master wrote it out for me."

"Give it here," the woman said. She scanned the list quickly. "I don't have them all. No foxglove, and only a little deathleaf. But I've plenty of bloodroot and wolf lichen. And of course verdigris."

Orya watched in silence as the woman gathered her order. Trading in textiles was an excellent cover. Plenty of dyes and some of the mordants used to color cloth were poisonous. Orya's skills were not limited to poisoning, but it was convenient to be able to travel with some of the tools of her trade without raising any eyebrows. It was much harder, for example, to carry a crossbow or a pistol without someone noticing.

"There you are. Comes to two rin six nir."

Orya counted out the coins the woman named, thanked her, and left. She went back the way she had come, running through her mental list. She'd already purchased the rope and grappling hook she needed, and now she had the poisons. She'd packed two daggers in a false bottom for her trunk, along with an ornate garrote that looked like jewelry. She had all the supplies she needed. Now came the hardest part: figuring out how best to dispatch Princess Azmei.

Orya's instructions were clear: Assassinate Princess Azmei and pin the blame on Strid. None of the situational details mattered, as long as Azmei's death could be very publicly attributed to Strid, and preferably the elder of the two Strid princes. No one could be allowed to suspect the Prince of Amethir. As the only heir of his kingdom, he was useful alive. No one could afford to have the wealthiest, most powerful nation in this hemisphere collapse into chaos over succession. Azmei, on the other hand, was only useful dead--at least in the minds of Orya's superiors.

Orya was not yet senior enough in the family to make decisions of such magnitude, but she believed Azmei could be a helpful ally to have in Amethir. Perslyn attention was currently wrapped up in the Strid-Tamnese War, but war was an unstable economy at best.

It was unfortunate, in a way. Orya had known since before they met that she would have to kill Azmei, yet she'd still allowed herself to come to care for the woman. But the Perslyn family worked for coin, not ideals; she could no more go back on an assassination contract because she liked the princess than a leather merchant could go back on tanning a hide because he had been fond of the cow.

Tucking her purchases safely away, she turned her steps towards the university. She had plans to dine tonight with the two owners of Tamnese dress shops. The sun was already nearing its apex, and she had much to do.

Later, Azmei would look back on that day as one of the happiest in her life. The sun shone warmly on Ranarr, and the dry breeze cooled them as they walked the wide, steep streets of the White Stone. They admired the brilliant spectrum available from the ink dealers and judged how each hue might look on the various parchments and papers for sale. Azmei bought herself a pen carved from the bone of a sea dragon and chose a bottle of violent red to ink it with. For Guira she purchased a hair comb carved of the same bone. They pored over books with names like, *Diplomacy and End Games*, *Safely Transversing the Sea of Stars*, and *Once Across the Blades*, debating what each book might be about.

When they tired of the university market, they wandered between stone planters overflowing with flowers and fountains that burbled and laughed. Carefully tended palm trees grew in larger stone planters, shading the streets from the hot midday sun. Guira told stories about Azmei's mother when she was a young woman: how she had met Prince Marsede at a Year's Turning ball and spilled her drink on him; how the whirlwind courtship between the Prince and Lady Izbel of the Fifth Family had set the court on its ear; how Izbel had doted on Razem and Azmei when they were babies. Azmei bought candied nuts and tepid tea from a street vendor and they found a chocolate shop for dessert.

After lunch, they wended their way through a colorful park with luscious grass and bushes full of huge fuchsia flowers. A central fountain caught the sunlight and drew them to dabble their fingers and wish over the little bronze coins called nir. Azmei had never thought Guira particularly sad or stern, but she had never seen her handmaid smile so much, or heard her laugh so often, as that day.

As they strolled along the main thoroughfare, peering into shop windows and amused by the raucous cries of gulls overhead, Azmei heard someone say her name. Surprised to have been recognized, Azmei turned and saw it was Orya. The cloth merchant was laden with packages, which struck Azmei as odd. Didn't she have a servant with her?

"Azmei, isn't the city beautiful?" Orya stepped closer, smiling. "I don't mean to be disrespectful," she murmured. "I use your name only so no one will realize who you are."

Azmei laughed. "Am I so transparent to you already, new friend?" she asked. "But I thank you. One can learn so much by observing unrecognized."

"Indeed." Orya pushed back her wide-brimmed hat and patted delicately at her forehead. "It is so hot here! Wenda has a bad foot, so I offered to run her errands for her, but if I had known how hot it is, I would have just paid for a chair."

"You would do so much for a servant?" Guira's tone was cool, polite, but disbelieving.

"Oh, she isn't a servant," Orya said carelessly. "She's a cousin. Just a different branch of the Perslyn family. I will not keep you, my lady," she added. "I only thought it would be rude to pass by you without speaking." She ducked her head respectfully as Azmei and Guira said their farewells and left her.

She had been right about one thing: it *was* hot. Azmei liked the heat, but she wasn't so fond of the sticky way the air clung to her skin. She wondered if it were sticky like this in Amethir. Or did it get hot there at all? Perhaps, since they had no snow, they also had no heat.

They ducked into the dim coolness of the Shrine of Peace, where Azmei left an offering of ten ran, and they both lit candles to shine in the still air. Azmei wondered again what it must be like to serve a god of peace. When one of the clerics walked up to the front of the shrine, she saw the man was barefoot; he knelt before the stylized candle flame carved into the wall and apparently sank into meditation. So perhaps she had been right about that, at least.

Finally they found themselves in the fruit and spice market. They picked a path between carts piled high with oranges and heartfruit and delightberries and goldenseed, Azmei buying two of every fruit she had never seen before. "We'll try them together," she told Guira, who tucked them into a bag she carried on her shoulder. On a terrace below they could hear the shouts of fisherfolk as they unloaded the day's haul at vendor stalls. The sweet astringent of citrus disguised any stink of fish, but without discussion, Azmei and Guira turned away from the fish market and began the long trek back to the university at the peak of the White Stone.

CHAPTER TWENTY-THREE

LATE IN THE AFTERNOON, after returning from the market, Lo pulled aside two of his best soldiers for the Chatty Raven detail. He'd already sent someone out for clothes an Amethirian ex-patriate might wear. Skaya and Espen would look like a couple in civilian clothing. They could spend the evening dicing and gossiping at the Amethirian tavern, and Lo could use their report to decide how to prepare for the meeting in two days.

He would take a squad of soldiers to the tavern ahead of the meeting, of course, but he was too recognizable for reconnaissance work. Besides, he was thinking about making his own plans for dinner.

At some point during the day, he'd come to a decision. He couldn't keep pining for Arama if she could never return his feelings; they both deserved better than that. And since they were here trying to establish a new balance in world power, it seemed a good time to establish a new balance in his own life. By the time they sailed from Ranarr with their new princess on board the Dawn Star, Lozarr would have Arama's love—or he would know he must cut himself free.

During a quiet moment in the afternoon, he found Arama studying a map of the city. She looked up. When he didn't speak right away, her expression turned quizzical.

His heart thudded once, twice, and then he forced the words out. "Would you join me for dinner this evening? The prince has expressed a desire to dine alone in his rooms so he can read over those grievances, and one of the Diplomats has recommended a fine place for Ranarri cuisine."

Diplomat Revalis provided two suggestions, but made it clear that Forenna's was superior to any competition. The Diplomat provided directions to the dining house and an assurance that the name Revalis would ensure the hostess welcomed them.

Arama tucked a strand of hair behind her ear. "Not checking out the Chatty Raven?"

"I've got someone on that already. They'd recognize me—or you, I'm sure."

She gave him a crooked grin. "All right, then. I'd like that."

Lo nodded. "I'll come by your room at the seventh hour."

For the rest of the afternoon, his heart kept jumping into odd rhythms, his chest tightening at the strangest times. He wasn't sure if his sudden impulse was a good idea or a horrible one, but he had to know, one way or the other. Arama owed him nothing for the years he'd spent pining for her; he must be clear with her about that. But he couldn't go on sustaining a love that was unwelcome. And if his love for her wasn't unwelcome...

But he didn't let himself think much on that. If he got his hopes too high, he might only be crushed the worse by falling further. He busied himself with fencing practice until it was time to get ready.

He was wearing his dress uniform when he reached Arama's room. The university bells tolled the seventh hour as he rapped on the door, less firmly than he would have liked. He didn't want to sound tentative or diffident, not tonight. He respected Arama, and he would accept her decision as final, but he would not apologize for loving so fierce and clever a woman.

The door jerked open and Arama blinked several times at him. "Oh!" Her gaze traveled down his tunic and her eyes widened. "I'm sorry, I'm not ready," she blurted. "Give me five more minutes." The door shut again before he could respond.

Lo's stomach seemed to jerk inside him. She hadn't realized the nature of his invitation. He could kick himself. He hadn't exactly been clear about it, and while he'd intended that to put her at ease, now he felt like he'd blind-sided her. She wouldn't appreciate it.

But when her door opened again several minutes later, Arama was dressed in a burgundy silk tunic over a sleeveless ivory shirt. Her loose silk trousers were tucked into the tops of her boots, and the short curls of her hair were ever-so-slightly tamer.

"I'm sorry," she said. She swallowed and stopped talking, her lips still parted.

"No, I should have said..." Lozarr trailed off, because he didn't know what exactly he should have said, just that he should have.

His heart jumped as Arama laughed, the sound clear and happy. "Never mind," she said, tugging the door closed behind her. "Where are we going to eat?"

He led the way down through the university to the city streets. Evening was darkening into night and the lamplighters were out. Some night-blooming flower gave off a heady scent as they walked through a public garden towards a fountain. The air was pleasantly warm, the occasional breeze keeping it from being too warm.

Lozarr glanced down at Arama and was pleased to see she looked relaxed. Her stride was loose, her hands swinging easily at her sides. He wondered suddenly if he should put aside his plan and simply enjoy the evening with her.

But no, he'd done that so many times before, telling himself to simply enjoy what he had without asking for more. He was torturing himself, and he wasn't being fair to Arama, either. He let a soft sigh escape and she looked up at him.

"It's a nice night," she said.

Lo smiled. "Yes." He pointed to their left. "There," he said. At the end of a short street was a warmly lit courtyard full of people sitting at tables; a cloth banner proclaimed the establishment to be Forenna's. "I'm told this is some of the finest Ranarri food to be had."

"I hope they have goldenseed wine," Arama said. "I had one glass of that last time I was here, and I've never forgotten it." She smiled. "Liquid stardust."

Lo let her lead the way into the courtyard, where a serving girl in a sleeveless gown greeted them with a faint smile. "Welcome," she said.

"Good evening. Diplomat Revalis recommended your establishment, and I hoped you would have a place we could eat." Lo wasn't used to places like this, with its elegantly-dressed customers and the quiet ripples of a harp or other stringed instrument in the background. He hoped he wasn't being uncouth.

The serving girl merely smiled some more. "Very good. I shall inform Mistress Forenna you are here, General Algot."

As she walked silently away from them, Arama glanced up at him and pursed her lips in a silent whistle. "General Algot," she murmured. "Hobnobbing with Diplomats now, are we?"

Lo felt his cheeks heat. "I merely asked him for a recommendation. He must have sent a message..." He trailed off as a generously-built Ranarri woman approached them.

"Good evening, General," she said. Her smile was only a shade bigger than the serving girl's, but Lo reminded himself that the Ranarri culture wasn't as demonstrative as Amethir's. "Diplomat Revalis asked me to reserve a private sea-view balcony for you. I hope you will be pleased."

"I am certain I will be," he assured her. "My companion is fond of the ocean." Arama flashed him a warm glance and he inclined his head a little, hoping she wouldn't see him blushing.

Forenna led them through the main room of her establishment to the other side of the building, where they found themselves on a small balcony. Lo could just hear the waves breaking against the rocks far below.

"Diplomat Revalis suggested I treat you to a traditional meal," Forenna said. "I have prepared several courses, but if anything is not to your liking, please say so." She bowed her head to Lo and Arama in turn. "We begin with tepid tea and small dishes of salted, bitter herbs. It whets the appetite." She gestured to the dim area beyond the balcony entrance. A moment later a servant appeared, carrying a tray laden with food and drink.

"Thank you," Lo said, startled. He wondered why the Diplomat had gone to such great lengths for him when they barely knew each other. Then again, perhaps all Diplomats extended such hospitality to their political guests.

"We will follow with wine and rice bread and soup, and the third course shall be a second wine and fish." Forenna unloaded the tray with graceful efficiency as she explained. "Then for dessert, goldenseed wine and heartfruit pastries in a decadent spice sauce."

"It sounds magnificent," Arama said, taking her seat. "Thank you for all your effort."

Forenna gave them another smile. "I am happy to serve two of the Amethirian prince's closest companions," she murmured as she set fingerbowls full of scented water in front of them. "And now I shall leave you to enjoy your first course."

As she bustled away, Lo and Arama exchanged a look. Arama started laughing. After a moment, Lo gave in to a chuckle.

"I suppose it was foolish to hope no one would care who we are," he admitted. He dipped his fingers in the scented water and dabbed them dry.

"Forget it," Arama said, her voice warm. She'd stopped laughing, but her lips were still curved in a smile when he looked back up at her. She opened her mouth and then tilted her head to the right and closed her mouth again. "This looks delicious."

Lo decided to take advantage of the reprieve. "Yes," he agreed, and loaded his plate.

They conversed idly as they ate, mostly about the food, the dining establishment, and the city. As they sipped their soup, a high, clear voice rose from another part of the restaurant, accompanied only by the faint plucking of harp strings. The words were in another language, but Lo felt his chest swell a little at the yearning in that voice. Arama fell silent and listened, gazing off over the sea.

They only had a bit of their heartfruit pastries left when Lo realized he'd allowed the entire meal to pass without bringing up the most important issue. He lowered his fork and took a sip of the delicious goldenseed wine, and then he sighed.

From the corner of his eye he could see Arama shift in her seat, but she didn't seem tense, only attentive. He looked up, forcing a smile even though his heart suddenly wanted to pound through his chest.

"I have to speak, Arama," he said. His voice was low; hopefully that would keep her from noticing how unsteady it felt. "I can't...I can't go on living in hope if there is none."

Arama set her fork down and folded her hands on the table in front of her, eyes steady on his face. She didn't speak.

"If there's never to be anything more between us than this..." He waved a hand between them and suddenly wished he'd practiced this speech. "This is good. What we have, it's good. But it isn't as good as it could be. I just need to know, one way or another, if you can ever love me."

Arama didn't look away, but she still didn't speak. Lo almost wished she would interrupt, just to cut short his exquisite embarrassment.

He took a deep breath and looked directly at her. "I love you, Arama. Not only as my friend, but as a companion, as a—as a different sort of man might love a wife. I know neither of us is the marrying sort," he added hastily, "but we could have something more than this without compromising who we are. Couldn't we?" He gave her an unhappy smile. "I don't want to chain you, Arama. I just want—you."

Seven hells. That had been the most ineloquent jumble of tripe he could have come up with.

Arama drew in a shaky breath. "I want—I don't want to lose you, to lose what we already have," she whispered.

"We wouldn't." Lo's heart jumped into a gallop, but he spoke evenly. Was she hinting that—

"I don't know," she murmured. She traced circles on the tabletop with one finger. "I feel—but I'm afraid. And we're never in the same place for long, anyway."

"That's true," Lo said. "But we could make the most of the time we have."

"I saw what love did to Raszel," she said. "How it hurt him, being away from his family so much. How he blamed himself when his son died. And—it's a weakness."

"Captain Raszel wasn't a weak man," Lo said. He'd met Raszel a few times, once when they'd made this same trip some fourteen years ago when Lo was just a major and

Arama the first mate of Raszel's ship *Bounder*. "Love isn't a weakness, Arama. It makes you stronger."

She bit her lip and looked away. "I—It scares me," she whispered. Her voice shook. "Giving something of myself away."

"It doesn't have to be that," he argued. "It's giving to each other, if anything. But you'd still be you. You'd still be the fierce, clever, strong woman I've always admired." He paused. "You can't truly be surprised by how I feel."

"No. I just..." Arama straightened and cleared her throat. "Give me time to think," she said. The words were emphatic and obviously pitched to carry, so Lo didn't jump when Forenna appeared at their table, smiling gently at them.

"I hope the meal was to your satisfaction," she said, bowing her head slightly.

"Very much," Lo replied quickly. He gave her a smile that he hoped didn't look too forced. He should have brought this up over the main course to give them more time without interruption. "I will be certain to advise Prince Vistaren to dine here when he is able."

Forenna actually bowed at that. "I am honored, General. Would my guests like another bottle of wine? We have fine entertainment here, and the harpist would be glad to play for you."

Lo knew Arama would refuse before he looked at her. She lifted a hand, her smile looking easy. "Thank you, no," she said. "We have a long day ahead of us tomorrow and should return to the university soon."

"Of course." Forenna bowed again and lowered her voice. "I am honored to have had the Storm Petrel dine at my establishment." She gave them a slow smile and left.

Lo stood and fished out the gold for their meal and a hearty extra to be divided among the servers. He offered Arama an arm, which she accepted without hesitation.

As they walked back to the university, the streets lit by small flickering braziers, Lo looked down at Arama, admiring the curve of her jaw and her petite, muscular build.

"I must know, Arama," he said softly. "Before we sail home, I must know. Whether it is yes or no, nothing will ever make me less your friend. Nothing will ever change my deep respect and regard for you." He drew in a slow breath. "But if you can't love me, you must say so. I cannot part with you again still wondering."

She looked up at him, her gaze troubled. "I'll—I'll give you an answer before we leave Ranarr," she promised. Then, to his surprise, she tugged him to a stop and stood on her toes to brush his jaw with her lips.

Heat flashed through him. He cupped her cheek and dipped his head to kiss her properly. Arama's breath caught against his mouth, but she returned the kiss tentatively.

When she pulled back, she gave him a shaky smile. "Thank you for being so patient with me, Lo."

Azmei had intended for them to share one or two of the fruits for an afternoon repast, but when they reached their apartments in the university, she could see that their long walk had tired Guira. After all, she had been Izbel's nurse before Azmei's, and must be nearing her sixtieth year, and their lives back in Tamnen had not involved so many hills.

Azmei sat in the window seat with a glass of cool white wine. Guira allowed herself to be chivvied into resting. When Azmei was certain her handmaid was sleeping, she refilled her wine glass and silently left their apartments to seek a shady courtyard where she could soak up the last day of her freedom.

The courtyard she found was pleasantly warm, the sun's rays slanting in from the west. The air was humid without feeling sticky, and she wondered if it was anything like the air in Amethir. Perhaps she should have spent more time studying practical things like the climate and economy of Amethir, and less time on their folklore.

She settled on a bench and closed her eyes, listening to the rustle of the breeze through the fragrant vines that grew up along stone columns. Was it always so peaceful here in Ranarr? Perhaps she would stall the marriage agreement until she had explored all of the city-state. That would give her and Vistaren both time to be certain they weren't making a colossal mistake.

But what other choice did either of them have? Vistaren didn't need the peace, as she did, but he did need heirs, and treaty aside, Azmei was of royal blood and therefore a proper match for him. As second-born child of the king, Azmei would have a single estate as her inheritance, unless her brother died untimely, and she did not wish for that. She might as well marry Vistaren. As much as she loved her life in Tamnen, she had always yearned for something more, and perhaps this marriage would give her that.

"Oh, I'm s-sorry, I didn't realize anyone was here."

Azmei's eyes popped open and she sat up. Heat washed over her as she realized the way she had been sprawled had likely displayed a great deal of skin around her bosom, arms, and legs. The boy stammering his apologies was pudgy, with dark olive skin and blue-black hair tied back neatly. No, not a boy, she revised as she took in the evening shadow along his jawline. He was come to manhood, though she didn't think he was any older than she, if he was even that old.

"It's all right," she said in a low voice. "I was only enjoying the sunshine. You're welcome to use the courtyard too, if you want." She smoothed her split skirts down in a show of demureness. "Our apartments haven't got a private courtyard, so I just came looking for one that wasn't being used."

The young man's posture was relaxing, and she realized that his skin tone wasn't quite as dark as she'd thought--he must have been blushing. It made her smile. "You have the look of a Crelin about you," she said.

"Aye." He perched on a bench across from her, his movements graceful despite the extra weight he carried. "I've just come from Amethir."

Azmei straightened. "Oh! You must be with the prince's party!" She forced herself to take a deep breath. She didn't need to make her curiosity so obvious.

He ducked his head. "I...did sail on the prince's ship," he agreed. "And are you a visitor as well? You don't look like any Ranarri I've ever met."

"That's because I'm not Ranarri. I sailed from Tamnen with the princess. I--I'm Orya," she lied. If she told him her real name, he might realize she was the princess who had come to marry his prince, and she didn't want him to be formal or awkward. She wanted to speak openly with him, to learn things about his country and his prince.

"I--you can call me Lo," he said. He bit his lip and studied her, and Azmei hoped desperately that he hadn't seen more of her than he should have. He would discover her true identity before long, she was sure, and it would be mortifying to have the first Amethirian she met think poorly of her.

"I'm pleased to meet you, Lo," she said. "Tell me, did you have a pleasant journey?"

"It was...eventful," he said. He scooted back in his seat. "Have you ever heard of stormsingers?"

Azmei tilted her head. "I thought they were called stormwitches?"

"No--I mean, yes, people are called stormwitches. But there are old stories about the folk we humans first learned stormwitchery from. They were always called storm-singers, but there was never any description of what they looked like. Well," he temporized, "nothing credible, any-way. Some of the descriptions involved great wings and long, barbed tails, and teeth that could crack up a ship with a single bite." He snorted. "Anyway, we brought a stormwitch with us on the ship, because every Amethirian vessel of any size has one, you know. And she caught some sort of witchery echo." He grinned. "Don't ask me what that is, I haven't a clue, but she noticed it, anyway. And when she investigated it, this--" He shook his head. "This amazing, gorgeous behemoth came to us. It was singing, and it called up a storm straight out of season."

Azmei leaned forward. "Behemoth?"

He nodded. She liked the spark of enthusiasm in his eyes. Whatever Lo did for the prince, he was obviously an intelligent young man. "Arama--that's our captain--she said she'd seen behemoths before, always at a great distance. But she'd never seen anything like what this one did. He was singing, and the stormwitch said his song was off--and that was odd, too, because our stormwitch is deaf, but she could feel his song with her magic, you know--and she fixed it for him." He beamed. "And next thing we knew, we were surrounded by them, on all sides of us, dwarfing the ship and churning up the sea all around us..." He trailed off, shaking his head. "It was beautiful."

It sounded awe-inspiring. But Azmei couldn't miss the note of wistfulness in his voice. She wondered if she would ever see something so amazing. "It sounds like it," she said. "I envy you."

He twitched, as if he'd forgotten he was telling the story to an actual person. Then he shrugged. "I don't think I'll ever forget it, as long as I live."

"What did the prince think of it?" she asked curiously.

He tilted his head. "I think he was similarly affected. But I don't understand him very well, you know. I don't think anyone really understands the prince."

"Why is that?" Azmei had almost forgotten the goblet of wine by her hand until her fingers brushed the cool brass. She lifted it to take a sip, then held it out in offering to Lo. "I'd offer you your own glass, but I only brought this one," she explained.

He gave her a startled look, then accepted the glass and took a sip. "Thank you. That's very nice. Like a burst of goldenseed and sunshine on the tongue."

"I like it too," she said, pleased. "I'd never had it before last night. It's something local, but I've forgotten the name."

"I haven't had any local wine," Lo said. "Of course, we just arrived last night, and we dined quietly in our quarters after getting settled."

Azmei nodded. "Did you have trouble getting your feet back under you?" She looked down at her own feet. "I had never been on such a long sea journey."

"Nor I," he replied. "I'm clumsy anyway, when I'm distracted. I didn't know everyone had trouble."

She grinned at him. "I didn't either, the first time I sailed. We were less than a week on ship that time, but my brother told me it must have broken my grace. He had no trouble at all, and I cried for an hour before I realized he was only teasing me."

Lo's plump cheeks made his eyes squint when he laughed. He had a friendly face. She wondered if he knew the prince well. Perhaps he didn't know him at all. He might be a stormwitch, for all she knew. Then again, he might be the prince's valet. Would he talk about Vistaren? There were so many things she wanted to know.

"Why do you think no one understands the prince?" she asked, going back to their previous topic.

Lo pursed his lips. He tilted his head back and stared up at the sky for several moments. "I think the prince is lonely. He's no brothers or sisters, nor even cousins, and he's been sent to marry a princess he's never met. I'm sure your princess is a lovely woman," he added quickly, "and I know it isn't at all uncommon for royals and nobles to have arranged marriages. But I think it weighs on him."

"I can imagine," Azmei murmured. "Perhaps he and Princess Azmei will like one another."

Lo's expression was thoughtful. "I hope so." He took another sip of the wine and handed the glass back to her. "She may need the peace, but he needs an heir."

Azmei smiled at the echo of her earlier thoughts. "And a friend, perhaps," she suggested.

He stared at her a moment. "And a friend, perhaps," he agreed.

Their talk turned to lighter matters then, comparing the differences between Ranarr and their respective homelands. She told him about the doves that woke her in the mornings at home. He told her about storms that rumbled thunder across the land, murmuring him to sleep. When the bell chimed to warn them of the approaching dinner hour, Azmei was startled to find they were sitting in twilight, and servants were lighting lamps around the courtyard.

"Oh! I must go," she said. "My--Guira will be looking for me. I'm to attend her at dinner tonight."

Lo stood and reached out to take her hand. "I am pleased to have made your acquaintance, Orya," he said, bowing over it. "I hope your princess and my prince may speak as easily tomorrow as you and I have this evening." His smile was friendly. Azmei couldn't help but return it.

"That is my hope, as well. Good night, Lo."

"Good night, my lady," he murmured as she turned and hurried from the courtyard.

Chapter Twenty-Four

"Ouch, not so tight!" Azmei protested.

Guira huffed but repinned the looping braid. Her hands gentled to keep from pulling Azmei's hair.

"I hate that everything has to be so elaborate," Azmei complained. "The Diplomats won't be impressed by the ceremony, and it'll only be me and Vistaren and a handful of companions each. Do you think Vistaren cares about my dress? If I'm not pretty enough for him, all the silk and lace and jewels in the world won't make him love me better." She scuffed her thin-soled slipper against the floor. "Not that that matters."

"It matters," Guira said grimly. She was silent as she poked a jeweled pin through the next braid. Azmei swallowed, trying to push down the tight feeling in her throat. "Besides," Guira added, "Your father gave me strict orders to present you as formally and respectfully as possible. You wouldn't have me disobey your father, would you?"

Azmei sighed. That was playing dirty, and Guira knew it, but Azmei couldn't protest. Her father *would* want her to be presented so, and Azmei always wished to please her father. "Well, you might as well use the rouge and lip color, while you're at it," she grumbled.

"Your highness is gracious." Guira's tone was dry.

Azmei glared out the window, wondering if Vistaren was the object of this much fussing in his apartments, wherever they were. Destar had said the prince was a tidy man. Perhaps that meant he actually *liked* all the fussing over his appearance. *Well,* she thought ruefully, *I suppose one of us might as well enjoy it.*

"There." Guira stood back and gripped Azmei's shoulders to turn her. "Very pretty. The trim color brings out your eyes, and with your hair up like that, they look larger. Smile for me."

Azmei bared her teeth. Guira clucked and reached for the cosmetics. "Behave."

She did her best not to flinch as Guira stroked the rouge across her cheeks and darkened her eyelashes. Harder was not squinting her eyes closed when Guira poked the kohl at her, but she managed it, and as the lip color stroked across her mouth, carrying the refreshing scent of peppermint, Azmei congratulated herself. She hadn't even tried to bite.

Guira's expression said she knew full well what Azmei was thinking, but thankfully she said only, "You look lovely, Azmei. Like your mother, but with your father's eyes."

Azmei pressed her lips together and swallowed. She knew all the reasons why her father and brother had been unable to travel with her. They would have presented too tempting a target for the Strid--or any other nation hoping to profit from a Strid victory. Besides, with the Kreyden District still occupied by their enemy, the king must not appear more interested in personal matters than in matters of state.

Still, it would have been nice to have at least one of them here when she met her future husband.

Guira must have seen some of this in her eyes, because her expression softened and she wrapped her arms around Azmei, mindful not to muss her. "You truly are lovely," she murmured. "Your father and brother would be proud of you, as I am. And your mother. I know I have been demanding, but you have never disappointed me, my dear girl. You will not disappoint me today, no matter what the outcome of this meeting."

Azmei worked an arm around Guira's waist. "I love you, Guira," she whispered. "Thank you for all your patience."

Guira held her a moment longer, then put her gently away. "There, now, no time for sentiment. We must get down to the presentation room before the Amethirians. The bride-to-be always arrives first."

Azmei let Guira settle a thin yellow-gold cape across her shoulders. "Why is that, do you think?"

"Perhaps so she has a chance to flee if he turns out to be an ogre." Guira flashed her a conspiratorial smile and led the way out of the room before Azmei could suggest it might be the other way around.

Azmei was properly seated in a high-backed chair, with Guira on one side of her and Destar on the other, when the prince's party arrived for their meeting. Apparently Guira hadn't made up the rule about grooms arriving last. A man with spiky hair the same blue-black shade as the boy from last night stepped into the room. His eyes flickered to Azmei's face for an instant before he bowed deeply.

"General Lozarr Algot of His Highness Prince Vistaren Doth'Mara's honor guard, at your service," he announced.

Guira stepped forward to address him. "Guira Sundarel, Handmaiden of Her Serene Highness Azmei Corrone," she replied. "Welcome and well met, General Algot."

"My thanks, Handmaiden Sundarel."

Azmei liked the general's voice. It was self-assured and calm with no hint of arrogance. This man, general though he was, understood gentleness, she thought.

"My lord prince approaches, desirous of meeting the honored lady to whom he has pledged his troth." Algot was still carefully addressing Guira. It was maddeningly fussy and correct of him. Azmei longed to urge him to get on with it. She looked over at Guira.

"He is most welcome to approach and share wine and food with my lady princess." Guira's shoulders, straight and tense, spoke volumes; Azmei should exhibit patience and decorum. Azmei held in a sigh.

Algot bowed again and turned on his heel as he rose. Several long strides carried him to the door. As soon as he disappeared through it, Azmei hissed at Guira.

"Will it all be so drawn out? I shall fall asleep before I even meet the prince." She was careful to keep her voice low enough that the Diplomats wouldn't hear her. She wouldn't want them to think her ungrateful.

"Yes," Guira said. "Now hush."

Azmei sighed silently but straightened her posture and clasped her hands in her lap.

The doors opened again. This time several people entered. Algot and the woman Azmei had seen in the hall yesterday morning strode in, each of them flanking a man in the front. Azmei looked at him, expecting the prince, and had to stifle a gasp.

It was Lo, her companion in the courtyard last evening. He was dressed in purple and gray finery, and his hair was tidier, but he was unmistakably the plump young man who had introduced himself to her using what she now realized must be a diminutive of his general's name.

His gaze, fixed on hers, was apprehensive. Well, good. He should not have lied to her.

"To Princess Azmei Corrone, daughter of the royal house of Tamnen, I present Prince Vistaren Doth'Mara, son of the royal house of Amethir and heir to that throne." Algot was fortunate, Azmei decided. He had a script with little room for deviation. Azmei had no idea what to say to the man who had lied to her only the night before. Very well, let the rules of decorum be of use to her for once.

Guira extended the Princess' welcome for her and introduced her as Azmei cast around for some reason he might have lied. She could think of none.

"We are pleased to greet our royal cousin the prince," she intoned, "who has traveled across seas and under skies to meet with us here." She was unable to tear her gaze from Vistaren's. She truly was pleased to see a blush creep up his dusky olive skin. She hoped she wasn't glaring daggers at him, but it was too late to worry about that now.

"We welcome also the noble sea captain Arama Dzornaea, of whom we have heard so much." Noble sea captain, or pirate? The Storm Petrel had captured or sunk many ships, both Tamnese and Strid. Barely in her thirties, the Storm Petrel was younger than Azmei had expected, and prettier. She bowed like a man, though, one hand on her hip where her sword belt might usually be.

Azmei glanced at Destar to see if he had noticed, but his gaze was polite, if wary. "Let us present our honored friend, Lord-Captain Destar Thorne, Commander of our father's Royal Tamnese Navy." Destar bowed to the Amethirians. "Lord-Captain Thorne has our full confidence and is tasked with securing our safety on this voyage." There. She had gotten through the protocol without any mistakes, and they were all free to sit.

The Diplomat who had been seated next to her at her welcoming dinner stood then, holding up a scroll before his face. In weighty tones, he read out the terms of the treaty between Amethir and Tamnen, complete with a surfeit of whereases and therefores. Azmei didn't listen; in the past three months, she had more than memorized the text of the treaty.

Instead she used the time to observe the way the general, the pirate, and the prince sat. There was an air of togetherness to the three of them, for all that their chairs were carefully placed and they sat with straight posture. Perhaps it was the way the general's gaze rested on the prince, or the glances the pirate darted every so often between the general and the prince. Their expressions betrayed nothing, yet Azmei felt almost excluded by this trio.

Oddly, it made her think better of them all. Angered though she was about the lie, she suspected Arama or Lozarr would understand at once why Vistaren had done so. And if they would understand his reasons, there was hope that Azmei might one day understand as well.

The Diplomat wound down and intoned, "Thus come Azmei of Tamnen and Vistaren of Amethir to discuss the final terms of this hard-forged peace. Welcome, and may the spirit of peace inspire your words." He bowed and sat down.

This was the moment one of them would have to speak. Protocol would dictate that the bride speak first, except that Vistaren was younger than she. As a result, either could speak first without giving insult. Yet Azmei was uncertain what she wanted to say, so she remained silent and waited for Vistaren to speak.

The silence drew out. Someone coughed. A breeze carried the scent of jasmine and goldenseed through the open windows. Azmei folded her hands more tightly on her translation of Rona and Fann. Her eyes grazed Vistaren's. She had lied to him, too, she scolded herself. And they had shared a cup of wine already. Very well. She would relent.

As she opened her mouth to speak, however, Vistaren stood.

"Princess, cousin. Betrothed. Well met, and a hundred times well met." His voice was husky but carried well enough. Azmei sighed minutely; she suddenly regretted not being the first to speak.

"My heart knows your face already, my prince," she said. "It is as if we were meeting not for this first time."

She felt ashamed of the barb as soon as it left her lips. There was no recalling it, but perhaps she could mitigate it. Standing, she held out the blue leather tome she had made for him. "I bring you a token of my esteem." She switched to Amethirian as she said it, though they had been speaking the Common Tongue until then.

Vistaren stepped forward, a tentative smile touching the corners of his mouth. "You are most generous," he said, and held out a wooden case. "I, too, wished to bring my betrothed a gift." Must he keep using that word? It was technically correct, but it unsettled her every time it left his lips.

Azmei traded burdens with him and held the box level, staring down at the rich sheen of the wood. It was a polished burgundy-gold color and reminded her of a sunrise. The color looked to be a natural one; the lacquer on the box was clear. There were no visible tool marks, but the grain of the wood was visible around a pearlescent inlay of green, blue, and white. Azmei found herself smiling though she hadn't meant to; it was beautiful.

"The box is only part of the gift," Vistaren murmured. "Pray open it."

Azmei's cheeks burned. She had forgotten they had an audience until Destar chuckled. "Of course," she whispered. She slipped her fingernail under the catch and lifted the lid. As soon as she glimpsed the box's contents, she knew her relationship with Vistaren could at least be built on mutual respect.

He had given her a knife.

Not that the gift was at all warlike or threatening. On the contrary, it seemed innocuous enough. The box held not only a knife, but also a crystal inkwell, several colored sticks of ink pigment to be ground and mixed as needed, and a lovely pen carved of the same burgundy-gold wood, adorned with a gold nib and more of the pearlescent inlay.

It was the perfect gift for someone with whom one had been corresponding and was now expected to marry.

But the knife!

It was meant to look like a letter opener made of the same wood as the box and pen, but a cursory inspection told her that was artistry. The blade was beautifully crafted of steel; the hilt alone was carved of the sunrise wood. There was no inlay, but the hilt was wrapped in leather dyed the same colors as the inlay on the box. That was what told her this was no decorative piece. That, and the obvious keenness of the blade's edge.

She could not test it, not in front of so many people, even trusted as they were, but she was confident it would part the finest silk with nary a whisper. It would do the same for paper, certainly, but this knife had been designed for the princess to act in her own defense, if necessary.

She didn't know what she looked like when she turned her gaze up to meet the prince's again, but she heard Arama inhale and then cough in what sounded like startlement.

"Thank you, Prince Vistaren," Azmei breathed. "Your gift is most insightful and beautiful."

His lips were full and well-suited to a smile, which he bestowed upon her now. "A beautiful gift to honor a beautiful lady," he said, and bowed.

Azmei hesitated. "I fear my own gift is pale in comparison to this," she admitted. Especially, she added to herself, since she had never quite figured out what those few tricky words meant about Rona's relationship with Fann.

"I doubt that greatly, lady," he said, and unwrapped the bound papers. Azmei watched his face, forcing herself to breath evenly.

Would he see it? Would he understand? Azmei sucked the inside of her lower lip, her fingers tightening on the box he'd given her. What if he didn't enjoy literature as much as he'd implied in his letters?

She had finished copying her translation into the fine navy leather and stitched with gold thread. She tried to forget about why she had ended up with the navy instead of the red. Perhaps one day she would tell him that tale, but not today. She hoped he would overlook the plainness of her handwriting and see instead the personal intent behind her gesture.

"*Rona e Fann ha Non Marro*," he read aloud, tracing his fingers over the golden inscription. His brows furrowed and he switched back to the Common Tongue. "I confess, my Tamnese is rustic at best, my lady. Does this say 'Rona and Fann...' er, 'The Exploits of Rona and Fann'?" He opened the makeshift book and studied it. His expression smoothed and his lips curved up just slightly.

"I wished to acquaint myself better with the legends of your country," Azmei said. She looked at his hands, holding the book almost tenderly. "I thought it would be a worthy task to translate the stories of your most famous heroes into my language."

Vistaren looked up at her. "A worthy task indeed," he said, his smile taking over his face. "I shall enjoy improving my skill with your language while I read this. What did you think of the stories?"

"They were so exciting," she said, forgetting about their audience. "My favorite was when the fisher lord Goula insulted Rona by stealing Aevver, and Fann swore to help Rona rescue her, only to discover Aevver had poisoned Goula and escaped herself!"

Vistaren laughed. "Somehow that doesn't surprise me," he said. His eyes sparkled when he laughed, reminding her of their conversation in the courtyard the evening before. She found herself wishing to overlook the way he had lied. It was pleasant just to talk like this, as if they were simply two people who happened to share interests, rather than two royal heirs who were pledged to marry.

Of course, their companions couldn't allow them to forget for long. Someone cleared his throat, and when Azmei looked over, she saw the Diplomat was standing.

"It is proper for the witnesses to stand out of earshot while the prince and princess withdraw to speak privately." He held out both of his hands, indicating the balcony that opened out from the audience room.

Azmei sighed, but she heard Vistaren sigh at the same time, and it startled a laugh from her. He looked at her and chuckled, too. "Very well," he said, and bowed, extending an arm. "Princess, will you join me on the balcony? The view is sure to be fine."

Azmei managed not to giggle as she placed her free hand on his arm. "Thank you, Prince Vistaren, I am sure it shall." She clutched the box close to her with her other hand as they walked out to stand in the sunshine.

When they reached the half wall surrounding the balcony, Vistaren sighed again. She felt his shoulders slump as she drew her hand from his arm. Azmei looked at him, a question forming on her lips, but she decided he was just relaxing. That was reassuring.

"I'm sorry I lied to you yesterday," he said quietly. "I didn't realize who you were until it was too late, and...well, I rather liked the idea of talking to someone who had no idea who I was." He gave her a rueful smile. "Perhaps you understand how tiresome it can be, having everyone remind you what an important person you are, when you don't truly feel like you're all that special. Er, not that you aren't special. I mean, I think *you're* special--but I don't feel as if *I'm* all that special." He paused. "Oh, damn."

Charmed, Azmei laughed aloud. "Vistaren, I know exactly what you mean, and honestly, I'd just as soon someone think I am special because of who I am, not what I am." She looked up at him; he was about four inches taller than she, which was a pleasant distance. She was used to men being a great deal taller than she.

Vistaren looked relieved. "Oh, good. It's just--ah, hells. We both know neither of us would marry like this if it weren't needed by our kingdoms. I feel all wrong-footed. I'd never even thought much about marriage until my father brought it up, and...well..." He shrugged.

"While we're being completely honest with one another," Azmei said, "I'd never thought to marry an Amethirian. I always expected to marry someone of my own country. But I find the idea isn't unappealing." She smiled wryly. "Or, at least, no more unappealing than the idea of marriage in general. Which also isn't exactly unappealing, but..."

Vistaren laughed. "Very well, we are both of the same mind, I think." He tilted his head, light gray eyes studying her. "But are we both willing to move forward with what our fathers have arranged for us?"

Azmei lifted her chin in determination. "I am. I would not have traveled to Ranarr if I were unwilling."

He raised his eyebrows. "Even if I'd turned out to be an ogre?"

Azmei snorted. "You would have had to be quite offensive indeed for me to prefer war over marriage," she said. "But I find you not offensive at all." She didn't feel any particular attraction to him, it was true, but that wasn't grounds for refusal. And perhaps she would grow to feel attracted to him once they had known each other for longer than a day.

His smile twisted in amusement. "Thank you, I think." He wet his lips, a thoughtful expression coming into his eyes. They were very expressive eyes, Azmei thought. He seemed a pensive man, which she liked. What was it he was considering now? "Princess--"

"Call me Azmei," she interrupted. "It's ridiculous of us to stand on ceremony when we're discussing whether or not to marry."

He nodded, his gaze solemn. "Azmei, then. I am willing to move forward with this courtship. But I would ask that we take our time. I would have no secrets between us when we wed, but it takes time to establish trust."

Azmei swallowed, her heart beating faster. What he asked showed how seriously he took this. And it was good--this *was* serious, after all--but it was daunting as well. "Yes," she whispered. "I agree. We should move forward carefully and honestly."

Vistaren's expression lightened and he clasped his hand on hers. "Thank you." He lifted her hand to his lips. It felt right, but sent no shivers down her spine. "I like your gift very much," he added.

She smiled despite a sudden tightness in her throat. "And I yours." Very well. Their future would be bound together. She would just have to get used to it. "Let's go tell our people what we have decided."

CHAPTER TWENTY-FIVE

KINNET ARDELIS HAD BEEN a stormwitch for fifteen years, a master stormwitch for five of those. She had spent too many of those years pushing against everyone around her, striving to show that she was as intelligent, capable, and powerful as any hearing person. It had become exhausting.

She had been delighted when she experienced, upon their arrival in Ranarr, total acceptance exactly as she was.

There was even one Master Diplomat who spoke the finger language Kinnet used with her family and closest friends. There were many gestures and symbols that were slightly different from the ones used in Amethir, but it had made communicating with others vastly easier. That

Diplomat had gone out of her way to make sure Kinnet knew she was available at need.

But the place Kinnet had spent the most time in during the few days they had been here was a place well-suited to her for many reasons. The university library was a vast space, and well-used, but no one thought it strange for Kinnet to present her requests in writing instead of speaking aloud.

Stifling a yawn, she set aside the book she had been perusing and stretched. She had been in the library all afternoon, and from the number of empty chairs she could see, she had stayed straight into the dinner hour. She would regret that later; she often suffered from headaches if she skipped a meal.

Kinnet made her way back to the suite of apartments that had been assigned to the royal party. She was in the empty main room, just reaching for a piece of fruit, when the door to the prince's room opened and he strode in.

"Kinnet!" he said, smiling broadly at her. "I haven't seen much of you since we got here. I hope you aren't bored waiting while we settle things."

She smiled back without meaning to. The prince was charming, almost despite himself. "Not at all," she said. "I have been given access to the university library. It is even bigger than the Academy's!"

Vistaren paused in the act of scooping up a roll. "Have you been researching something in particular?" he asked.

"Stormsingers, of course," she said promptly. "Qiaru shared much of himself with me, but he has been alone a very long time."

Vistaren took a bite out of his roll and chewed it slowly. "How long is long for stormsingers?" he asked finally.

Kinnet closed her eyes for a moment, casting her thoughts back to the dark whirl of experience the stormsinger had thrust at her when they met. "I do not know for certain, but from his impressions and memories, he must be at least a century old."

Vistaren gaped at her. "And alone all that time?"

Kinnet saw the sorrow in his eyes, and it made her like him even more. It meant much that he was the sort of man who ached for the pain of others, even others so mysterious and unknowable as a stormsinger. She lifted one shoulder in a shrug. "He had parents. But I don't know where they are now." She paused, remembering the fleeting impressions Qiaru had shared.

A dark sky filled with scudding clouds. A black, boiling sea lit only by intermittent lightning. Two other stormsingers—or were there three? Shrieking and wailing, and other noises that muddled everything. Again, Kinnet strained to remember if there had been a ship.

"Human hunters?" Vistaren asked.

She shook her head. "He did not say." She couldn't get any idea from the memories he had shared. They were too frightening and he had been too young, she thought.

Vistaren tipped his head, studying her. "Can you still talk to him?"

She stretched out her awareness, not calling to Qiaru, just stretching toward him with her thoughts and being. "I can sense a *sense* of him," she said finally, knowing it was a confusing statement. "But he is at the very edge of my awareness. We cannot exchange thoughts or ideas at this remove."

Vistaren nodded.

Kinnet didn't feel the need to shove worthless chatter into a moment. She liked having space to think, and she could only suppose Vistaren did, too. They both sat, unspeaking, for several minutes. Vistaren finished his roll and reached for another. Kinnet began peeling a heartfruit.

When Vistaren did speak again, he touched two fingers against her forearm first, to get her attention. "Have you learned much about stormsingers from the books you have found?"

Kinnet grimaced. "Not as much as I should like. The librarian has been very helpful, but I have found books in mythology, religion, history, and biology. There are so many of them."

"Biology?" Vistaren frowned. "It seems odd to classify them as if they are simple animals."

That made Kinnet laugh. "There are books about humans in the biology section," she told him. "It is not only for dumb beasts."

"Doubtless I would know that if I were studying to be a medic rather than focusing on statecraft," Vistaren agreed. He grinned at her, and she found herself grinning back.

To her surprise, Kinnet found herself asking, "Has your time here been...all that you hoped, Prince Vistaren?"

As soon as the question was out, she chided herself. Who was she to pry into the personal life of her prince? It wasn't her business. He hadn't confided in her while they were on the ship; why should she expect him to confide in her now? But as she looked at his thoughtful expression, she found herself hoping he would answer her.

"It is early to say," he said finally. His gaze found hers. "I believe I like Princess Azmei. I believe you would like her, too. She has a deep appreciation of books, for one thing." He smiled faintly.

"That is very important," Kinnet agreed.

"Her gift to me was the Rona and Fann Cycle, translated into her native tongue. She did the translating herself, and wrote it in her own hand. It's a very thoughtful gift."

Kinnet agreed, but found herself saying, "I am surprised she did not choose the Daughteriad. Why choose Rona and Fann when she had four very strong princesses to translate?"

Vistaren hitched a shoulder. "Perhaps the *Four Daughters of the Storm* aren't as well-known outside of Amethir."

"If I see her in the library, I shall make sure she finds a copy," Kinnet said.

They laughed together, and it gave Kinnet a warm feeling in her stomach. She had friends at the Academy, of course, but there were not so many. How strange to have made a friend in the prince.

"Is there anything you need to further your research?" Vistaren asked. "Ink and paper? Someone to carry your research materials?"

Kinnet smiled. "I am well supplied. The Academy does not send us out penniless."

"Of course not."

He looked embarrassed, and suddenly Kinnet found herself wishing she had given him something. He seemed to want to be useful. She cleared her throat.

"Perhaps...perhaps you would allow me to join your party for any balls? I enjoy dancing."

"Of course." Vistaren was nearly successful in hiding his surprise, which made her like him even better. "We would be delighted for you to join us."

His pretense that it was normal for a deaf girl to enjoy dancing kept her from bristling. How was he to know anything about deaf people if he had never met any before her?

"I can feel the rhythm," she explained. "If there are drums or other low-pitched instruments. And my witchery lets me sense vibrations in the air."

He gazed at her, eyes shining. "I hope you will save a dance for me when it comes time."

Kinnet smiled and nodded, feeling as if she had somehow done him a favor.

Arama shifted in her seat, trying to refocus her attention on the report she was reading. She had requested an update on the store of supplies on the *Dawn Star*, after all, and if the quartermaster had gone to all the trouble to compile the report, she owed him the courtesy of reading it.

She made it another paragraph in, twitched as a stray breeze blew hair across the back of her neck, and sighed explosively. She pushed herself to her feet. Dropping the report on the seat she had just vacated, she gazed around her.

The prince's apartments were generous, with bedrooms for Vistaren, his manservant, Arama, Lozarr, and a number of guards. There was a common seating area, where Arama now stood, and it was kept well-stocked with refreshments. It served as a hub for the bedrooms and had a large table that was suitable for private meals as well as conferences. There was a private bathing chamber for the prince and a shared one for the rest of the bedrooms. The way the rooms were laid out provided space for only one window in the common area, but it was a large one. It was through this window that the errant breeze had blown.

Arama strode over to the window, intending to shut it. Instead, she found herself leaning her elbows on the wide stone sill.

They were on the side of Ranarr that faced the Amethirian coast. The bay between looked calm from this distance, large birds wheeling and soaring above the water—though she had to look down to the see the birds. They were probably frigatebirds, she thought, and perhaps seaskimmers as well. Seaskimmers were a good omen to sailors, indicating good sailing and good fortune, though Arama didn't know why.

She yawned, which made her eyes water, and then blinked. She hadn't slept well the past two nights, her thoughts whirling about the Amethirian expatriates that had approached them in the market, then to Princess Azmei and the tangle of concerns about the marriage treaty. She'd woken in the middle of the night last night from a nightmare of the *Bounder*. She'd woken drenched in sweat and shivering, convinced she could hear the creaking groans and shrieks of the sirens.

With a gust of breath, Arama dropped her head onto her arms and uttered a heartfelt, "Fuck."

None of those reasons, bad as they seemed, were the true cause of her restless discontent. The real reason, she knew, was Lozarr Algot.

"Damn him, anyway," she muttered, straightening and shoving her short curls out of her face.

What right had he to say things about love and longing? What gave him the idea that she would welcome such words? Why could he not see that the way they had lived all these years, not together but not separate, was safest?

A door closed behind her, footsteps entering the room. Arama whirled, fumbling for an excuse to leave if it was Lozarr looking for her.

To her disappointment, it was Vistaren, and that made her crankier. She hadn't been *hoping* it was Lozarr. It was just irritating to tense for a confrontation only to be denied it.

The prince stopped walking and eyed her. "You look as if you'd bitten into a sea sour."

"Good afternoon to you, too," she snapped.

His eyebrows shot up, and guilt washed through her. She didn't have any right to take out her nerves on Vistaren.

"I cry you mercy," she said. "I slept ill last night, but I can't seem to settle down to read or to rest."

He still stood with his shoulders cocked as if he expected her to blow up at him again, but his expression smoothed. "I can certainly understand that," he said wryly. "Though I, at least, know I slept ill because of betrothal nerves."

The look he gave her was humorous and oddly shy. It made Arama feel even worse about snapping at him.

"I don't know about you, but I could stand to burn off some of this nervous energy," the prince continued. "Lozarr showed me the way to a practice room, if you'd do me the honor of sparring with me."

She held in a snort. She wouldn't be honoring him by sparring. She was decent enough with a cutlass, but she preferred to do her fighting with her gunnery crews and, in closer quarters, her pistols. The cutlass was more for show these days. Most encounters these days involved her running up the Storm Petrel flag underneath the Amethirian one, firing a shot or two across an enemy ship's bow, and then accepting their surrender.

Then again, it wouldn't do to lose her fighting edge. And perhaps if they sparred hard and long enough, she would wear herself down enough to get a good night's sleep tonight.

"That sounds like just the thing," she agreed, and gestured for him to lead the way.

As soon as they were in the practice room, wearing padded tunics and weighing wooden practice swords, she felt better. This *was* a good idea.

They took their places, saluted, and then began circling, each taking time to size up the other. Arama waited for Vistaren to make the first move, which she met and replied to. Then it was her turn to test him, and his response was quick but not overly powerful. After another brief exchange, they fell to it in earnest.

Vistaren was a big man, not overly tall, but solid, with powerful muscles underneath a layer of softness. It didn't surprise Arama, because she knew Lozarr's opinion of the prince's fighting skill, but she could see how an opponent might underestimate the prince. Arama, by contrast, felt child-sized against him; she had to rely on her quickness and cunning to meet and match his strokes.

"You sent some sailors 'round to the tavern where we're meeting Yadian Shemma, didn't you?" he asked after a while. "The Chatty Raven, wasn't it?" He wasn't winded, which pleased Arama.

"Aye, but they won't learn aught," she replied. She took advantage of his attention to try a bit of footwork and sent him stumbling back two paces. "I've no doubt that group of malcontents knows each and every person of Amethirian blood on this cursed rock."

"Oh well," he said, righting himself and regaining his footing. "Even if they don't learn anything, their presence can show Shemma we aren't worried he'll suborn our people." He thrust and, when she parried it, spun away to come at her from the other side.

"That's clever," Arama said in admiration, meaning both his move and his comment.

He shrugged and withdrew a few steps, studying her. "I don't know enough of our policies regarding our folk here. For that matter, I didn't realize General Balahar had a Diplomat brother. That has to make for awkward family reunions."

Arama chuckled. "I daresay."

She was beginning to feel the strain in the big muscles of her legs now, and a slight tightening across her chest. Vistaren's cheeks were dark with exertion, and she could see a sheen of sweat building on his forehead. They exchanged a quick succession of blows and then parted again, Arama with a new bruise on her forearm.

"You're skilled at the blade," she observed.

Vistaren's chuckle sounded bitter. "I've drilled so much I can move fast for a fat man."

Arama frowned in surprise. "I wouldn't call you fat," she said, darting in and tapping his chest with the flat of her blade. "You're big, aye, but you're strong." She ducked back out, just missing another bruise.

Vistaren didn't speak, his own expression screwed up in concentration. He wanted her to think he was too focused on the fight to answer her, she thought.

"You've much to recommend you, lad. You're good-looking enough, skilled with a blade, thoughtful. Not to mention being a prince. I don't see Princess Azmei finding fault with you."

His cheeks flushed even darker and he missed an easy parry. "Am I that easy to read?"

Arama smacked his ribs smartly. "It's obvious enough, all things considered, but only because I've had a fortnight to study you."

He grunted and drew back, rubbing at his abused ribs.

"She's said she's open to the treaty," she continued, and saw that didn't cheer him. "Or would you rather she say no?"

"No, of course not," he said. "I just...I...oh, I don't know what I want. Freedom, maybe."

Arama grunted. "Freedom's blessed lonely sometimes."

Vistaren lunged, the tip of his practice sword gouging her wrist. She gritted her teeth against the sudden pain, hoping it hadn't broken the skin. A moment later, a thrill of cold heat ran down her spine. *Freedom's blessed lonely*—what had she been thinking, to speak so openly?

"And freedom's not for the likes of princes born into obligation," she added, and got another smart rap on his ribs.

"It doesn't have to be lonely, though," Vistaren protested.

Arama narrowed her eyes.

"Sorry," he said quickly. "Not my business."

They fell to sparring in earnest, Arama pressing him harder than she had been. The irritation that had been fading with their exercise flared back up, making her want to beat him. Vistaren's blocks became more urgent. His breath came faster.

"But why don't you let him in, Arama?" he burst out finally. His face was twisted in confusion and unhappiness. "I'd have killed to have him look at me like that!"

Arama stepped back, lowering her blade to her side. "Freedom," she said coldly. How *dare* this boy prince presume to know her situation?

"Is even freedom worth that?" he asked softly.

Oh, that was the last straw. Arama straightened to her full height and caught his gaze with hers. "I like you, Vistaren. But this match is over. I do not allow even princes to speak to me like this."

She spun on her heel and strode away, pausing only to rip off her padded tunic and hang it with the practice blade in their spots by the door.

She had to fight to keep her shoulders from twitching. She had come to know Vistaren well enough to know he would be chagrined by her reaction rather than angered, but she knew full well that any other royal—or noble, even—would have her flogged for the discourtesy she had just shown him.

Well, sod him, anyway.

Slamming the door behind her, Arama went in search of the largest bottle of rum she could find. There was more than one way to get thoughts of Lozarr Algot out of her head.

CHAPTER TWENTY-SIX

ORYA DIDN'T HAVE TO pretend to be pleased when the princess announced her acceptance of Prince Vistaren's courtship. The Perslyn family might have amassed their fabulous wealth through assassinations, but one branch of the family was dedicated to their legitimate business. Every assassin trained for six intensive months to be able to discuss cloth intelligently. Wenda had taken on the trade responsibilities, but the betrothal and subsequent set of parties would provide the family plenty of cover once Orya struck.

"Fortunate Prince Vistaren!" Orya squealed, beaming at Azmei. "Oh, my lady, you shall be a hero to your people when they learn of it."

Azmei's smile seemed tremulous, but her response was good-natured. "I'm only a potential hero until Vistaren and I have had our blessings spoken and contract signed and witnessed." She took a long sip of wine. "Sit down, Orya. I've no desire to dine alone tonight. Tell me what you've been doing since we arrived."

"Oh, it will bore you," Orya protested, but she launched into a long, unfocused discussion of unpacking her wares, securing warehouse space, seeking out buyers, and trying to find an appropriate property to serve as office and housing for the Ranarr branch of Perslyn Textiles. She could almost see Azmei's eyes glazing over as the princess nibbled on rice cakes and fish rolls, flatbread, herbed fish steaks, and figs.

"What dressmakers have you secured to purchase your cloth?" Azmei interrupted at one point.

Orya paused. *Had* they secured any dressmakers? She'd ordered her cousin to do just that, of course, and Wenda would not have disobeyed her. But she could think of no reports regarding that order. "I will write you a list," she offered, stalling.

"Mmm, no. Tell me which one you don't have but want. Who is the most famous dressmaker on the island?" Azmei smiled wryly. "I might as well be useful to you."

To her great consternation, Orya felt a flash of liking for the younger woman. It didn't make any difference in the long run, but by the seven hells, it was uncomfortable.

"Ah, that would be Eustra, I think," she stammered. "She's quite skilled, and famous for her vision, but she is vocal about her adherence to Ranarri cuts and fabrics."

Azmei finished her glass of wine and lifted a hand for a refill. "Let us correct that, then," she said, as Guira moved forward to serve them. "I like the way Ranarri women dress. That hooded sleeveless dress seems eminently practical for the heat and sun." She glanced over her shoulder at Guira. "That will be proper enough, will it not? If I dress in the clothing of local custom?"

"Indeed, my lady."

"There, good. Ranarri cut and style, but only Tamnese silk will do. I have such sensitive skin." Azmei grinned at Orya, who grinned back.

"I hope your highness will not be offended," Orya said, "when I say you would excel in my trade."

Azmei laughed. "Indeed, I take it as a compliment." She pointed at a bowl containing a blend of diced fruit. "I believe this would taste better with sweetbread, but Eustra the Dressmaker would likely disapprove--I find I like Ranarri cuisine so well she would probably have to let my dresses out after only a week."

They laughed together and lingered over dessert, talking of how different Ranarr was from Tamnen. Orya wasn't as steadying as Razem, nor as comforting as Guira, but she was entertaining and acerbic, and Azmei offered a silent thanks to the gods for providing her with a friend here. That made her wonder what gods the Amethirians revered, and when she asked, Orya didn't know.

"I don't think much about the gods." Orya's tone was careless. "If they wanted us to regard them highly, perhaps they shouldn't have turned their backs on us. Whatever gods the Amethirians worship, they can't be any worse--or better--than ours."

Azmei just hummed and took a sip of her wine. She would have to ask Vistaren. It would give them something to talk about while they were gaining one another's trust.

Vistaren gazed around him, trying not to show how bored he was. He normally enjoyed formal banquets, but tonight he was preoccupied with so many thoughts, and he wanted nothing more than to be alone with them.

Lozarr was seated to his right, next to Azmei's handmaiden, Guira. On Guira's right sat the princess herself, which meant they had no chance to converse. Though in his present state of mind, that might be more a blessing than a curse, he reflected.

Arama had begged off, and Vistaren had been more than happy to let her stay behind. Eyes puffy and bloodshot, she'd also looked to be a bit green. Vistaren felt guilty about that; he had no doubt his words during their sparring match had angered her. She'd obviously turned to drink the night before and was feeling the effects today.

A Diplomat Vistaren had never met was sitting next to him, and while they made intermittent polite conversation, it was not enough to keep Vistaren's thoughts from pulling back around to think about the Amethirian expatriates who had approached him in the market.

Their meeting was set two days from now, and Vistaren wanted to be prepared, but he also wanted to approach them with an open mind. He kept alternating between thinking he should ask Ambassador Renat what he knew and asking one of the Diplomats. If he had been seated next to Revalis Ingan, he might have taken the chance. Revalis was Amethirian, but he was a Diplomat, and they were famously unbiased. It was a point of pride for them.

Vistaren was sure he could trust Revalis for an accurate summary of the situation.

Whatever that situation was.

He had read the documents Yadian Shemma had given him, but mostly they were meeting requests with increasing urgency but little detail about their grievances. The final letter had enumerated some of them: taxes, tariffs, and trade agreements chief among them.

Amethirians living in Ranarr were taxed the same as Ranarri citizens, because they benefited from services such as the fire brigade, local security forces, and improved roads. At the same time, they were taxed the same as Amethirians living in Amethir, despite not placing any burden on Amethirian services. Vistaren had to admit, it didn't seem fair, though he wasn't sure of the best way to work it out. The Ranarri government deserved to be reimbursed for some of the services they provided to Amethirian citizens living there. On the other hand, the people *were* Amethirian citizens, not Ranarri. Perhaps an arrangement could be made so they paid only Amethirian taxes, but Amethir would reimburse the Ranarri government a set amount of those taxes per citizen living in Ranarr.

"You're deep in thought," Lozarr said, jolting Vistaren back to the present.

Vistaren shook his head. "Thinking about Shemma and his grievances," he said.

Lo gave him a sour look. "You've got other things to worry about. You could have told them to talk to Renat."

"Renat doesn't seem to be listening to them," Vistaren reminded him mildly. "Anyway, having that to distract me from this whole courtship and betrothal thing isn't necessarily a bad thing."

Lo snorted. "I'm glad you can see the silver lining to that cloud. Though I think you made a good start yesterday with the courtship. She certainly liked your gift."

Vistaren grinned at him. "And you thought a knife wasn't an appropriately romantic gift."

"I said nothing about the knife," Lo said. "I just worried she would look at a correspondence set and find it..."

"Boring was the word you used."

Lo's lips curved slightly. "I gave Arama a knife, years ago. It's made of a sirenstooth. She told me it saved her life when the *Bounder* went down." He huffed a soft laugh. "She still wears it on her hip. For too long, I've let that give me hope."

"I know she cares for you, Lo," Vistaren began, but his friend held up a hand.

"Let's not, tonight. She isn't here, and I'm trying to put her out of my mind."

Vistaren had his own thoughts as to how successful that would be, but he glanced around for a change in topics. He took a slow sip of his wine, then nodded slightly beyond Lo. "Who's that sitting next to the princess? She wasn't presented as part of Azmei's company, but she seems familiar with her."

Lo didn't have to look. "She was introduced to me earlier as Orya Perslyn. A well-heeled cloth merchant, and I understand she's been attempting to seal some trade agreements with various dressmakers and tailors in Ranarr. She sailed on the *Victorious* with the princess and her party."

From this distance, Vistaren couldn't tell if Azmei liked Orya or was annoyed by her. The princess was keeping up her side of the conversation, but it looked like Orya was considerably more enthusiastic about it.

"What do you know about the others in Azmei's party?" he asked Lo.

"Dester Thorne is the most capable sailor Tamnen has," Lo answered. "I asked Arama about him, and she has nothing but respect for the man. She told me she wouldn't raise her flag against him if they met on the sea, and that tells me a lot."

"Indeed it does." Vistaren decided one more sea-diamond wouldn't hurt. He waved for a servant, and when it was delivered, he opened the delicacy with care. "And her handmaid? Guira Sundarel."

Lo leaned a little closer, lowering his voice. "From all reports, she's been like a mother to the princess since Queen Izbel died. She had served Izbel first. If you want Azmei to like you, you'll definitely want Guira to like you."

"I hope she does," Vistaren said, surprised. "She seems protective of the princess, and I saw the love in her eyes when she looked at Azmei during the ceremony yesterday. It gives me a good opinion of both of them."

Lo smiled. "I know you're worried about all of this," he said. "But honestly, Vistaren, I think you do yourself too little credit. You have a clear eye and a good heart, and I think you are doing well."

Vistaren took a bite of his sea-diamond so he wouldn't have to answer. All the same, the praise warmed him and carried him through to the end of the banquet.

Chapter Twenty-Seven

T HE NEXT MORNING, Azmei and Guira called on Eustra the Dressmaker, where Azmei used all the royal airs she could summon to persuade Eustra to take on the challenge of sewing traditional Ranarri garb from silk. The feel of the cloth was pleasing, Eustra allowed, but she complained of the extravagant cost. Azmei shrugged off the argument, carelessly declaring she would pay whatever price necessary to have something more appropriate to wear in "this beastly heat". Royalty--and gold--prevailed, as Azmei had known they would. Eustra promised two gowns by the end of the week, one in pale gold and the other in white and rose. Azmei had held a violent hatred for pink since her babyhood, but she couldn't argue when

Eustra said it went well with her complexion, even with Guira smirking at her from behind the dressmaker's back.

They returned to the University in time for Azmei to prepare for her first intimate lunch with Prince Vistaren. Intimate lunch, she thought, because there would only be two servants and four retainers. But she and Vistaren would have their own table, well apart from the others, so no one could eavesdrop. She was both looking forward to and dreading the meal.

She knew Guira noticed that she protested less than usual about all the fussing over her appearance. Guira, may all the gods bless her, was wise enough to keep her mouth shut. Azmei was too old for tantrums, but she was fairly certain she would have shouted if anyone commented on her sudden eagerness to impress the prince.

When she was almost ready, someone tapped on the door to her suite. Guira bustled off to open it and returned a few minutes later, bearing an armful of flowers. They had long, naked stems and wide white blooms with deep pink spots in the middle. Azmei had never seen anything like them before, but they reminded her of the fuchsia blossoms they'd seen at the park down in the city.

"Well, they don't match your dress, but they're close enough to the ribbons," Guira said, holding one next to Azmei's face and studying it with a critical eye. "I'd be happier if you were in the rose silk already, but I don't think you allowed me to bring anything that shade."

"*Pink*," Azmei said.

"No, of course you didn't." Guira's voice was serene. "Very well, we shall make do with what we have." She snapped the stem halfway down and tucked the flower into Azmei's hair. "Actually, I believe the balance is perfect. You look pure and innocent."

"How dreadful--" Guira glared and Azmei amended what she was going to say. "--ly boring for him." Guira sniffed and let it pass.

Captain Dzornaea opened the door to the prince's apartments. Vistaren was standing at the balcony with General Lozarr. When Vistaren saw Azmei, he smiled. "Do you like the flowers? They only grow here on Ranarr. They're called peaceblossoms."

Azmei told herself it didn't matter that Vistaren wasn't struck dumb with her beauty, as Rona was when he met Aevver. It didn't matter that she felt no leaping of her heart within her, as Aevver had felt when meeting Rona. This wasn't a hero tale, it was true life.

"They are very pink," she said before thinking. "Beautiful, I mean," she added. "They have a lovely shape."

Vistaren looked rueful. "You hate pink," he said. "I should have known."

"No, of course not!" she protested. Then she thought about how she had promised herself she wouldn't lie to him again. "Well...yes. It's such a soft color."

Vistaren nodded, almost to himself. "And you are not a soft person. That much I did know."

"I'm sorry," she said, suddenly miserable at how utterly she had failed to be gracious about his gift. "I am grateful that you thought of me. Your gift is very appreciated."

General Lozarr looked like he was choking on swallowed laughter. Vistaren glowered at him and took Azmei's arm, curling their fingers together as he led her away from Lozarr. "I hate yellow, if you want to know," he said, his voice low. "It makes me feel like I'm going to purge."

She shook her head. "I think you would look very handsome in yellow. Why do you hate it?"

"I don't look handsome. I look like a big puff-skin. Do you have those? They live in tide pools, and they're absolutely worthless. They taste dreadful, their barbs are poison if they pierce your skin, and they eat sea-diamonds, which are possibly the most delicious food we have in Amethir."

Azmei couldn't stop the giggle that spilled out of her. "I've never heard of puff-skins, but we don't have sea-diamonds either. I've heard of them. Are they really that wonderful?"

"They're amazing. Possibly more blissful than se—" He stumbled. "—several of our other delicacies all wrapped into one."

She smiled. "So really you just object to puff-skins because they compete with you for your favorite food."

"No." His voice was sharp for a moment, but before she could react, he softened it. "I object to the color yellow because no one wants to look like a puff-skin, and I do when I'm wearing it." He gestured at himself.

Azmei wondered if he were being self-deprecating about his weight. He was plump, but that didn't necessarily mean he was soft. And what if he was? Destar Thorne had already told her Vistaren didn't care for war, but Destar seemed to think well enough of Vistaren despite that. Azmei had had her fill of war, even at a distance.

"Well, when I wear pink, I look like I'm perpetually embarrassed," she said. "And people expect me to be silly and sentimental and embroider perfectly."

Vistaren feigned a look of shock. "You mean you don't embroider perfectly?"

"No indeed. The only thing I pierce with my needle is skin."

"I didn't realize embroidery was a matter of state," Vistaren remarked.

"Precisely what I've been telling Guira all these years," Azmei agreed. "No crisis was ever solved by embroidery."

"Ah, but have you read all of the tales about Aevver? How do you know she didn't embroider a secret message in code to someone who prevented an uprising as a result?" Vistaren's left cheek dimpled, though he was valiantly trying not to smile.

"There are more tales about Aevver? I want to read them all!" In Azmei's opinion, there should be more hero tales about women. For that matter, Azmei's love of reading probably had something to do with why she had grown up so unwomanly; there weren't enough stories that glamorized embroidery and painting and dancing.

Vistaren was chuckling. "There are floods of stories about Aevver and her sisters. Did you know she had sisters? Three of them, and each of them almost as brave and clever and beautiful as Aevver." He glanced sideways at her. "One of them was a spymaster disguised in her life of silk and perfume and embroidery. One of them was a scholar who discovered the secrets to healing the human body. One of them was a bard whose voice could charm the most savage of enemies and tame the most fractious of beasts. And, of course, one was Aevver."

"You'd better not be lying to me." Azmei glared at him. "If you're making this up—"

"I wouldn't be brave enough to lie to you again," he replied. "I'll find a copy of *The Four Daughters of the Storm* for you. It might have been a better gift than the letter-writing set."

She stopped walking. "Oh, no. The gift was perfect. Just—perfect."

Vistaren beamed at her. There was no other word for it. His face lit up, his eyes sparkled, and his dimples dimpled at her. It struck her suddenly just how young he was. She kept forgetting he was only twenty. "I'm glad," he said. "It was my idea, and my mother thought it a good one. Lo thought it was too boring, but Arama looked at the knife and said it would serve."

"Arama knew exactly why I would like it," Azmei said. "I hope I shall get to know her. She's so brave and exciting."

"Aye, I think you'd like her." Vistaren looked over her shoulder and she turned to look as well. The pirate captain was standing with General Lozarr. They were talking, but she wasn't quite meeting his eyes. The general looked unaccountably sad.

"Gods, I wish they'd just get on with it," Vistaren muttered. "It's the only thing I don't understand about her. Lo looks at her like she discovered seaglass, and she knows it, but she won't—won't accept it." He scowled. "I know she loves him too."

Oh. *Oh.* Azmei tilted her head as she stared at them. Yes, she could see the awkwardness now that she knew to look for it. The way the general leaned in a bit too close, the way Arama seemed to be holding herself away. The tilt of her shoulders away from him—but her hips were turned toward Lozarr, her eyes brushing his cheek and jaw and the top of his head, but never quite meeting his.

"She wants to," Azmei murmured. "Perhaps she's afraid of losing herself." She felt Vistaren go still beside her. Did he realize she had just confessed her own fear? "Maybe she's afraid of how hot his love burns. The hottest flames sometimes die soonest."

"Not Lo." His voice was fervent. "They've known each other for years, and I think he's felt that way all that time."

"Then she'll come to accept it eventually." What would it be like, she wondered, to have someone know you that long and still feel as though you were the brightest star in the sky? Would Vistaren ever feel that way about her?

Vistaren's expression was somber. "I hope so." He sighed. Then he seemed to realize they were no longer laughing. "But enough of them. We're supposed to be talking about our own epic romance." He spoke the words lightly, his lips curving up again. Azmei couldn't tell if it was pleasure or humor. Did he relish the idea or mock it?

She slanted a glance up at him. "I suspect we shall not have as long a courtship as your friends, anyway."

He laughed, which she'd been hoping for, and she didn't think she was imagining the relief in his eyes. Perhaps he was as nervous about this as she was. Perhaps this might turn out well, after all.

Chapter Twenty-Eight

Thunder rumbled in the distance. Orya tugged her hood tighter over her forehead and slipped into a narrow alley between houses. According to her observations, the dressmaker's shop was at the end of this alley. She should be pleased. True to her word, Princess Azmei had persuaded Eustra the Dressmaker to purchase Tamnese silk from Perslyn Textiles.

Orya had been banking on the likelihood of Azmei's success. Eustra was a vain woman. The same pride that had made her speak loudly about the inferiority of Tamnese silk had not allowed her to back down when the princess challenged her to use it to create a thing of traditional Ranarri beauty; the fact that Eustra held the silk in such contempt only heightened the challenge.

Dust and grit blew into the mouth of the alley, hissing against Orya's shoes. At the noise, she looked over her shoulder. No one there. She shrugged her shoulders and loosened her dagger in its sheath on her belt. Thunder growled, closer than it had been, like an angry dragon roused from slumber.

Orya wanted to hurry along the alley to her goal, but she crept forward, pausing every few steps to listen and look around. There was little light in the alley. The moon had been barely a crescent when the clouds shrouded it. Orya had a lightbox with her, but she would only use it in extreme need. The textile shops on this block had all closed hours ago. If someone spotted a light down this alley, there would be trouble.

As she inched forward, Orya found herself wondering what Yarro was doing at home right now. Would he be asleep? His Voices kept him awake late into the night far too often, but once he slipped into dreams, he slept soundly. He might be reading. He could read, despite the fractured concentration that made him such a trying companion.

Something shifted underfoot. Orya flung out a hand, slapping it against the limestone wall beside her. It made no noise, but she froze, holding her breath. What had she stepped on? She leaned down to inspect it.

Only a stone. But kneeling gave her a better angle from which to view Eustra's shop windows. On the second floor, which was supposedly only a storeroom, a light was burning behind closed shutters.

"What?" she muttered, narrowing her eyes. It was a warm, flickering glow. Candles, then, or perhaps an unshuttered lantern. But who would be up there at this time of night? The first hour past midnight had come and gone. Eustra had a very nice home several streets from here. Could she still be awake and working on Azmei's dresses?

The princess had told her over an early lunch this morning that Eustra had promised delivery today. Could the dressmaker have overcommitted herself?

Orya shook her head. It didn't seem characteristic for a woman who took as much pride in her work as Eustra did. The flicker intensified as a shadow passed between the light source and the window. "Curse the Vigilant!" The woman must have a guard.

Very well. Orya could deal with that. She had herbs that would set any guard to dreaming, and make him forget what he'd been doing when it took effect. As long as she was careful, she could arrange for the guard to fall asleep without piquing anyone's suspicion.

She crept forward again, slipping to the side of the alley underneath the window. People looking out windows rarely looked straight down. She slipped one hand inside her belt pouch, touching small bags made of differently textured cloth until she found the one she needed by feel. It was a trick she'd learned from one of the shop cousins, a girl who was so nearsighted she had learned to identify cloth by texture alone.

By the time she had reached the back entrance to the shop, she had coated a dart in the sleep dust. She would be able to take the guard down without even showing her face. Orya's lips curled up as she reached out a gloved hand to test the door.

It was locked, which was to be expected. Orya went to one knee, slipping a pick into the lock. It took her longer than she had expected to get the door open. When she felt the tumblers click into place, she let the door swing ajar. She waited, listening, but nothing stirred.

Orya took a few breaths and stepped into the back entry hall. No one raised the alarm. The entire first floor was dark. She waited in place until her eyes adjusted, then made her way to the showroom. It was always possible Eustra had been stupid enough to display the princess' dress for all her customers to see.

But Eustra proved cannier than that. The showroom held cloth of all varieties along with a handful of dummies displaying samples of Eustra's work. That was all. Orya clicked her teeth together and headed for the stairs.

This was trickier. While most of the buildings on Ranarr had limestone walls, the interior floors and staircases were often made of wood. Such was the case with Eustra's shop. Orya had to ease her weight onto each step while easing her weight off the step before. It was a painstaking process, but at last she reached the head of the stairs.

The upstairs hall appeared to be straight. There were two doors on the left and one on the right. The furthest door on the left showed a thin line of light underneath. Orya smirked. Perhaps she could gain access to the dress without even risking an encounter with the guard.

But the door on the right led into a sewing room strewn with scraps and half-finished dresses. None of them were silk, and none of them fancy enough to be under consideration for Azmei.

Orya went to the next door. It was locked, but when she got inside, the room turned out to be Eustra's business office. A desk took up most of the inadequate floor space. A shelf behind the desk held ledgers and order books.

Very well, the guard was in the room with the dress, then. Orya grudgingly revised her opinion of Eustra. The woman might have little experience sewing for royalty, since Ranarr had none, but she was canny enough. She must realize someone might wish the princess ill. Or perhaps she was merely afraid someone would sabotage her work for the princess. Either way, Eustra had had the good sense to post a guard on the work intended for the princess. Orya had to admire her foresight, even though it made Orya's job more difficult.

The problem was that the door to the lighted room was locked with the most difficult lock Orya had encountered on Ranarr. The city on the whole was remarkably trusting, which she found useful but incongruous, considering that Diplomats were said to trust few outside their company. Orya had had free reign of the city's buildings. Even inside the university, where she exhibited a great deal more caution to keep from destroying her assumed persona, she had little trouble entering any room she wished.

The lock on Eustra's door outstripped all of them. It was more than unusual, it was unbelievable. What would a simple dressmaker need with such an expensive lock? When Orya knelt to inspect it, though, opening her light-box to allow a faint glow from the ember within, she saw faint scarring in the wood around the lock. So the lock had been replaced, and recently. That made more sense.

Unfortunately, it probably meant Destar Thorne was cleverer than Orya had credited him. No one else would have been so thorough in protecting the princess.

She breathed in slowly through her nose and took out a better set of lockpicks than she had been using. The pick slid in silently, but when she caught the first tumbler with it, the lock clicked loudly. Inside the room, wood scraped against wood, as if the guard had pushed his chair back. Orya jerked away and retreated to the shadowy end of the hall.

Footsteps thumped inside the lighted room. The door swung inward and a strapping, bronze-skinned man peered out. Orya held her breath before remembering her training. The guard swept the hallway with his gaze, more thoroughly than Orya liked. She turned her face away. Only her dark clothing kept her hidden, and her skin, while not pale, was still more visible than her clothes.

The guard swore and reached inside the room. He drew out a sword and a lantern. Stepping into the hall, he pulled the door shut behind him. Orya heard the lock click into place.

This was an unfortunate turn of events. From the color of his skin, the man looked to be from Strid. Sleep dust wouldn't work on the Strid. Common belief was that so many of the Strid handled the lazyflower from which sleep dust derived that they had developed a racial immunity to it. Orya didn't know if that was true, but she knew she wasn't equipped to take on the guard.

Thunder cracked overhead. Orya jumped. Fortunately for her, the guard jumped too. As Orya was reeling to regain her balance, the guard was swearing and shaking his head. Any other time, Orya would have laughed. But she couldn't afford to kill him, which was what she would be forced to, should she attract his attention.

Orya put a fingertip in her mouth, hooking the nail on her teeth but not biting it. Killing a guard would raise the wrong kind of suspicion. Of course, even if Orya succeeded in poisoning the dress without killing the guard, there were possible complications. What if Eustra checked the dress a final time before handing it over to the princess? If the woman died of the poison, the dress would never reach the princess, and Thorne the watchdog would realize someone intended Azmei harm. All of Orya's work would be more difficult from that point.

The guard heaved a deep sigh and walked towards the stairs. Orya waited, pressed against the wall, until the guard's footsteps retreated down the stairs. She could try to pick the lock before he returned. She probably should try. Orya wasn't optimistic about her chances, though. She was an excellent assassin, but only a mediocre lockpick.

And if she were honest with herself, she didn't want to try. Poisoning the dress has been an ambitious plan, especially considering Orya was trying to assassinate a royal. If it had only been one of the Ten Families, the security might not have been as tight. With Tamnen's only princess, it stood to reason that Thorne would cover all weak spots.

Rather than wait for the guard to finish patrolling the building and possibly catch her on his return, Orya let herself back into the business office. It had a small window overlooking the alley. Orya eased it open, scanned the alley below, and, seeing nothing stirring, climbed through. The window ledge provided enough support for her to ease the window shut behind her. She sidestepped her way along the wall, clinging to the slightest rough spot in the limestone, until she had reached far side of the shop next to Eustra's. Then, judging herself far enough away, she lowered her body until she was hanging from the ledge.

She dropped, knees bending to absorb the shock of landing. Her boots gripped instantly, telling her the storm hadn't yet broken over the island. Orya didn't want to get wet. She tugged her hood forward again and moved towards the main road more rapidly than she had come earlier.

As she slipped out of the alley, Orya's shoulders twitched. She paused and looked around her, but no one was visible. Not even an alley cat or stray dog could be seen. The hair on the back of her neck was crawling, though. Something wasn't right.

It's just the storm, she told herself. *Get on your way.*

She wanted to believe it, but with all the other precautions Thorne had taken, wouldn't he have guarded the shop from without as well as within? Orya put her fingertip in her mouth again. How best to handle this?

She hunted in the refuse along the side of the alley until she found an empty bottle. She kicked it hard and made a retching noise. There were no taverns along here, but a person could get strong drink nearly anywhere. It would at least disguise her true intentions here. She stumbled out into the main road, reeling but being careful not to overdo it.

There--she saw the movement from the corner of her eye. Rather than spin to face it, she paused, staring down at her feet as if she had stepped in something. Without moving her head, she scanned her periphery. Yes, there was a figure swathed in dark cloth. To hide her triumph, Orya reached down and touched her shoe.

"Ugh! Dog shit." She lowered her voice and roughened it. Her observer would think her male and give it less thought. "Sirens take 'em." That was a nautical oath, not one most Tamnese used. Orya's shoulders relaxed. Her watcher, whomever he was, would never see through her disguise.

As she stumbled and bumbled her way uphill towards the university, she tried very hard to ignore the last glimpse she'd gotten: a dark beard streaked with gray, a cowl that dipped to obscure eyes and nose. He wasn't Destar Thorne, certainly. But who he was, Orya had no clue.

Chapter Twenty-Nine

THUNDER RUMBLED IN THE distance. Vistaren's stomach rumbled in answer. He looked up from the book he was poring over.

Earlier in the afternoon, he had gone to the library with Kinnet in search of copies of the Amethirian tax code, as well as information on the latest census numbers. There were nearly a thousand Amethirian citizens living on the White Stone for various reasons, and he suspected that number wasn't large enough for the ambassador to risk rocking the boat.

It was large enough for Vistaren.

He opened the door that separated his sleeping quarters from the common room in time to hear someone with a Tamnese accent say, "—just what my folk have heard. No proof, of course, but I thought it credible enough to pass it along to you."

Vistaren stopped just outside his door. Lozarr was facing Lord-Captain Thorne, who had brought Azmei from Tamnen to Ranarr. Lozarr looked relaxed, but Vistaren could tell from the set of his shoulders that he was troubled. Thorne was shorter and broader than Lozarr, and had his head tilted up a little to speak to him.

"I'm gratified you chose to inform us," Lo said. "And impressed at your skills, honestly. I've had my own folk out and about, but they haven't heard any of this."

Thorne shrugged one shoulder. "Oh, well, I went to the expense and trouble of hiring a Shadow before we arrived. No room for risks when it comes to our princess, you know." The expression on his brown face was affectionate.

"Shadow?" Vistaren asked, curiously.

Lo turned as if just noticing him, though Vistaren couldn't imagine neither of them had heard the door open.

Thorne bowed deeply, one fist pressed to his chest and the other propped at his left hip. "Your Highness. I've shared all I know. Doubtless you'll all want time to confer. I'll take my leave."

Vistaren opened his mouth and caught Lo's expression; Lo was afraid Vistaren would display his ignorance again with another question. He pushed down the sense that he'd disappointed his friend. "My thanks for your cooperation, Lord-Captain Thorne."

Thorne bowed again and allowed Lo to show him out. When Lo turned back, Vistaren was waiting, arms folded across his chest.

"All right, what was that about? And what's a 'Shadow'—for hire, apparently?"

Movement by the window caught his eye and he realized Arama had been present for the conference, as well. His cheeks heated. Had they thought he wouldn't care about security? Or did they just not trust him with this sort of information? The thought made his stomach hurt.

"Shadows are folk in service to the Diplomats," Lo said. "As I understand it, they can be contracted to act as special protection for those who are in dealings with the Diplomats."

"Did we hire any?"

Vistaren was surprised to see Lo's cheeks darken. "I was…not aware of their existence until tonight, Vistaren. I apologize for that ignorance."

Vistaren waved it off, feeling abruptly better. "Well, at least Thorne is of a mind to share information. What did he tell you?"

"He knows of the unrest in the Amethirian Quarter, for one thing," Lo said. He was frowning. "I'd have preferred that information stayed under wraps."

"It sounds as though there have been signs of it, for those who pay attention. Anything else?"

Lo's frown deepened. "Thorne's source is convinced there is an assassin watching the University, though it isn't clear whether we or Azmei's party are the target."

Vistaren snorted. "Who would want to assassinate me?" It was a disconcerting thought, but he tried to ignore the emotion and think logically about it. "My father's bloodline ends with me. It would cause a succession nightmare." That was something he didn't like to think about for a number of reasons, but he pushed that away, too. "That wouldn't benefit the lords. The stormwitches have no reason to remove the royal family; they don't answer to us. Tamnen certainly can't want me dead—they need me to marry their princess."

And that thought sent his stomach rolling again. He still hadn't thought of a good way to tell Azmei that he would never be attracted to her, that he couldn't give her the adoration and passion she deserved.

"There's always the Strid," Lo said dryly.

"They can't possible hate me more than they do Azmei or her brother."

Arama spoke up then. "I wouldn't discount them entirely, Highness," she said. Vistaren met her concerned gaze and nodded. She had certainly had more exposure to the Strid over the years than he and Lo put together, and he respected her opinion.

"And I haven't written off Yadian Shemma and his group, either," Lo said darkly.

"Oh, they just want to be listened to. I'm doing that." Vistaren couldn't see any reason to consider them a danger. They'd set up a meeting, albeit through unconventional methods.

"You really think that's enough?" Lo's voice was more severe than it had been. "Don't be naive, Ren. If they've been planning this—"

"Thank you for that vote of confidence," Vistaren said icily. "I have taken Shemma's measure. He is an honest man."

"Even honest men can be driven by desperation."

"I will not hear it, Lo. We will deal fairly with him, and I won't suspect him of ill intent when I've seen no malice in the man."

"I agree," Arama said unexpectedly. "Shemma's not a villain. If he had intended to assassinate Vistaren, he wouldn't have gone to all the trouble to approach us in the marketplace and arrange a meeting."

"It's my duty to protect you, Vistaren," Lo said. "You can't ask me to ignore possible threats—"

"I'm not *asking* you, Lozarr," Vistaren interrupted. "I'm *telling* you."

The words were like cold water dashed in their faces. Lo drew himself up, clearly angry. Arama went still. Into that tense silence, the door opened and Kinnet came inside, her face alight. She faltered at the expression on Vistaren's face, then recovered.

"This storm is glorious," she announced too loudly. "It is so strange and fascinating to experience it and know I am not permitted to alter it!"

"I know the feeling," Lo growled, "but I wouldn't call it fascinating."

He spun on his heel and stalked off, letting the door slam shut behind him.

Kinnet looked around, confused. "What did I do?"

"He'll calm down, Vistaren," Arama said, finally stepping away from the window. Her gaze was troubled, but she smiled in an obvious attempt to be reassuring. "I daresay we're all a bit on edge."

"I don't know why he's so surly, anyway. He isn't the one who has to marry someone he's not suited to," Vistaren grumbled.

"You did agree to it, my lad," Arama pointed out. Her smile strengthened. "Azmei seems quite a clever and reasonable young woman. I have confidence it will all work out."

"You might be the only one," Vistaren snarled, and headed back into his bedroom, leaving Arama and Kinnet to stare at each other in bemusement.

Thunder rumbled in the distance. Azmei sighed and leaned against the stone windowsill. Last night's storm had missed Ranarr. She'd watched the lightning in the distance, counting the heartbeats from flash to crash, and thought about how the old wives at home had predicted how long it would take for a storm to arrive: *Count ten beats of your heart for every mile you and the storm are apart.*

She wondered if it were the same calculation in Amethir, or if stormwitchery fouled the calculation.

She hadn't been able to see Vistaren today. General Lozarr had said something about protocol and political obligations. It sounded legitimate, but Azmei suspected the general had plenty of practice at making flimsy excuses sound like earth-shatteringly plausible circumstances.

What if Vistaren had decided he didn't like her after all? What would Azmei tell her father and brother? How could she face them again?

At least Eustra's delivery of her dresses had served as a distraction for the better part of the morning. She had been insistent about Azmei trying each of them on, making final tucks and adjustments.

"Princess?"

Azmei turned to look at Guira, who hovered in the doorway. "What is it?"

"Orya Perslyn wishes to call on you." Guira frowned. "I told her Captain Thorne will be arriving soon for an appointment with you, but she is set upon seeing the dress Eustra made for you."

Azmei sighed. "Oh, it's all right. I should have made a point to show her, as it's Perslyn silk. Tell her I'll be out in a moment."

She was pleased with the dress Eustra had made. The golden silk emphasized Azmei's tawny eyes while complementing her skin. The cut was pretty but still practical. And the silk was very fine indeed. Azmei stood in front of the mirror to be certain she was presentable, then went out to the sitting room.

Orya broke into applause as soon as she saw Azmei. Her enthusiasm brought a genuine smile to Azmei's lips. She executed a slow twirl in response, spreading the skirt for full effect.

"It's a pretty dress, isn't it? The quality of your wares is exquisite."

"It is a *beautiful* dress," Orya said, smiling. "I predict my entire stock shall sell out before your wedding. Everyone will be vying for a copy of the dress Eustra created for the future queen."

"We don't know for sure yet that I will ever be Queen of Amethir," Azmei protested. She knew it was ridiculous to argue--she was marrying Amethir's only heir, after all--but she wasn't quite ready to consider being queen. "And besides, what do the Ranarri care about the queen of another country, especially when they have no queens of their own?"

"Everyone expects you shall be queen, whatever is yet to happen," Orya said, with a wry twist of her lips. "And you, of all people, should know that everyone cares about the royalty of every country. You're royal. Born with special position and privilege. People are always curious about that. Especially people who have no experience of royals of their own."

"Curious," Azmei repeated, tilting her head. She supposed being royalty was interesting to outsiders, but it carried with it a great deal of responsibility. She had never been tempted to throw away her palace life to go live as a shepherd, certainly, but she wished she knew more of how the common folk lived. "I suppose so. And here am I, curious about how silk merchants from Meekin live."

Orya snorted. "Nothing so glamorous as a princess' life, I can promise you." She flicked her fan open. "It's warm today, isn't it?"

Azmei settled into a chair. "The Ranarri say it's the heat that has fueled these storms this week. But I rather like the heat," she said. "For that matter, I like all of Ranarr. I hadn't expected to, but it's a lovely city. I only hope I shall like Amethir as much as I do Ranarr."

"And what about the prince?" Orya probed. "Do you like the prince as much as you like Ranarr?"

Azmei felt herself blush and hoped Orya was not watching for it. "He...isn't as bad as I had feared he would be," Azmei said. She flicked her own fan open and fanned herself. "He's very young. I'm a year older, did you know that? You wouldn't think it would make such a difference, but it does."

Orya laughed. "It just means you'll be able to train him into the husband you want." She slanted a look at Azmei. "Especially in private matters. Younger men are so eager to please."

Azmei's face grew very hot. How dare Orya speak to her of such things? "You're impertinent."

"What are friends for?" Orya grinned slyly at her. "Princesses are so carefully guarded. You've probably never been with a man."

"Of course not!" Azmei stared at her, mouth dropping open. "My virtue belongs not to me, but to my kingdom."

"Ridiculous." Orya waved her fan lazily and leaned back in her seat. "Your honor might belong to your kingdom, but your virtue is yours alone, to keep or give away as you see fit. And honor and virtue are not, despite what some would say, the same thing."

Azmei shook her head. She didn't want to talk about this. Not with anyone, but particularly not with Orya. How dare the other woman judge her own ruler! "I've never met anyone I would want to be with, anyway. And once I am married, I shall belong to my husband, as he will belong to me."

"Do you really believe princes are faithful?" Orya shrugged. "But I suppose this one might be. Your brother has always been very discreet, if he has affairs. The Strid prince, though--the elder, I mean--is notorious for his womanizing."

Azmei turned away. "I don't want to know anything about my brother's past. Or Vistaren's. It is their business, not mine." She didn't think Razem had ever been in love. She wasn't so naïve as to think that meant he had never been with a woman, but she didn't want to think about it.

Orya made her laugh gentle and somewhat condescending. "And yet your virtue is your kingdom's business?"

"Well, it certainly isn't yours," Azmei snapped. She stood and stalked away from Orya. She was fanning herself faster now.

"Do you not see they hold you to a different standard than they do princes? For all your vaunted independent thought and playing with daggers, they all still see you as a pretty thing to dress up and give to whomever pays most for your virtue."

Azmei whirled on her. "How dare you--" she began, and Orya interrupted. She *interrupted* her *princess*.

"I apologize," she said quickly. "I have offended you." She stood. "I will withdraw."

If she expected Azmei to call her back, she would be sorely disappointed. Azmei watched her leave without giving her the dignity of a response. As soon as the door shut behind her, Azmei called to Guira.

"I will see no one until Destar arrives. Orya Perslyn is not welcome to return this evening."

She stormed into her sleeping chamber, angry at Orya, but also angry at herself. Why had she allowed the other woman to upset her? She had no reason to feel ashamed of her choices. Royalty should live as a sacrifice to the kingdom. Was it asking so much that she abstain from certain pleasures?

She threw herself into the cushioned window seat and propped her chin on her hand. Lightning flickered and she automatically began to count her heartbeats. Then she stopped, feeling stupid. Her heartbeat was faster than usual, so it wouldn't be accurate. Besides, what did it matter? The storm would hit or it wouldn't, and either way, she was inside solid stone walls.

She had never cared one way or another about storms before learning she would be going to live in a kingdom where storms could be used as weapons by a select few people. Vistaren had brought a stormwitch with him, hadn't he? What would she think of this storm? Perhaps it was her doing that last night's storm had deflected to the north.

Azmei sighed. What if Vistaren *had* loved other women before? Would he have abstained out of fear of having bastards, or would it matter in Amethir? She couldn't think of any kingdom where it would be a good thing for royalty to have illegitimate children. Succession could be such a cloudy issue anyway.

No, surely Vistaren wouldn't have taken that chance. But what if he had?

He had said he didn't wish to have secrets between them when they married. Could this be what he had meant? What if he already knew about children? Azmei had never given the prospect of becoming a mother much thought; it would happen because it was the role of a princess to marry and bear children. But was it something she craved? What if Vistaren had been with other women who gave him children? Even worse, what if he had children by others, but could have none with Azmei?

She slumped down, laying her arms on the windowsill and her head on her arms. It didn't matter. She would marry him regardless. She *must* marry him. And she would worry about his past only if and when it mattered.

Whatever else happened, she could not let Orya's crass insinuations drive a wedge of mistrust between her and Vistaren.

Lightning flashed outside and Azmei counted only fifteen heartbeats between that and the crash of thunder that rattled the pane of glass in its setting. The storm was getting closer. She tilted her head so she could watch the black clouds roil in. The sun hadn't set, but the clouds had darkened the sky so much it looked like twilight outside. It was beautiful, in a powerful, almost frightening way.

Rain spattered against the windowpane. Azmei flinched at the first unexpected drops, then smiled and watched them roll down the pane. She got up and found the glass of wine she had abandoned when Orya arrived. Refilling it was perhaps not a good idea, but she had only drunk half of it, anyway. She took her glass back to the window seat and settled back against the cushions to watch the lightning show.

Twenty minutes later, the storm was still working itself into its strongest. Guira's knock was nearly drowned out by the crashes of thunder overhead.

"Come!" Azmei called.

"Captain Thorne is here, my lady."

"Show him in. You might as well come in as well, Guira. He may have news or instructions for us both, concerning security for the upcoming betrothal celebration."

Guira disappeared for a moment, then returned, leading Destar. He came in and bowed deeply without even a glance at the folding screen that hid Azmei's bed from the rest of the chamber.

"Sit down, Destar, and let us talk," Azmei said. "Guira will pour you a cup of wine. Have you eaten?"

"I have no need of supper, princess. A cup of wine wouldn't go amiss, though, I confess. The weather gets my knee all tight, and wine does help."

Azmei nodded. "Is all well, Captain?"

"As well as I can make it. My soldiers are pleased with how the Ranarri are conducting themselves. These Diplomats mean business when they say they believe in peace. My thanks, Guira." Destar took the wine Guira handed him and sipped. "Many of my security requirements are redundant because of university policy. I won't complain about that, though I do hear a bit of grumbling from the men since I don't let them slacken their own duties because of it."

Azmei shrugged. "If the Ranarri are doing your men's work for them, why not let them?"

"You want me to rely on the diligence of folk we aren't sure of? Oh, nothing against the Ranarri," he added, "but I'm sure of myself, and I'm sure of my men and women. I've been diligent about weeding out the bad well before now. Can we say the same about the Diplomats?"

"I suppose not. But I hope you aren't being obvious about it. We wouldn't like to offend them, either."

Destar bobbed his head. "Protocol's protocol," he said. "If there's one thing these Diplomats understand, it's that. They don't take any offense. Matter of fact, I've had more than one issue praise at our diligence."

Azmei laughed. "Well, I have no further complaint myself, then. And what of the Amethirians? Is all well there?"

"As far as I know." Destar took another drink of his wine. "The prince is busy, but then, the Amethirians and Ranarri are close neighbors, after all."

"The mainland north of us, across the bay?" Azmei said.

"Aye. All of the mainland is Amethir, now. Parts of it might not have been, a century ago, but the Ranarri Diplomats have been in power here for many centuries. None of the mainland ever belonged to Ranarr."

"Why would they want the mainland?" Azmei said. She waved a hand at the window. "They have all they could want here."

Destar chuckled. "You'll do well in Amethir. Their dry season is supposed to be much like the weather we've seen here, this week's storms aside."

Azmei's stomach fluttered. She sat straighter. "I'm glad to hear it. I suppose the wet season will grow tiresome, but at least the dry season will be pleasant."

"I'm told the palace is a lovely building, every bit as grand as the university here, and then some," Destar said. "I've done some asking around, looking for those who've actually been there."

"Good." Azmei lifted her cup to her lips and was surprised to find it empty. She held it out to Guira for a refill. It wasn't at all wise, but she didn't care tonight.

What if Orya was right about Vistaren? What if he was nothing like he seemed now once they returned to his home? What if Azmei was agreeing to a life of misery?

Don't be ridiculous, she told herself. She gulped her wine. "How long before the storm season arrives in Amethir?"

How long did she have before she must stop stalling and sign the treaty that declared them married?

Destar scratched his chin, blunt fingers rasping against evening shadow. "Let's see, the rainy season ended perhaps six weeks ago now. I'd say another twelve weeks before the storm season arrives in force. But the Storm Petrel won't sail with royalty on board anytime close to storm season.

I'd say the *Dawn Star* will have to leave port in another eight weeks, to stay on the lee side of things."

Eight weeks. How could she hope to discover enough about Vistaren to be sure of her decision in only eight weeks? Azmei gulped her wine again.

"You needn't make up your mind in that time, my lady." Destar's voice was low. "If more time is what's needed, you can wait until the rainy season to travel to Amethir."

Azmei looked up at him. "Oh, Destar." She closed her lips on the complaints and doubts that bubbled up. "No, I have decided. The Diplomats are already planning our betrothal celebration, after all."

"That doesn't bind you." He leaned forward. "Nothing binds you until you sign the treaty with your own hand."

Azmei lifted her chin. "Which I have said I will do. Would you have me forsworn, Destar?"

His gaze was warm as he looked at her. She hoped it was pride. Nearly as much as her brother and father, she wished to make her teacher proud of her. "Nay, lass," he said at last. "I would not. I will say again, it is a brave and noble thing you do for Tamnen."

She gave him a wan smile. "Thank you for your confidence, my friend." She lifted her cup to wet her lips. "Now go, if you have nothing further. I wish to be alone."

Orya was in a foul mood by the time she hauled herself over the windowsill and dropped inside her bed chamber. She was soaked through, and on her way back to the university she had missed a step and plunged into a gutter ankle-deep with storm runoff. Her right boot squelched every time she took a step, and it had made scaling the wall more difficult than usual.

Her argument with Azmei had been designed to sow the seeds of doubt in the princess' mind concerning her betrothed. It had certainly worked, if Azmei's reaction was any indication. But any extra time it might have bought Orya was time she sorely needed.

Her initial plan abandoned, she was also reevaluating her fallback plan. And on top of that, she was not beginning to doubt her activities had gone entirely undetected.

She remained convinced Destar Thorne thought of her as nothing more than a silly cloth merchant, but there was no sense in foregoing common sense. Whether or not Thorne saw her as a threat, he could not observe her leaving her quarters in the middle of the night if she left by uncommon exits.

But Thorne wasn't the only possible threat. The Diplomats might not suspect her, but they couldn't fail to be aware there had been threats against the princess' life--and the prince's, for that matter, though Orya hadn't been able to discover anyone working towards that end.

And then there was that tall, hooded figure she had seen the night before. She'd glimpsed him again tonight while she skulked through streets steaming from cold rainfall on sun-heated cobbles. The mist had shrouded her from view, wrapped as she was in thin gray wool, but it had also prevented her from getting a good look at the man. She'd caught a glimpse of a white-streaked dark beard, but that was all. At least he hadn't seen her this time.

"My lady?"

She gasped, whipping out her dagger as she whirled around to stare into the darkened room. The moon was waxing, but its light wasn't strong enough to illuminate more than a pace or two inside the window.

"Oh, Orya, I'm sorry!" She could hear the shock even through the sudden rushing in her ears. And she could recognize Wenda's voice now.

"What are you doing waiting for me in my room?" she snapped. "I might have killed you first and only seen afterwards that it was you. Have you no sense?"

"I am so dreadfully sorry, cousin." Sulfur burned Orya's nostrils as Wenda lit a candle, illuminating her contrite expression. "I was only thinking that someone might get suspicious if they noticed a light in your room so late."

"Perhaps, but not as suspicious as they would be if I accidentally murdered my cousin in the middle of the night," Orya muttered. "Why are you sitting in my room anyway?"

"I wanted to pass along some of the tidbits of information I've collected." Wenda shrugged. "It can wait if you'd rather sleep."

Orya waved a hand. "No, go on. I want a glass of water. Shall I pour two?" She went to the table where a small stone vault kept drinks chilled and began pouring.

"Please." Wenda settled on the padded bench at the foot of the bed. "I trust your errands were fruitful?"

Orya lifted an eyebrow. "You may trust so if you like. You know I won't tell you."

Wenda folded her hands, casting her gaze down at them. "Of course. I forgot."

"You know the rules as well as any," Orya snapped. There were actually whole branches of the family that knew nothing of the true nature of the Perslyn trade.

Orya poured the second glass. She didn't think Wenda was truly interested in Orya's murderous errands. As if the crippled girl could learn how to be an assassin, even if she wanted to! Wenda was good with fabric and she ought to be content to create the intricate patterns decorating some of the trim pieces they sold.

"Here," Orya said, holding out the glass. "Tell me what you've learned."

"First of all, there's nothing to indicate that the prince is anything less than whole-hearted about his courtship of the princess. He spends a fair amount of time alone in his courtyard, but the servants say no one visits him there alone. He has had several appointments with Amethirians living here in Ranarr, and I have heard there is grumbling about taxation. The rest of his time he spends with Azmei. Oh, or his advisers, Dzornaea and Algot." Wenda lifted her glass.

"Is that so?" Orya took a long gulp of her water and unfastened her knife belt. "Is there something between the two advisors? Arama Dzornaea is famous for her refusal to marry. I don't know anything about this General Algot."

"Everyone agrees he's hopelessly in love with her. No one can agree about how she feels, though." Wenda curled both legs under her. "The kitchen servants think she spends her nights in the general's bed. The chambermaid denies it, but chambermaids can be bought off."

Orya hummed and untied the scarf from her hair. "What does Vistaren think, I wonder. And how can I best use that?" She tapped a finger against her glass. "Perhaps a better angle to pursue would be the Amethirian unrest. I'll have to look into that tomorrow. It will be several days before I am ready for the next stage in my plans, anyway."

Wenda's mouth turned down. "I could help you better if I knew what you were doing."

"I'm already bending the rules close to breaking by telling you what I have," Orya snapped. "My grandfather may have no high opinion of me, but I am a loyal daughter of the Perslyn despite that. Cease asking me, or I shall thrust you outside my plans altogether."

Wenda sighed, but her eyes sparkled in a way that told Orya she was uncowed. Perhaps she would stop asking, but she wouldn't stop wondering. Orya supposed that was the most she could hope for, anyway. Wenda had turned out to be both more spirited and more resourceful than Orya would have reckoned. In some ways, it was almost too bad she had the crippled foot. She could have been so much more than a cloth merchant.

Orya gentled her voice. "Leave me, now. I'm tired." She shrugged out of her vest and went to pour another glass of water. What she wouldn't give for it to be something stronger, but she must keep her wits about her until this contract was fulfilled.

Wenda's uneven footsteps paused. "Good night, cousin," she murmured, and then the door closed behind her.

"Good night," Orya whispered. She shaded the candle and went to stare out the window. So much more than a cloth merchant, she thought again. And yet, was assassin truly better than merchant?

Orya had always been proud of her skills, honing her reflexes and balance with hours of practice. But in the end, what did she do with all those skills? She sold them. Worse--she allowed the patriarch to sell them for her. She wasn't truly in control of her own destiny. She was merely a weapon in someone else's hand, used to dispatch whatever target the patriarch chose.

Perhaps the Wendas and Yarros of the family actually had it better than Orya. They belonged to the family, true, but they were also, for the most part, beneath the notice of the patriarch. He only cared about Yarro as a way to manipulate Orya. He had never realized that, with Orya, he needed no leverage.

Orya turned and blew out the candle.

Chapter Thirty

Azmei was going to be late. Guira had fussed at her about it but hadn't shortened her preparations. She'd braided Azmei's hair and brushed on the cosmetics as if she and Vistaren hadn't already seen each other half a dozen times by now. The whole time, Azmei had huffed out remarks about the time, but Guira merely snorted and said perhaps Azmei shouldn't have stayed up so late last night reading.

If only Azmei *had* been reading. As the storm diminished into a steady rainfall, Azmei had lain awake in bed, staring blankly into the darkness and brooding about how little time she had left and how much was still unknown about her betrothed.

Now Azmei was all but running through the university halls. Her silly, girlish slippers kept falling off her heels, making her pause to fix them back in place. Every time she paused, Destar Thorne, her security for the afternoon, snorted. How nice that someone got amusement from her predicament.

As she paused and slid her index finger inside the back of the shoe yet again, Azmei heard an angry voice from somewhere off to her right. "--I know what he told you, and he had no right--"

"He was trying to do what's best." That was a more placating tone, a man's voice.

"He should have asked what was best before he started shoving his nose in things he doesn't understand." The woman's voice had gone from hot to cold. And it sounded familiar. Azmei lowered her foot and twisted it gently, trying to get the slipper seated more firmly on her heel. It was her own fault for wearing them. She'd complained about all the fussing, but she'd wanted to look particularly nice today when she saw Vistaren.

"It's only natural, considering the situation he's in."

"Oh, stop being so reasonable!" the woman snapped. Footsteps rang on the stone floor, approaching Azmei rapidly. Whoever the woman was, she was about to catch Azmei eavesdropping on her. After a quick glance at Destar, Azmei shrugged and waited for whoever it was to show up. Why did the voice seem so familiar?

When the woman came into view, her short stature and blue-black hair identified her immediately. Azmei blinked. "Arama?"

The pirate captain, so intent on getting away from her conversation, had obviously failed to look where she was going. She stumbled to a halt in front of Azmei and said, "Oh, shit."

"Thank you," Azmei said, though she wasn't really offended. "I am late to an appointment with Vistaren. However, we have had little time to talk, you and I, and I regret that. I am eager to ask your advice on a matter that concerns us both." She smiled. "I would speak with you, tomorrow perhaps, if you have no other duties."

She saw the consternation cross Arama's face, but it was the prerogative of princesses to ignore consternation when it was convenient. She smiled pleasantly at the pirate and tilted her head, awaiting the older woman's answer.

"Of course, princess. It would be my pleasure to attend you whenever you like."

Azmei nodded. "Very good. Come to see me tomorrow afternoon, then. Good day, Captain."

Arama bowed as Azmei swept past on her way to Vistaren's quarters.

The prince seemed out of sorts that day, though he perked up when Azmei asked him to tell her about his home. He spoke so eloquently about the palace, with its sweeping terraces overlooking the capital city, Maron, that Azmei suspected he was homesick. He talked about the central Gehb River Estuary and how the estuary folk tended to band together on political issues. He told her about stormwitches whose primary duties were to ensure the Gehb flooded just perfectly, enough to fertilize the farmlands every year without destroying any property.

"And there's the Sandswamp, which I've never seen. I'd like to, though. It's supposed to be covered with knee-deep water for miles in every direction, with just sandy hummocks rising up out of the water here and there. There are swamp folk, I've heard, but not many of them, and none of them have any real villages or anything. I'd like to learn more about them."

"Perhaps they are isolated because they choose to be," Azmei pointed out.

"Perhaps." Vistaren tapped his lower lip. "Have you read the tale about when Aevver went into the Sandswamp?" Azmei shook her head, and Vistaren grinned. "She was looking for magic to heal a fouled spring, and the fisher lord's daughter told her of a wise woman who lived in the Sandswamp. Some people think Aevver's quest to heal the spring is how we got stormwitchery."

"Is it?"

Vistaren shook his head. "I don't think so. I told you--the night we met--about the stormsingers."

Azmei nodded. "I remember. Great behemoths."

"Yes. I've never heard anything that says they can change their shape. But the water of the Sandswamp would be too shallow for them unless they could become very small, or perhaps change to look like us."

"They're the ones who taught stormwitchery to humans, you said," Azmei recalled.

"Yes. So I think, whoever it was Aevver found in the Sandswamp, she wasn't a stormwitch."

Azmei leaned her chin in her hand. "I cannot wait to read more about Aevver and her sisters."

"Oh, you'll love the stories," Vistaren promised. "I haven't got a copy for you yet, but I have someone looking. There must be good booksellers here on Ranarr."

"There are! Some of them had stalls at the market." Azmei launched into a retelling of her exploration of the Ranarri markets the day after she arrived. Vistaren seemed content to listen, though she could sense him growing more distant the longer she chattered. What was he thinking about? Someone he had left behind when he came here to meet her? Azmei's throat grew dry thinking about it. Finally she trailed off.

"I beg your pardon," she said. "I find I am rather tired."

He looked ruefully at her. "I was inattentive."

"No, not at all!" She pulled her lips to one side. Even polite lies were still lies. "Well, not much."

"It is I who should beg your pardon, Azmei. I am taking advantage of this visit to Ranarr to look into certain situations here, among Amethirians who live here on the island." Vistaren rubbed a hand down his jaw. "I fear some of them said things that have me rather preoccupied. Will you forgive me?"

"Of course. But I feel bad for distracting you."

"Not at all," he said, then laughed. "Well. We are falling all over ourselves apologizing to one another. Perhaps instead we should agree to part as friends tonight and meet again tomorrow." He broke off and swore. "No, not tomorrow, I have an engagement I cannot break. The day after tomorrow?"

An engagement? She bit back the question that sprang to her lips. It was not her business who Vistaren might be spending time with while he was here. She surely knew him well enough to be confident he would not carry on an affair while arranging their betrothal.

Trying not to let her disappointment show, Azmei smiled. "Of course, that sounds lovely." She stood. "I will see you then."

Vistaren took her hand in his and bowed low over it. "Dream well, Azmei."

CHAPTER THIRTY-ONE

L OZARR HAD LOW EXPECTATIONS for the Chatty Raven, but he was pleasantly surprised when his advance party arrived in the tavern yard. The Raven was constructed of the same white stone as the rest of Ranarr, but it had been painted a deep blue color, and the sign was fresh painted. The yard was swept clean; though there were few horses on the island, there were plenty of other sources of refuse. He could hear, inside the tavern, the patter of a hand drum.

He gestured to the guards he had brought with him. Four would remain in the yard, four more would circle around to guard the back entrance, and two would come inside with Lozarr and Arama, to be at hand if they were needed. Arama was accompanying the prince with another squad of soldiers. Lo stepped inside, his gaze flicking around the room.

The interior of the tavern was well lit and clean. More than a dozen people of various Amethirian ethnicities were gathered inside, most of them at two tables in the center of the room. Yadian Shemma sat at the head of one of those tables.

He rose when Lozarr came into the room. "General Lozarr," he said. "You're early."

"I came ahead of the prince." Lo made his voice curt. "I will brook no disrespect to the prince, Shemma. He has already given you more attention than I would have spared in his place. After he arrives, you will remain seated at all times. One of my soldiers will carry any food and drink you have ordered, and it will be tested before the prince partakes of any."

Shemma glowered at him. "Weapons are all on the table," he said, gesturing at them. "Would you like your men to gather them for safekeeping?"

Lo raised an eyebrow, surprised.

"We're in earnest, general," Shemma said. "We genuinely love our country and our king, but our lives have brought us here—many of us for our trade, or for our studies. Some of us because we're restless. Some for their own reasons. But none of us are rich enough we can pay taxes to Ranarr and to Amethir both, not if we're to be ignored by the ambassadors and charged high tariffs for the goods we send back home."

Lozarr didn't smile as he gestured for Skaya to gather the weapons and move them to an empty table across the room. "Prince Vistaren is the one you must convince of your earnestness," he said. "I require only that you be harmless while the prince is here."

Shemma folded his arms across his chest. "I think we can agree on that," he said. He gestured to his companions. "This is Marka, a basketmaker whose husband fishes. Shoanna there is a dyer. Her brother is at the university and she came with him because they've no other family. Yasbon makes beer. I'm a drygoods merchant."

Lozarr nodded as a clamor of voices rose in the tavern yard. "That'll be the prince," he said. He nodded to one of his soldiers, who stepped out the door. A moment later, he returned, Vistaren and Arama behind him.

Shemma and his companions rose and bowed to the prince. Lo noted that Shemma's bow was deeper than it had been in the market. "Your Highness, you are our honored guest. Thank you for coming."

"I've reviewed the complaints you documented," Vistaren said. "I find that some of your arguments have merit. The issues are too weighty for me to address in a single meeting. Indeed, I am of the belief that at least you, Yadian, should return to Amethir with me to discuss these issues at length."

Lo only paid cursory attention to the conversation that followed. He was more interested in the body language of the prince's companions, as well as any possible outside threat. Arama, who had taken a position against the back wall, was likewise engaged. Vistaren didn't actually agree to anything, as far as Lozarr could tell, but when the conversation was over and they left the Chatty Raven, all parties seemed satisfied that progress had been made.

"That was well done," Arama murmured as they walked back towards the hired chairs that were waiting for them.

"There will have to be more meetings to hash out the details," Vistaren said, his tone self-deprecating. Then he huffed. "But thank you. I think it was well done."

When Vistaren disembarked from his chair at the university, he almost bumped into Princess Azmei, who was looking lovely and impish in a blue silk tunic with a darker blue skirt. Her sandals were gold, and she wore a bracelet around one wrist, but no one would take her for a princess, Lo thought. He found himself thinking warm thoughts about the Tamnese princess. Between her adventurous nature and the fact that she'd obviously chosen the Rona and Fann adventures because she was aware of—and accepted—Vistaren's love of men, Azmei seemed the best person for Vistaren's marriage alliance.

Vistaren's cheeks darkened in a blush. He bowed hastily. "Princess, my apologies. My feet are clumsy."

Azmei had light brown skin and long black hair, which was currently twisted back in an intricately braided style. Lo couldn't help but smile as she swept a polite curtsy. "It is I who must beg your pardon, Prince Vistaren," she said. "I was in too much of a hurry, and did not watch where I was going."

The stilted, polite language made Lo grit his teeth, but he couldn't help thinking that Vistaren and Azmei at least liked each other. He found himself smiling as he and Arama turned away from the conversation.

"What is going on inside your head?" Arama asked, her voice soft.

When Lozarr looked at her, her blue eyes were intent on his face. He smiled and rubbed a hand across his hair. "I am just glad they seem to like each other," he said, pitching his voice to match hers. "It could be much worse."

She nodded. "I don't know what the Tamnese in general think of same-lovers," she said. "It's good that she doesn't seem to care."

Lo pursed his lips. "That isn't exactly what I meant," he said. "Though it's part of it, I suppose. But Vistaren's always known he probably wouldn't marry for love. I don't say he's resigned to it, of course, but at least it comes as no surprise."

Arama tilted her head, watching him.

"Well, if they can be friends, that's more than many in arranged marriages can claim, isn't it?" Lo shrugged. "Just because our king and queen fell in love after their wedding, that doesn't mean everyone can. It's a rare thing to find someone who sees you for who are and still chooses you."

"Chooses." Arama's voice was strange. When Lo glanced back down at her, she was looking down the long passageway. "But they didn't choose each other."

"Not as spouses, perhaps, but they might still choose each other as companions. It's enough to build an alliance on."

Vistaren knew Lozarr would chide him for slipping out of their apartments without a guard, but he was beginning to feel stifled by the level of security Lo had enacted. When Lo was occupied checking the duty roster for his men and consulting with Arama, Vistaren had grabbed a full flask of whiskey, Azmei's translated book, and a bag of mixed delightberries and nuts.

His meeting at the Chatty Raven had gone well. Vistaren had taken time to speak with each of the individuals who came to the meeting, and he had liked most of them. One or two were overly concerned with their own problems and less interested in working with their fellow expatriates, but they had all been respectful and courteous.

Yadian Shemma, in particular, struck Vistaren as a good and honest man. He had spoken knowledgeably about the Amethirian tax code, tariffs, and shipping schedules. He had known more about the Ranarri tax code than Vistaren had, despite the research Vistaren had done to prepare. His explanations had been concise without being condescending. He had also taken the time to introduce Vistaren to the others.

Shoanna, a pretty Sterr with light gray eyes, had moved to Ranarr with her brother, who was studying languages at the University. He hoped to become a translator with the Diplomats. In the meantime, Shoanna had brought their family's trade of dye-making to Ranarr. She was successful enough to rent a set of rooms, but there was little money to spare.

Yasbon made the beer for the Chatty Raven. He brewed it in Amethirian style using important Amethirian grains, but between the shipping costs and the tariffs, his craft wasn't cheap. He sold it exclusively to the Chatty Raven because the innkeeper did thriving business with the upper class of Amethirian expatriates. If that relationship ever failed, though, or if business slacked off, Yasbon would be in trouble.

Meeting these people, seeing their faces and hearing their individual stories, had only cemented Vistaren's desire to do right by them. He and his father often discussed state issues, and he was confident his father would listen to him. He still felt strongly that Yadian Shemma, at least, should travel back to Maron City when Vistaren returned—hopefully with a marriage treaty signed and sealed.

A jolt went through Vistaren. Sleeping gods, if he returned to Amethir, he would hopefully be returning with a *bride*.

"Gods give me strength," he muttered. "A wife is the last thing I want." He sighed and rubbed his hands over his face. Just like that, he was back to thinking about Azmei.

What would she think about the unrest, if she knew about it? Would she think Vistaren weak for meeting with them and hearing them out? Or would she appreciate his cleverness and generosity?

It's not as if you're trying to make her fall in love with you, he reminded himself. *Sooner or later, you're going to have to admit you're marrying her only for heirs. You'll have to find out if she's willing to settle for being only your friend and consort, mother of your children.*

He fished the whiskey flask out of his pocket and took a long drink.

The most damnable part of it was that he *liked* Azmei. He had enjoyed their months of correspondence before they agreed to meet. He had appreciated her frank good humor about the nature of their tenuous relationship. They hadn't yet spent much time together in person, but the evening they had spent in the courtyard before they knew each other's identities had been one of the best evenings in his recent memory.

He glanced down at the blue leather cover of her translation. She was intelligent, thoughtful, and kind. He thought she would approve of his dealing with Shemma and the others. At their next luncheon engagement, he would ask her opinion. Even if he ended up disagreeing with her suggestions, it would be a good exploration of her thoughts on policy. It might be a good way to see if they would have compatible ruling styles.

He traced a finger across the design embossed on the book. She seemed curious and compassionate. Was she perceptive? Had she read between the lines—or perhaps heard something about him—and realized why their marriage posed him such a dilemma? Whas that why she had chosen Rona and Fann to translate?

He hadn't finished reading her translation, of course, and his Tamnese was not as strong as he would like. She had included the story when Rona married Aevver, with Fann standing by his side. Azmei used what he believed was the romantic form of love for Rona's relationship with Aevver. She had also used it, on at least one occasion, to describe Rona's relationship with Fann.

The mythology was clear about Rona's love and desire for both his wife and his best friend. There was no record of jealousy between Aevver and Fann. When she and Rona bore children—all daughters—she named her eldest Fiahna, which was the feminine of Fann. Vistaren truly believed she had understood her husband and made allowances, and that Fann had done so, too.

Sleeping gods, he hoped Azmei understood all that, too.

Footsteps and a soft gasp were all the warning he had that his introspection had been interrupted. Vistaren looked up to find a woman curtsying deeply to him. She had dark hair and wore Tamnese silk, but he could already see that she was taller than Azmei. When she spoke, he recognized her.

"My apologies, Prince Vistaren. I did not realize anyone was here. I did not mean to intrude."

"No apologies are needed, Mistress Perslyn," he said, guiltily relieved that Azmei herself hadn't interrupted him while he was thinking about her. "Had I sought true solitude, I have a private courtyard. But I enjoy the fragrance of these flowers, and they do not grow in my courtyard."

She glanced up without straightening. "They are very pretty, Highness."

"You traveled with Princes Azmei, I believe," he said, gesturing for her to rise.

"Yes, Highness." She smiled, revealing a dimple in her right cheek. "We first met at her leave-taking ball in Tamnen. But ships can make for quick friendships." She paused, a flicker of uncertainty crossing her face. "Or quick acquaintances, at least."

"Indeed." Vistaren hid his amusement, but he found it interesting that she was attempting to imply a close friendship with the princess while overtly doing the exact opposite. "What brought you to Ranarr, if you are not part of Azmei's entourage?"

"I am a cloth merchant, Highness," she said eagerly. "Perslyn House is well known for its silks in Tamnen and the Long Coast. The princess's voyage here seemed a propitious time to expand our trade."

"Silk, you say?" Vistaren smiled. "I am fond—perhaps overfond, I confess—of silk shirts. I must find a tailor to commission one with your wares. Have you anything in dark green?"

"Certainly, Highness! My cousin and I have made agreements with two of the best tailors in Ranarr—as well as some of the best dressmakers, of course." She dimpled at him again.

"I am pleased to hear it." He rose, suddenly tired of the conversation. "I will send someone out tomorrow to get me a shirt."

Fortunately she took the hint. With another curtsy, she backed away. "I hope you have a peaceful evening, Prince Vistaren."

As soon as she had disappeared around the corner, he headed back to his apartments, taking with him even more to think about.

Chapter Thirty-Two

Azmei was disinclined to receive Orya when the merchant called two days after their argument. Azmei had been plagued by doubt and confusion since their conversation, and Vistaren's behavior yesterday didn't help. But Azmei wasn't one to hold a grudge. She would hear what Orya had to say. If the woman continued to be insulting, Azmei would cut their friendship.

She had Guira serve drinks and sweet pastries while she made Orya wait. She would not hold a grudge, but she would remind the merchant of her place in the world.

Azmei tapped her fingers against the windowsill as she listened to the clink of cup against serving tray in the next room. How long should she wait? Guira had spent so much time drilling promptness into her that deliberately dawdling over her preparations rankled.

Instead of retreating to the entry hall of their chambers, Guira tapped on Azmei's door and let herself in. Her lips were pressed together. She crossed the room in silence. When she reached Azmei, a chuckle escaped her.

"It is probably safe for you to go out now. Orya has dropped a pastry and spilled her wine. I would venture to declare she is nervous."

Azmei smiled grimly. "Good. She and I did not part on friendly terms. I will have her apology before we return to familiarity."

"Well done, princess," Guira said. She squeezed Azmei's hand. When Azmei went out to meet Orya, Guira followed silently.

Orya was studying the contents of her cup. While Azmei watched, she crossed her ankles, then uncrossed them, then reached up to pat at her hair. She only looked up when the sleeping chamber door clicked shut behind Azmei.

Orya jumped to her feet. "Princess!" Her cup clutched in one hand, she swept into a curtsy. "Thank you for being willing to see me."

Azmei lifted her chin. "I am willing at the moment," she said, her voice cool. "As to whether I shall remain willing ...Well, we shall see."

"Please allow me to tender my strongest regrets and sincerest apologies," Orya said. It was impressive how she managed to hold her curtsy and speak at the same time without her balance wobbling.

Azmei would not make this easy for her. "Continue." She sat, spreading her skirts around her.

Orya didn't even falter. "I was beyond impertinent. I was insulting. I freely admit you are within your rights to hold my words against me. I had no right to speak of your brother Prince Razem or your betrothed Prince Vistaren as I did. I had no right to presume such a close friendship between us that would allow me to speak so freely of such personal matters." She wet her lips. "I should not have dared to speak so to you."

Azmei ought to draw this out, but she wasn't interested in punishing either of them more than was necessary. "You may rise," she informed Orya. "I shall consider your apology."

Orya straightened. "Please forgive me, your highness. My words were unforgiveable, but my motive was love. I would see you happy, and in my eagerness to give you advice, I failed to consider how unwelcome and unnecessary that advice would be."

Azmei softened. "Or how ill-mannered," she suggested. "Very well, I invite you to remain here and speak with me for a time."

"Oh, thank you, Princess Azmei." Orya dipped another curtsy as a smile ventured across her face. "I confess, I was greatly troubled when I saw you last, and my uncertain frame of mind no doubt contributed to my poor judgment."

It was an obvious attempt at excusing her impertinence, but Azmei decided to go along. She tilted her head to one side. "Why were you troubled, Orya?"

The other woman looked down. "I should not trouble you with it, princess."

"And yet you will, because I ask it of you," Azmei said.

Orya dipped her head in obedience. "I was thinking of my brother, your highness."

"Your brother." Azmei held out her hand and Guira placed a cup in it. "You have three, I think you said."

"Your highness remembers well." Orya's lips curved in a brief smile. "I don't care for my two elder brothers. They have made a sport of trying to best me in our business. But my youngest brother, Yarro... He is different. Special." Her lips curved up again.

"Tell me about him." Azmei sipped her wine. She would invite Orya to sit soon, but not yet.

"He is fourteen. He should have been prenticed already, but he has always been...delicate." Orya's lips pursed. "Our grandfather has no use for anyone who cannot contribute. I agreed, many years ago, to take up whatever burden my brother left slack." Her hands knotted together.

Azmei wondered if she resented that agreement now. "Go on," she urged.

Orya sighed. "I worry about him. I worry what will happen if I fail to secure all the trade agreements my grandfather has demanded of me." She turned her face away, and Azmei heard a sniffle. "I fear my grandfather will try to force him into apprenticeship, and Yarro's health will not allow it. I cannot stand the thought of seeing my brother's frail body broken by the harsh demands of our trade."

"Is it so harsh?" Azmei asked, keeping her voice neutral. "I have seen your lame cousin's work, and she is quite skilled. Could Yarro not take on the same duties as she?"

"I fear not. His eyesight is poor, and he hears almost nothing." Orya looked back at her, and Azmei saw tears glistening in her eyes. "Delicate needlework would ruin whatever eyesight he has left, and without his hearing, he could not take directions."

She seemed truly distraught over her brother's situation. Azmei took a slow breath and waved her hand at the chair. "Be seated, Orya. There is no need for you to be so formal when you are distressed."

Orya's smile was tremulous. "My princess is most generous."

"Tell me more about your brother," Azmei said. "Perhaps my own brother could use a squire. Even if it were in name only, it would surely protect him from your grandfather."

She waved off Orya's profuse thanks and urged her again to talk about Yarro. It might take some time, but Azmei felt confident their friendship could be repaired.

Chapter Thirty-Three

The next day, Azmei met Arama in the courtyard where she and Vistaren had first met. She wore the brown silk tunic, which made her feel more confident and less silly, compared to the brave sea-captain. She didn't want Arama to think her nothing but a spoiled princess.

"Thank you for allowing me to sit in the sun for a while." Arama grimaced. "It's not easy on an old seadog, being trapped on dry land indoors."

Azmei laughed and sat next to Arama. "Come, you can't have any right to call yourself old"

"Mm. Perhaps not. I'm thirty this year. Feels old." Arama glanced over at her, lips pulling to one side. "You're just a bit older than the prince, aren't you?"

"Twenty-one," Azmei confirmed.

Arama nodded. "It seems late for royalty to wed. They didn't break a covenant to arrange this, did they?"

Azmei felt her face heat. She didn't think the other woman was being malicious in pointing it out, just blunt. But it was a valid question. "I believe my father was hoping for Prince Anderlin of the Strid, but..." She trailed off and shrugged. There had never been much hope for that in the first place, and when Anderlin had demanded the Kreyden as her bride-price, Marsede had done an abrupt about-face. The threats Anderlin had issued when Marsede broke off negotiations still made Azmei shiver.

"Ah. You wouldn't want Anderlin anyway," Arama said. "There's at least one illegitimate child already, and I don't doubt he would laugh at the notion of fidelity." She grinned crookedly. "That's one area where I can vouch for *our* prince. He's always been shy with women." Her blue eyes fixed on Azmei's. "It's one of the things surprised us about all this, honestly. He took to you right quick, and it seems you've taken to him. I hope I'm right in thinking that?"

Azmei tasted the peppermint of her lip color as she licked her lips. "I like him a great deal. He is a lovely man, and I hope we will grow to love one another."

Some of the brightness in Arama's gaze faded, but she nodded, her grin slipping into a chagrined smile. "I suppose it isn't easy, being thrown together so and told to make a go of it."

Azmei shrugged and turned her back to the sun, enjoying the feel of it against her back. "Did you know we met by accident before our introduction?" she asked.

Arama laughed. "He did mention it after that formal introduction. I don't know that I've seen him so nervous before then. He was glad you forgave him."

Azmei felt a pang of protectiveness that surprised her. Arama, of all people, likely had most right to criticize Vistaren, but Azmei jumped to defend him. "I lied to him before he lied to me. I told him I was just one of the princess' party. I know why *I* lied." She paused and wet her lips again. "But do you know why *he* did?"

Arama gave her a long, considering look. Her eyes were very blue, and startling in her light brown skin. Azmei felt her face heating again before the pirate even said, "Why did you lie?"

"I..." She scuffed the sole of one slipper against the stone paving. "I was afraid to face my future." She realized it as she said it. She wanted to pretend it was to have an honest conversation with someone lower in rank, but there was only a tiny grain of truth to that pretense. The truth was simple, as Guira had pointed out a fortnight ago: Azmei wished not to grow up.

Arama's head bobbed slowly. "I think that is probably why Vistaren lied as well." She tilted her head. "He is intelligent and mature, but in some ways he's very young yet."

She stopped speaking, her gaze tracing up something behind Azmei's back. When Azmei looked over her shoulder, she realized there was a trellis growing there, flowering with peaceblossoms. She wondered if Vistaren had cut the flowers himself that he sent to her. It seemed the sort of thing he might do. Azmei felt her lips curving. She didn't love him, not at all, but she was quickly growing fond of him. He was a very genuine person, despite being a prince. It was one of his most admirable qualities.

Arama sighed and Azmei turned to look at her, recalled to their present conversation. The pirate made a gesture of dismissal. "Then again, what does a harridan pirate know of love, eh?" She grinned.

That was an opening Azmei couldn't let pass. "Oh! I thought..." She trailed off as if embarrassed. "I mean, aren't you and the general...That is, I..." She wished she could blush on demand. She settled for glancing aside and down. "Oh dear."

There was an extended silence. Azmei gave Arama several heartbeats for the words to sink in, then glanced up at her again. She surprised the tail end of shock, but as she looked at Arama, she saw the shock begin to fade into rue. At least there was no outrage; Azmei had no desire to offend Vistaren's sea-captain, but she was wildly curious, now that he'd mentioned it, what the relationship was between Arama and Lozarr.

"Damn," Arama said finally. She sounded almost guilty. Azmei widened her eyes, hoping she would go on, and was not disappointed. "I was hoping you hadn't misinterpreted things when you caught me leaving Lozarr's room that morning. It wasn't what you thought."

Azmei's mouth dropped open as the realization hit her. The first time they'd met, Arama had been sneaking--and apparently sneaking *out* of Lozarr's rooms. But it wasn't what she thought? "What was it then? You two clearly fit together."

One brown hand lifted to scrub across Arama's face. "You have keen sight," she mumbled. "Ah hells. Lo and I...well, it's complicated." She twisted her mouth as if wishing she had a strong drink. Likely she did, Azmei thought.

"Is it?" she inquired, making her tone as innocent as possible. "As complicated as trying to fall in love with someone in order to stop a war?"

"An honest hit," Arama said drily. She arched an eyebrow. "You're a formidable match for Vistaren, I'll give you that. I don't know if either father knows what they've wrought in this treaty."

Azmei folded her arms and gave her an unrepentant stare.

Arama huffed a sigh. "We've been friends far too long. I can't stand the thought of losing that friendship. And Lo's an idealist of the first rank. He doesn't see me as I truly am, just as he wants to see me." Her eyes darted away and then back to Azmei's. "When he learned my true character, he'd regret it. And if things went sour, it would ruin what we have now."

"Oh, you mean him pining and you cutting him needlessly?" The words were out of Azmei's mouth before she'd thought them through, but she found she didn't regret them. Arama did love Lozarr, however afraid she was to admit it. How dare she throw that away? She, who had the freedom to love where she wished--what Azmei wouldn't give for that freedom!

Arama bristled, her small frame straightening, her shoulders going back. Azmei pictured this stance on the deck of a ship and understood how the slight woman commanded hardened sailors and pirates. "Now listen--" Arama began, but Azmei was in no mood to let her off lightly.

"Perhaps you should listen to me, captain," she said, injecting every bit of imperiousness she could muster. "Have you considered how short and uncertain life is? Lozarr's fervor for you is clear. Many people live their whole lives without such devotion." Azmei felt a sudden shudder of anxiety.

"Some of us have little say in our fate," she went on. "But those who can choose their own path?" She shook her head. "It is arrogance to take such a privilege for granted. What I would give for the freedom to--"

Azmei broke off. Arama wasn't meeting her gaze now. Her jaw was still tight, but her shoulders slumped. Azmei drew in a quick, shaking breath.

"Shame on you, that you would use such a good man so." Azmei stopped speaking. She was afraid if she went on she would begin shouting, and calling the prince's sea-captain a fool, no matter how well deserved it was, would not endear her to the Amethirians. Instead she knotted her fingers together in her lap, tracing them with her eyes and trying to get her breathing back under control.

A flutter of wings brought a bright yellow and green bird down onto a branch that reached out from a stone planter next to her. Azmei blinked several times and pursed her lips at it, trying to make a chirping sound. She failed miserably. It cocked its head at her and flew away.

"Perhaps I am being a bit of a fool," Arama said at last. Her voice was low. She wouldn't look at Azmei. "It isn't quite as simple as you want it to sound, though."

Azmei cleared her throat. "Neither was Fann and--I mean, Aevver and Rona." Damn. Now her own ridiculous speculation was creeping out into her conversation.

"Hm." Arama glanced up at her through the blue-black wave of hair that fell across her forehead. "Why did you choose that epic, in particular?"

"Because I didn't know about *The Four Daughters of the Storm* when I set out to translate something for the prince," Azmei said, flippant. After reading a sampling of Amethirian tales, she had been drawn to Aevver. It wasn't until she began reading the cycle of tales more closely, with an eye towards translation, that she'd discovered the strange undercurrents between Rona and Fann.

"Huh." Arama rubbed a hand across her forehead. "I'm not a kind person, Azmei. If Lo sticks around long enough, he'll realize it, and I'll fall off the ivory pedestal he's put me on."

Azmei lifted her chin. "I can't pretend to know General Algot well, but I doubt he is quite as blinded to that as you wish to think." She twitched her lips into a smile. "Besides, it seems to me Lozarr doesn't care about that, or he wouldn't be in love with a pirate."

Arama gave her a reluctant smile. "Brat. I'm a privateer. I have my letter of marque from King Rekel."

Relieved that Arama wasn't angry at her meddling, Azmei laughed. "Ah, but you're talking to a Tamnese princess, remember. To me, you're nothing but a pirate until I marry Vistaren."

"There's nothing," Destar grumbled. "Nothing set in stone, nothing I can point to and say, 'Yes, this proves someone is watching you.' But something is not right here."

Azmei, dressed in her favorite brown silk, was examining the knife Vistaren had given her. The more she looked at it, the more she liked it. She had tested the edge already and found it keen. "Very well," she said. "Forget set in stone. What do you think? What do you *feel*?"

He grunted. "I think the fact there has already been one attempt on your life proves there are those back home who want this wedding not to go forward. If there are Tamnese who wish the wedding averted, there must be double that number of Strid. Our kingdom will only lose by your death. Strid stands to gain a great deal by it, if you're assassinated before the wedding."

"Because until Vistaren and I actually marry, my death won't offend Amethir," Azmei said, looking up at Destar in time to see him grimace.

"Exactly. No one wants to offend Amethir. The Strid may be powerful, but the Amethirians, quite frankly, rule the sea."

"What, the great Destar Thorne can't stand against them?" Azmei teased.

His eyes crinkled at the corners. "Impertinent girl." His voice was warm. "I actually consider myself fortunate that I've never come up against Arama Dzornaea on the open sea. The *Kerava* was supposed to be unsinkable, and she took it down without even using a stormwitch against them."

"She's very impressive."

"Aye, she is that. More so in person." Destar scratched his chin. "She lives up to the legend and then some. Though I admit, she's shorter than I expected."

Azmei laughed. "I like her. Her and the general both, though I haven't spoken to him as much."

"He's a canny one. Young for his rank, but then, there was that uprising west of the Garn Mountains ten years back or so. The Shroudling War, I think they called it. I seem to recall they lost more than a handful of ranked officers putting that down."

"Garn Mountains..." Azmei frowned. "They're in the middle of Amethir, aren't they?"

"More west than middle. The region west of 'em isn't big, but it's more isolated from the rest of the kingdom, and they were only brought into the empire a couple of generations ago. They're restive, you might say."

Azmei sighed. "I should have read more Amethirian history. I don't suppose I can get a book about it here in Ranarr, so it will have to wait until I'm actually there."

"No, there are hundreds of Amethirians living here on the White Stone. Large stormwitcheries are outlawed here, but folk of all nations are welcome to settle here. Even stormwitches, if they keep their magic to themselves for the most part." Destar stood and went to his chest. "I'll send someone out to look for a history of the kingdom for you. In the meantime..." He rooted around for a moment, then came back with a slender volume. "This is the past hundred years. It'll give you a good idea of recent history of your new home."

"I should have known you would have something," Azmei said, smiling. She took the book and stroked a fingertip across its pebbled leather surface. "Thank you, teacher."

He snorted. "Old habits die hard." He hesitated, rubbing his jaw, then sat on the edge of his chair, leaning towards her. "There's something else you might want to know. It may have no bearing on things between you and the prince, but there's no harm being forewarned."

Azmei set the book down in her lap and straightened. "What is it?"

"There's been some unrest here in Ranarr, among the Amethirians who've settled here. Seems they're being taxed the same as Amethirians living in the kingdom *and* they're taxed the same as Ranarri citizens. Needless to say, they don't like it. I'm not clear on all the particulars, and I don't think there's any danger from it. The Diplomats are pretty strict on keeping Ranarr a safe place to live. But Vistaren has—well, not enemies, exactly. I'd call them detractors, perhaps. I only thought you ought to know." Destar scratched his ear. "Mayhap the prince will want a sympathetic ear from time to time. I know he's been spending time in the Amethirian neighborhoods while he's been here."

"Thank you." Azmei looked down at her hands. She wasn't sure if Vistaren would confide in her about the unrest, but at least she would know. "Do you have anything I could read to learn more about that?"

He chuckled. "I'll see what I can find. I can tell you, it's got General Lozarr on alert. He seems to fear violence from them, but my understanding is that the prince himself has spoken with them and scheduled more meetings. I don't know what the Amethirian ambassador has been up to, if they're speaking straight to the prince, but it sounds like Vistaren is giving them his ear."

"That would suggest he is approachable, then," Azmei mused. "And interested in fairness. Thoughtful. It speaks well of him." She glanced at Destar to see if he agreed with her.

"Aye, it does." His gaze was warm. "See if that book has anything you're looking for there, but as I said, I'll have someone dig up more from the University library. And in the meantime, I'll keep a weather eye out for anyone who looks at you askance. As I said, there's nothing in stone, but things don't feel right. And I've learned a long time since to trust my feelings in these matters."

Azmei stood. "I applaud your diligence. I have complete confidence that I am safe in your care, Destar."

He stood as soon as she did. When she finished speaking, he bowed. Azmei touched his shoulder briefly and left. She had a book to read and much to think about.

CHAPTER THIRTY-FOUR

ORYA RESISTED THE URGE to twist on her stool to see what was taking Wenda so long. The rhythmic tugging at the hem of her skirt had slowed, but there were two hidden pocket slits to put in.

"You're a much better dummy than I'd expected," Wenda said, her voice bright with humor.

Orya exhaled. If her cousin expected her to take offense at the term, she was mistaken. "I have a lot of practice at being still."

"Oh, yes, I expect so. Do you train by sitting about on rooftops or in cellars, waiting for everyone to fall asleep?"

"Something like that," Orya said wryly. For one contract, she had spent an hour submerged to her neck in frigid canal water. Her spare clothes, stored in an oiled canvas bag atop her head, had scarcely been enough to warm her when she was finally able to climb up from the boat slip into the house of the slaver she'd been hired to kill.

What was wrong with her, that she took pride in such things? She imagined telling Wenda just to see her good-hearted cousin flinch. She felt no real desire to do so, though. Something about her cousin's innocent world-view was still appealing. All too often, if Orya could not have something, she wished only to destroy it. It should be her reaction to Wenda. But it wasn't.

Perhaps if this mission failed, Wenda would look after Yarro for her. She tried to remember if Wenda had any brothers, but Wenda said surprisingly little about herself. For all her seeming openness, she was actually something of a mystery to Orya.

"What is taking so long?" Orya snapped.

"You clearly commissioned this dress from someone here." Wenda's voice was unruffled. Her needle slid into the fabric and tugged again. "Any of our own dressmakers would have designed a proper ball gown instead of this restrictive prison of cloth."

"You ought to know how it's done. Give a dressmaker the opportunity to work with your fabric in exchange for a lovely addition to your own wardrobe." Orya paused. "Oh, of course. You probably have little use for ball gowns in your life."

She felt the sting of the needle against her calf before she could think of calling the words back. She stifled her yelp, knowing it was what Wenda wanted. In an odd way, though it felt good. At least now she knew Wenda had feelings to be pricked, and the self-worth to prick back when it was warranted.

"I have been to a ball or two in my time." Nothing in Wenda's voice indicated she had just deliberately stabbed her, but Orya knew better. "Just because I do not dance, you must not think I dislike music."

"That isn't at all what I meant," Orya said. She didn't bother trying to inject any feeling into her voice. They both knew it had been exactly what she meant.

"Don't underestimate me, cousin. I am not one of the foundlings or throwbacks, to have our family's true business hidden from me. I may not be fit for your line of work, but I am well suited as a helper to you." Wenda's stitches had resumed. "I've already deduced from the alterations you need that you will be carrying a brace of daggers and poison darts in the hem I am mending."

"It is--"

"Against the rules, I know. But can you not think for yourself?" Wenda's voice took on an edge of teasing. "Have we not grown to be friends on this trip, Orya? Tell me what you are planning."

It *was* against the rules. But Orya was uncertain enough that she wished to have an alternate plan for Yarro's safety. Her allies at home had sworn they would watch over him, and if anything looked amiss, they would steal him away from the patriarch's oversight. But there was always the chance Orya might fail at her assignment and the word not reach Tamnen until it was too late. It was unthinkable, but that did not make it impossible.

"You will have me punished for disobedience to the patriarch yet, won't you," she grumbled. "Very well, you are correct. My secondary plan involves carrying daggers under my dress and poison darts in my hem. I have rings with sleep dust in them."

Her jewelry was nearly all deadly. Her earrings had tiny claws on the backs that were sharp enough to puncture the skin; they could easily be coated in poison. The necklace she would wear was actually a braid of wire strong enough to suspend her weight or tie up a captive, if necessary. And her bracelet was an ornate but serviceable garrote.

But Wenda didn't need to know all that.

"Sleep dust?" There was a final tug and Wenda lurched to her feet. "There, the hem is finished. Turn so I can see where you want the pockets."

Orya turned obediently. "The sleep dust will put a grown man down with just a breath of it, and no ill effects afterwards. This mixture has Mindease blended with it to make him forget what he was doing before he slept. I don't mean to use it, but it's good to have in case I need it."

Wenda made a noise to show she was listening. "Put your hands down at your sides. No, not where you'd normally belt a dagger. Lower, where it's natural. You can't wear daggers on your hips, not under this dress. They'll need to be strapped to your thighs."

Orya glared down at her. "If I have to bend down to draw them--"

"No, not that low. But if you wear them too high, they'll create an unflattering silhouette. Everyone knows you have a slender waist and lovely hips. Extra bulk would make people suspicious."

She shouldn't feel so pleased at the casual compliment. "You act as though I've never done this before."

Wenda shrugged. "Have you?" When she looked up, her eyes were wide.

"You don't need to know that." Orya made her voice curt. She had actually killed three times before at fancy balls. One of her victims had been fatally poisoned by Orya's perfume, a toxic mist that settled into the victim's lungs and killed over the course of several hours. She had painted a coat of poison across her lips to deal with one of the others, and drawn back in shock and horror when he began convulsing mere minutes after stealing a kiss during their dance. Poison was so much easier when one had to kill quietly in public.

The first ball, though... She held very still as a shiver tried to crawl down her spine. The first ball had been her very costly failure. There had been daggers involved, which was why she preferred, to this day, to use poison whenever possible. When poison was impossible, she preferred crossbows. It wasn't the idea of personal contact with her victims that she minded. It was the smell of their blood as it washed across her hands.

She swallowed hard and pushed the feeling away. "You'll need to stay in our rooms all evening tomorrow. I might as well make good use of you, since you are so insistent on being a part of my plans."

"Of course! What do you need?"

Orya glanced down at her. "A witness. I have been the princess' friend on the voyage to Ranarr. Though she has been very busy since we arrived, it is still well known that I dine with her on occasion. I must be highly visible at the ball. I will dance as much as possible. With the prince, if I can manage it, and certainly with Destar Thorne and that Amethirian general. I want everyone to see me at the ball and know how very happy I am for my dear friend, Azmei."

Wenda nodded in time with her scissors as she snipped a slit into the side hem of Orya's skirt. "Of course, everyone knows how much you like the princess."

Orya caught her breath. Had Wenda realized just how true that was? "That was rather the point of my befriending her before leaving home," she said, trying to make her voice condescending.

"Oh, yes." Wenda fell silent. The cloth of Orya's skirt rustled as Wenda rolled it up, seeking the exact part of the underskirt that needed to be cut.

"I will spend as much time as possible talking to the princess, and at the height of the ball, I will dose myself with just enough redleaf to make me seem ill."

"Redleaf? What does that do?"

Her lips parted to answer, Orya caught herself. "Make me seem ill." It would raise her pulse and make her skin pale and clammy. She would have to feign a swoon as soon as she felt it taking effect; if she waited too long, she would swoon for real, and then she would have to take an antidote and rest before recovering. There was no way to treat herself ahead of time, though; the only antidote to redleaf was sunder, and if sunder was in the system, redleaf was harmless and wouldn't give her the illness she needed.

It was a shame Orya had no herbalist to brag to. She would have to remember to tell the story far and wide in the training hall when she returned home. She looked down at Wenda's bowed head and hesitated. Then she shook her head. She couldn't tell Wenda.

"This is the point where it's very important you be waiting up for me in our rooms," she said instead. "I'll need you to open the door when I come back. Someone will escort me from the ball, of course. If nothing else, the Diplomats are too blazing polite to let me return back to our rooms alone when I'm obviously ill."

Wenda nodded. "Those Diplomats are *weird*. I'm glad I've only had to deal with them once or twice. How do they go about their lives with no expressions at all? Is it a drug they take to freeze their faces?"

"I hadn't thought about it. I suppose it's just training." Orya grimaced. It was inconvenient, certainly. She was extra careful around the Diplomats; she suspected one of them could observe her make an outright assassination attempt and show no reaction at all. She wouldn't realize she'd been spotted until they arrested her. Diplomats, she assumed, were no big fans of assassination. Disturbed the peace and whatnot.

"In any event," she said, shaking her head, "I'll need you to be seen here when I arrive. Then on the off chance there are any questions about my whereabouts the rest of the evening, you can vouch that I was lying in bed with a cold cloth over my face, when I wasn't heaving into the chamber pot." She smiled down at Wenda, who giggled as she was supposed to.

"And instead you'll sneak out and wait for your moment to strike," Wenda said.

Orya hummed noncommittally. "Anderlin's threats are well-known by now. No one will be surprised to hear of a Strid agent attacking her."

"What did he say?" Wenda asked. She rocked back on her heels and lowered her hands.

"You didn't hear?" Orya shook her head. "He'd have been better off saying nothing but acting in silence. But it makes my work easier." She smirked. "He demanded the Kreyden as bride-price for the princess, and said if she rejected his offer, all of Tamnen would weep in mourning."

Wenda's eyes widened. "He all but admitted he planned to kill her?"

"It will make everyone think he decided to kill her and be done with it." Orya shrugged. "He's a fool, but a useful one."

"Mm." Wenda pursed her lips, her brows drawing together. Then her face twisted and she jerked to one side. She fell clumsily onto her backside, one hand clutching at her crippled foot.

Orya held out a hand. "Did you hurt yourself?"

Instead of answering, Wenda shook her head, ignoring the hand. Orya sighed and leaned over. "Let me help you up."

"I'm fine. I just forgot I can't sit like that for long." Wenda's voice was tight.

Orya decided to ignore it. If Wenda was going to pretend everything was all right, so would she. "If all goes well, in two days' time, we'll be ready to return home."

"You will, at least." Wenda sighed. "I'm to stay and establish our custom, remember?"

Orya hadn't forgotten exactly, but she hadn't thought about it either way. "I envy you, actually," she confessed. "I like it here. It's so hot and sunny."

Wenda's smile was lopsided. "It is nice, but my friends are all at home. Once you complete your assignment, you'll be free to go." She studied Orya's face. "Though...I'm not at all certain you really want to complete your assignment and return home."

"What's that supposed to mean?" Orya snapped as a thrill of fear rushed through her. Of course she wanted to complete her assignment! Yarro needed her! She would never abandon him.

"Why do you even have to kill the princess? Why this contract?" Wenda must have seen the gathering anger on her face, but she pressed on. "Doesn't the patriarch want peace?"

"Peace is bad for business," Orya said tightly. "Not for us, no, but for those who profit on war contracts and army supplies. War can be profitable enough for some folk that they're willing to pay us to prolong that war."

"Even if it isn't necessary," Wenda persisted. Orya glared at her and Wenda flinched but said, "You like the princess, don't you?"

"And what does that matter?"

"You don't want to do it. You don't want to kill her." There was a glitter of something stronger than curiosity in Wenda's eyes.

"It doesn't matter if I want to do it or not." Orya stepped down from the stool and began stripping off her dress. She was finished with this conversation. "I have no choice in the matter."

She tried to keep the bitterness from her voice, but she must have failed. Damn Wenda for disarming her so! Orya managed to get untangled from her skirt and stepped out of it. Wenda, eyes big, placed a hand on Orya's shoulder. It wasn't a steadying hand. She rested it there and squeezed, just tightly enough that Orya knew Wenda was trying to be sympathetic.

Orya jerked away. "I've broken enough rules for an entire lifetime. Take the skirt and finish making the alterations I need. The ball won't wait for your sewing."

She turned away quickly, but not quickly enough to miss the tiny flash of hurt and resentment in her cousin's eyes.

To his surprise, Vistaren was relieved to put aside his tax codes when Lozarr told him Azmei had arrived for their luncheon appointment. He had been thinking for several days about asking Azmei's thoughts about the tax situation, and this was his opportunity.

He glanced down at himself and stood, smoothing his clothes. He was wearing the green shirt of Tamnese silk that he had commissioned after his conversation with Orya Perslyn. His trousers were a pale yellow-tan, but he thought the contrast with the dark green prevented him from looking like a puffskin. He brushed his hands over his hair and raised his eyebrows.

Lo grinned. "You look very elegant, Ren. I'm certain she will be impressed."

Vistaren huffed, but he couldn't help being pleased.

"I'll show her in," Lo said, and left the room.

A few moments later, Azmei came in alone. She was wearing a blue dress that was less formal than most of the the dresses he had seen her in so far. She greeted him with a smile.

"I apologize for being so preoccupied recently," he said once they were settled across from one another at the table. "I would like to give you my full attention, but a matter has arisen that I would be remiss to neglect. Nevertheless, I do not mean to neglect you."

Azmei's smile widened. "I do not feel neglected, Vistaren," she said. "I hope it is not a serious matter."

They were interrupted by the servants bearing in the first course, a cold salad and refreshing white wine. Vistaren had directed the cooks to prepare Amethirian food, the sort of dishes they would eat during the dry season. He would bring in Tamnese chefs if necessary, to please his bride, but he hoped Azmei would like the cuisine he had grown up on.

"It is serious," he said finally, "but not dangerous, I believe. I learned there are nearly a thousand Amethirians here in Ranarr who do not feel they are well-represented by our ambassador."

"The scoundrel, to neglect his duty," Azmei said, though her gaze was on his face as if she were uncertain.

"No, I don't think so. I don't think he's been neglecting it. It is just that he has been so absorbed with the treaty you and I are attempting to cement that he has, perhaps, not had the attention to lend them." Vistaren took a small sip of his wine.

"How did you happen to learn of it, then, if the ambassador did not bring it to your attention?" Azmei asked.

His telling of meeting Yadian Shemma in the market and then going to the Chatty Raven carried them through the first course and into the second, which was a cold soup. Although most of his attention was on Azmei's reaction to the story, a small part of Vistaren noted that she seemed to relish the cold soup, and he was glad.

"So you have invited their leader to travel back with you?" Azmei asked after the servants cleared away the soup dishes and prepared to bring the main course, which was seasoned fish steaks. She paused, tilted her head, and added, "With us, I suppose."

His stomach swooped oddly. It was the same reaction he'd been having every time he thought about the fact they were planning to marry. Then he had a second thought. "That doesn't trouble you, does it? I truly believe Shemma is no danger."

"Of course not," Azmei said. She reached across and touched the back of his hand with her fingertips. Vistaren tried not to freeze. "They are your people. Soon they will become my people."

Her words pleased him, even though they also made him feel a little sick. *I have* got *to tell her the truth soon*, he thought. To which another thought said, *Not yet.* "How would you respond in my place, Azmei? What do you think of their grievances?"

She tilted her head again, thinking. "I haven't studied Amethirian taxes or financial policy, but the situation as you describe it does seem unfair."

"Life often isn't fair," Vistaren pointed out quickly. He knew it was the first thing his father would say.

"True." She sipped her wine. "But isn't it the task of those in power to attempt to make it more fair? Even a monarch doesn't have the power to create true fairness. But the responsibility is there, to ease oppression, to care and protect, to ensure the people do not live in want."

Vistaren gave her a slow smile. It was the sort of answer he wished he could think of. "Azmei, I believe you and I are going to do well together."

CHAPTER THIRTY-FIVE

A MONTH AFTER ISSUING his ultimatum, Lozarr finally got his answer.

His duties ended for the day, he had just removed his tunic and tugged off his boots when someone knocked at the door. Lo looked sideways at the door, wondering if he could pretend to be asleep already. But everyone had seen him take his leave of the prince, and that had only been a quarter of an hour ago.

Lo sighed and went barefoot to the door.

Arama was standing on the other side, her lower lip caught between her teeth. She was barefoot, too, though it wasn't uncharacteristic for her.

"Arama." Lo knew his voice warmed when he said her name. He couldn't quite help it. Just the sight of her short, muscular figure was enough to make his heart jump. Seeing her look so—well, not uncertain, but… conflicted, perhaps—made him feel protective, too.

She didn't say anything. She just walked past him into the room. Lo turned, watching her, and shut the door behind her.

"Is everything all right?" he asked.

She went still. Her gaze was pointed somewhere near his collarbone, which was exposed since he'd undone the front of his shirt. Lo felt a rush of heat go through him and he had to put his hand behind his back to keep from tugging his shirt together.

"Arama?" he said more softly.

She lifted her gaze to meet his, and then she surged forward, catching a hand around the back of his neck and tugging him down to crush her mouth against his.

Lo caught his breath, a flush of desire rushing through him. He rested a hand at her hip and returned her kiss eagerly. She hummed softly and pressed her body against his, her fingers slipping into the short hair at the nape of his neck.

He let Arama control the kiss. Was this a test? He knew she wouldn't toy with him, but she might be experimenting, testing him to see how he would react, testing herself to see how *she* would react. He couldn't control how she felt, but he didn't want to push her away because of his own reaction.

She broke the kiss abruptly, though she didn't pull out of his touch. "I don't know," she said, breathless, and the bottom dropped out of Lo's stomach. He sucked in a breath, but she pressed a finger against his lips.

"I don't know how this will go," she continued. "If it will end. But—" Arama paused, meeting his gaze with naked desire—and naked fear. "But I know I want to try to have more." Her tongue flicked out and wet her lips. "I want to choose you."

Lo drew in a slow breath. "I never asked you for promises of forever," he whispered.

"I know." Her lips quirked. "Maybe that's what frightened me most of all. You're always willing to take whatever I'm able to give. What if I give you everything, and it isn't enough?"

"The Storm Petrel? Not enough for me?" Lo smiled slowly. "I'm not worried about that. I choose you, Arama Dzornaea. As my friend and companion, and hopefully as my lover, but no matter what, always as someone who truly sees me." He raised his hand to stroke gently through her short curls. "And no matter what, I swear that I will always see you for exactly who you are."

Arama drew him down for another kiss. "And I choose you," she whispered. "So we can make the most of the time we have together."

Lozarr bolted the door behind him and guided her to the bed.

Chapter Thirty-Six

S OMEONE MUST HAVE TAUGHT the Diplomats something in the past month about how to throw a party. They were in the same ballroom that had held the welcome ball the month before, but the music was lively with complex rhythms and shaded harmonies. Perhaps it was because this was a betrothal party and therefore celebrated peace between Tamnen and Amethir. Azmei looked around as she paused in the huge double doors.

The crowd was large, billowing and shifting like a body that moved and breathed. She recognized some of those in attendance. Several Diplomats in their sober brown robes were gathered around a table of refreshments. There were two score Ranarri citizens, all important for one reason or another, congregating near the punch. That short, fat woman was the head of the bankers guild, and the tall, spare man talking to her was apparently a revered councilman--the closest the Ranarri got to nobility. Azmei recognized several other faces, though she couldn't put a name or occupation to them.

Prince Vistaren's party had already arrived, though she didn't currently see the prince. She did see Lozarr, resplendent in his uniform, complete with a scarlet sash from shoulder to waist. And beside him--she did a double take--was Arama, looking absolutely nothing like a pirate captain in the sea-blue silk gown she wore.

"I didn't realize the Storm Petrel knew how to wear a dress," remarked a mischievous voice behind her. Azmei glanced over her shoulder. Orya. She should have known. She liked the cloth merchant a great deal, but the woman had a sharp tongue, and she spared no one.

They had mended their friendship after the argument last week, but Azmei had chosen to take a more formal air with her since then. She didn't think Orya was deliberately hateful, but she could be casually cruel, and it grew tiresome.

"I expect long skirts would get caught in the rigging," Azmei said now. "It would be impractical for her to wear skirts most of the time."

"Most of the time, certainly. But she's been on dry land with the rest of us for a month now. It's about time she adapted."

"You've certainly adapted well to the high life," Azmei said, knowing the words were unkind and speaking them anyway.

The dress Orya wore was beautiful, there was no doubt. Made of a deep red silk, it highlighted Orya's dark beauty, contrasting with her black hair and matching her red lips.

Orya's dark eyes were wounded as she gazed at Azmei. "Surely you understand how a cloth merchant can ill afford to dress in anything but the best," she said. "I took a bolt of this silk to one of the cloth merchants I wished to win over, then promised if her design pleased me, I would wear the dress she made of it to one of the balls."

Azmei sighed. She shouldn't have tweaked the other woman. "Of course, you're right. I suppose I'm in a foul mood because I would rather be tucked into a cozy seat reading. I apologize."

Orya's gaze softened. "Truly, you have no reason to apologize to me, princess. I forget that, whatever pressure I am under to gain new custom here in Ranarr, the pressure you are under is far greater, and with far-reaching consequences."

Azmei could have done without the reminder. She grimaced and looked back out at the ball room. "I see the general and the captain, but I don't see Vistaren. Do you see him anywhere?"

"I don't. He isn't at the food table, nor at the drinks." Orya injected just enough surprise into her tone that Azmei could not reprimand her, but nor could she miss the meaning. "Perhaps he fainted from the shock of seeing the Storm Petrel in a dress." She giggled.

"Enough," Azmei said, striving to keep her tone friendly. "I am not in the mood for jests tonight, Orya. Let us simply have pleasant conversation of no importance."

Orya gave her a sympathetic look. "Are you nervous about the betrothal?"

Azmei lifted a hand to rub her eyes, but she fortunately remembered her makeup in time. She patted her hair and dropped her hand again. "Not nervous, really, but..." She flicked her fan open and fluttered it in front of her face. "I just wish everything was over and done. It's this dreadful feeling of being half-swallowed."

Orya laughed. "Half-swallowed?"

"You know, when you start to eat a pimmin vine that turns out to be longer than you expected," Azmei said. "And so you've swallowed half of it, and the rest is stuck in your throat. I feel like that pimmin vine. Why can't Amethir just swallow me whole and have done?"

"You think too much. You're the most beautiful woman at the ball, you're marrying a prince, and everyone is looking at you with admiration in their eyes." Orya shrugged. "Relax and enjoy it."

Azmei smiled, though it felt thin and strained. "Thank you, my friend." She reached out a hand, which Orya gripped. "You have proven faithful and true through this trying time. I am grateful."

Orya lowered her gaze, her lips curving demurely. "I am grateful to have had the chance to serve, even if only with my friendship."

Azmei squeezed her hand and dropped it. She turned her head, scanning the room again. Where was Vistaren? He wasn't avoiding her, was he? Perhaps she had been wrong. Perhaps he was uncomfortable with Anderlin's slurs against his betrothed. But surely Vistaren would be aware that the insult was aimed at him as well as Azmei. Wouldn't he want to discuss it with her, at the very least?

Her gaze skipped across brown and black heads, seeking out the particular blue sheen bestowed by the Crelin blood. She found none. Even Arama and Lozarr had disappeared. Then her eyes settled on the big double doors and her heart thumped. There. She felt her lips curving up, almost involuntarily.

"Ah, there he is," Orya said. She had followed Azmei's gaze. "He looks quite elegant, doesn't he? I wonder where he found such fine silk." Her tone was just smug enough that Azmei darted her an amused glance but said nothing. "Go on, then," Orya prompted. "He'll want to see you. You look magnificent."

Azmei gathered her skirts and crossed the room. Vistaren almost looked as though he had dressed to match her, though his colors were bolder. Azmei's dress was made of pale green silk, with a daring amount of throat and shoulders showing. Vistaren wore white silk trousers and a rich blue shirt with a deep green tunic flowing down to his knees. With his dark complexion and the blue sheen of his hair, it was a striking look. Azmei caught her breath.

Vistaren saw her coming while she was still some distance away. He abandoned his conversation with Arama and Lozarr and crossed the room to meet her, hands outstretched to take hers. As their fingers met, she thought she heard someone near them sigh. It must look like a scene from a play, she thought. Her heart gave another absurd thump. It made no sense; she wasn't in love with Vistaren, and yet the romance of the situation was affecting her even so.

"Princess, you are lovelier than ever," Vistaren said, his voice pitched to carry even though the smile in his eyes was reserved for her alone.

Heat spread through her body and Azmei replied, "You honor me, paying such compliments when you look so handsome yourself." Her voice didn't carry as his had. She considered herself lucky that she hadn't squeaked when she spoke. What was wrong with her?

He leaned in, lowering his voice. "They tried to put me in yellow. Can you believe it? Tonight of all nights?" He shook his head, full lips curving. "I had to insist on a completely different outfit, and so I am late. I apologize most sincerely."

Azmei laughed. "I thought you promised not to lie to me again," she said. "You will never get me to believe they wanted you to wear anything but what you have on."

Vistaren tipped his head in concession. "It is possible they attempted the yellow first to soften me to this. I am fond of fine clothing, I confess, but I was afraid the silk trousers were a bit much."

She snorted, feeling absurdly happy. "I feel better now that you are here," she confessed. "I thought perhaps something was wrong."

"Nothing of consequence. There are Amethirian citizens here in Ranarr, of course, and politics seem to follow me everywhere." He shook it off. "But tonight is for you and me. I won't let politics ruin the celebration that marks the official beginning of our betrothal."

Azmei swallowed as he brought both of her hands together and lifted them to his lips. "Dance with me, Azmei, my betrothed and my friend."

As she let him lead her into the center of the ballroom, Azmei concentrated on placing each foot where it ought to go. Her heart thudded hard in her chest. She knew Vistaren didn't love her, just as she didn't love him, but he was playing the part remarkably well, and she could feel herself being swept along. Then again, what would it hurt if she appeared to be entirely smitten with him, and he with her? That could do nothing but good for their two kingdoms.

The musicians struck up a lively tune that made her even more nervous about placing her feet properly, but Vistaren's strong arms closed around her and held her up, guiding her with his skilled lead. She surrendered, following his movements and mirroring them. He was a graceful dancer, though she had witnessed firsthand the clumsiness he had professed during their first meeting.

For a time they danced in silence. As she was no longer concentrating on her steps, she was able to enjoy the intricate way all the dancing couples wove around each other. She no longer felt everyone was whispering about what Anderlin had said. Almost everyone was watching her dance with the prince, but she thought--she hoped--it was because they made a pretty picture together. She was unaware that she had been smiling until Vistaren spoke.

"You truly are beautiful," he murmured. "I don't believe I deserve you." He gave a self-conscious laugh. "But at least I am cognizant of that fact, and it serves only to make me more grateful of the honor you are bestowing on me."

She jerked her gaze back to his, tilting her face up to study him. "Do you honestly not realize how nice-looking you are? Perhaps yellow makes you look like a puff-skin, but blue and green are very good colors for you."

He smiled, but there was a strange light in his eyes as he looked away from her face and over her head. "I am glad you think so. At least I don't shame you."

"Of course not." Azmei tried to think back to their last conversation. Had there been any clues then that he might be doubting himself? Well, no more than usual, anyway. But no, they had parted laughing, she remembered, over a story he'd told regarding his first time sailing with a stormwitch. At some point over their acquaintance, Vistaren had deduced her anxiety about stormwitchery; several times he had brought up experiences that made the strange weather magic seem natural and normal.

Given the way they had parted that evening, their last long conversation must not have made him doubt himself or her. What had changed since then? The political trouble he mentioned? She looked up at him again, opening her mouth to say something just as he spoke.

"Did I tell you Arama came to see me yesterday?"

Azmei closed her mouth and shook her head. Maybe that was what troubled him.

"Mm. She all but had her tail between her legs, asking if I would mind terribly if she attended the ball in a dress. A *dress*. Mind, I haven't known her all that long, really, but I've never even heard of her wearing something like that." A smile flashed across his face and faded just as quickly. "I told her what she wore was no business of mine. She was quick to point out that she's technically here as one of my bodyguards. I told her that if I needed my body guarded at the ball, I was certain she could do it just as well in a gown as she could naked."

Azmei snickered and he blushed. "Well, it's true," he protested. "I believe Arama is the most capable, frightening woman I have ever met. And I'm including my mother in that assessment." He smiled down at her and she realized he was holding her very tightly. "Though I suspect you will give Arama a run for her money," he said, lowering his voice.

Azmei tilted her head and pursed her lips. She didn't have to ask her question aloud, though. Vistaren chuckled.

"Do you know what she said to that? She said she was inclined to give you a sword and let *you* protect me, considering what a fierce little rock-cat you've proven to be."

"Rock-cat?" Azmei repeated.

Vistaren grinned. "They're small, not much more than thirty pounds, but they can take down a full-grown cliff ram. They scale rock faces you wouldn't think anything could get up. And the claws on them! Sharper than shark's teeth. No one who lives on the coast wants to get afoul of a rock-cat. Fortunately, they're more fond of rabbits and cliff sheep than people."

"You know, I think most women would be insulted at being called a rock-cat," Azmei said. She knew she looked as pleased as she felt, though. To have Arama say such a thing about her was fine indeed.

"Most women, perhaps, but not you," Vistaren said. He lifted one hand from her waist to cup his palm against her cheek. "You are quite unlike most women, Azmei of Tamnen."

He was going to kiss her. Her heart thudded hard in her chest, just once, and then settled back into a regular rhythm, though rather faster than usual. Azmei had never been kissed before. What if she did it badly? What if she turned her head the wrong way and made them look foolish in front of the others? What if--

Then his lips were pressing gently against hers. They were soft and rather moist, and she remembered how he'd licked them nervously just before they touched. She breathed slowly in through her nose and kissed him back, wondering if one were supposed to think about the scrape of evening shadow against one's chin when one was kissing a prince.

And then he pulled back and her heart refused to settle back into its usual rhythm. Vistaren looked uncomfortable but not flustered or excited. Azmei licked her lips, but she tasted nothing but her own peppermint lip gloss. Her chin felt a little sore and she hoped it hadn't reddened.

The music swirled and swooped and Vistaren guided her into the next arcing turn without missing a step. Azmei's cheeks warmed until they were burning. He seemed so unaffected. Was that how every man reacted to kissing someone he had just called beautiful and unlike other women?

Her mind felt as if it had continued spinning when they finished the dance turn. To break the miserable silence building between them, she blurted the first thing that came into her head.

"Have you had a chance to look at my translation of Rona and Fann?"

Vistaren twitched and missed a step. She stumbled with him and uttered a wordless exclamation as they clutched at each other to keep from losing their balance. By the time they had righted themselves and caught up with the others in the dance, she had almost forgotten her question.

Vistaren obviously hadn't. "Rona and Fann. I, ah, actually I've liked the tales you chose. I've had to ask what some of the words were, though. What version of the tales did you use?"

Trying not to be hurt that he was so relieved to talk about something unrelated to their kiss, Azmei said, "I don't really know. It's a leather-bound copy my brother gave me for my fifteenth birthday."

"Hm. I only ask because there are a few nuances that I wasn't sure if I was missing, or if your translation had left them out, or perhaps I'm just not good enough at reading Tamnese yet.."

When he didn't finish that sentence, Azmei took a deep breath. "Do you mean how Rona and Fann--that is, they, ah--well, the way they seem to be..." She trailed off, thinking. "Mmm, not merely brothers in arms?" she finished.

At the same time, Vistaren blurted, "Lovers?"

Azmei stumbled, but Vistaren was prepared and caught her elbow in a grip that was gentle but strong. He kept her with him, lowering his head until his mouth was very close to her ear. "It's one of the secrets I felt we shouldn't have between us, Azmei." His voice was low and steady. "I love men. I have as long as I've understood what it meant to desire another person. And the woman who is to be my wife must know that about me."

This time it wasn't just her mind that was spinning, but her stomach as well. He had promised not to lie to her again, and he hadn't, not exactly, but he *had* concealed this from her, and he had led her on, kissing her in front of all these people! What could have made him do that? Why would he marry her if he wanted someone else--someone male!--even if it was to end a war? Azmei stumbled again. She looked up, plastering a bright smile across her face.

"Oh, this heat! I am so unused to it," she declared in a loud voice. People were already staring, and more turned towards them at the sound of her voice. "It's making me clumsy. Vistaren, would you have someone bring me something cold to drink?"

His gray eyes were agonized as he looked at her, but she thought she saw understanding in them. She hoped that was what she saw. He bowed. "Let me help you to a seat," he said, guiding her to a cushioned bench near a planter.

She watched him walk away from her. Now that they weren't dancing, he seemed unable to walk a straight line. She folded her hands around each other and hoped desperately that no one could read her face. Everything she had been planning for, everything she had anticipated, suddenly seemed to be crumbling into shaky ground under her feet.

Why would Vistaren marry her? Was it truly for the reason he'd said, that he needed an heir? But would they even be able to have children? If he desired men, how would he give her children of his body? And she was certain there was no magic to make that happen; the Amethirian magic was only related to the weather.

Did Vistaren have someone at home? Perhaps he wished to marry her for heirs but keep his lover near him to make him happy. But was she capable of sharing? She had been trying to fall in love with him! Would he have let her? But if he couldn't feel the same for her, what would be the point?

He was coming back to her, a golden goblet in each hand. Her stomach flipped. Did the others know? Obviously it was not commonly known, but Lozarr and Arama? Surely they must know. What if Arama had been pitying Azmei as they talked in the courtyard?

She swallowed back a sob that swelled in her throat. This was certainly not the place for her to lose her composure. And this was not even the time for that. Vistaren was a good man. She had become convinced of that over the past month. She might not feel desire for him, nor he for her apparently, but she knew him for an honest, honorable person. He would not have told her about himself for no reason. And it could not have been easy to tell her.

She pressed an icy hand to one hot cheek. Perhaps she had inadvertently made this all worse! What if, by choosing the epics of Rona and Fann to translate, she had made them all believe she already knew about Vistaren's disposition? He would have been relieved that he didn't have to explain it to her. And then she told Arama how much she wished Vistaren to love her, and Arama realized Azmei didn't know. Arama would have gone to Vistaren, who must have felt that his life had just grown more complicated than he had expected. And here they were, at the ball celebrating the beginning of their official betrothal, and Vistaren had faced her knowing she didn't realize the truth about him.

Gods, poor Vistaren! The agonies he must have been going through made her own look insignificant. That realization gave Azmei the courage to smile at him when he arrived, goblets in hand. He exhaled and smiled back at her, handing her a goblet. It glistened with condensation, so cold was the wine inside.

"How is it so cold?" she asked. Surely there hadn't been time to fetch a bottle from the depths of the rock where it would be kept out of the sun.

Vistaren's smile strengthened. "Our stormwitch frosted it. Have you met Kinnet? I think you'd like her. She's prickly, but fierce and independent. Rather like someone else I know," he added, and sat next to her.

He was sitting so close their shoulders touched. Azmei wasn't sure if it was proper, and she wasn't sure why he did it, since he'd already told her that her beauty didn't affect him. But she found herself leaning into him ever so slightly. His presence was solid and so very, well, *Vistaren*-like that she felt comforted.

She sipped her drink. It was so cold it hurt her teeth, but the taste of sunlight and brisk winds and oranges and heartfruit hit the back of her throat and made her smile and then sigh. "You could have told me sooner," she muttered. "It would have been easier."

He opened his mouth to speak, but before he could say anything, the tall, spare, Ranarri councilman was bowing before them and requesting a dance with the princess. Azmei shot an agonized look at Vistaren, but she stood and joined the man on the floor. As they danced, she learned his name was Menerth and that he was one of the few non-Diplomats who had worked on the peace accord. He was polite and interesting and for the entire set, Azmei wished for nothing more than to escape him and go back to her conversation with Vistaren. She feared she offended him when she refused a second set with him, but she was too busy looking for Vistaren. When she finally found the prince, however, he was dancing with Orya, who appeared to be chattering gaily up at him without pausing for breath.

Another important person, this one wearing a turban, bowed before her, proclaiming his earnest desire to join the princess in a dance. Swallowing a sigh, Azmei pushed down her desire to talk through things with her betrothed. Tomorrow she could go back to being a confused young woman pledged to marry a man who loved other men. Tonight she must be a princess.

Through dance after dance, she managed some semblance of grace, though she never felt as comfortable as she had while dancing with Vistaren. She made polite conversation with merchants, councilmen, guilds-men, and scholars. She was beginning to truly feel over-heated and headachy and cross by the time a handsome brown-skinned man in a scarlet sash bowed before her.

"Princess Azmei, may a humble soldier request a dance with his future queen?"

She looked down into Lozarr Algot's sparkling gray eyes. The general's mouth was quirked with humor, inviting her to share in his joke. Azmei laughed and placed her hand in his. "It would be my delight," she said.

The general was very tall, but being so close to him for the first time, Azmei could see that he was actually young for his rank. He looked to be around thirty. Perhaps it was the mischief in his gaze that made her notice it. He was usually so solemn.

"Arama thought perhaps you would like a moment or two with someone familiar," he said, guiding Azmei into the dance. It was, to her relief, a less lively number than the last several.

"I would indeed," Azmei agreed. "I have long suspected ceremony and etiquette to be difficult as well as tiresome, and I confess myself disappointed, for the first time in my life, that I was correct."

Lozarr laughed. "I see why Vistaren and Arama like you so much." He smiled wryly at her. "I hope you will forgive my forwardness, princess. In the court of Amethir, we don't stand so much on ceremony as the Ranarri do."

"Nor do we at ho--" She caught herself. "In Tamnen, where I grew up."

His expression softened. "It cannot be easy to leave all you know behind you. I hope we are doing everything we can to make the transition easier on you."

Azmei lowered her gaze. She had thought they were, but then again, she hadn't realized the enormity of the secrets they were keeping from her. "I expect it is a transition for everyone," she temporized.

"It is indeed." He paused. "And even before we leave Ranarr for Amethir, you are changing those around you." She didn't know what he meant until he added, "I'm in your debt, Princess Azmei."

She looked up at him. His gray eyes were intense on hers. Of course. Arama must have changed her position on their relationship. Had she told Lozarr about their discussion, then? Hells, Azmei hoped she hadn't told him *all* of it. But she could see, from the mingled gratitude and sympathy in his gaze, that Arama had told him.

"Did you know?" she murmured. "About Vistaren?"

She felt the muscles of his back tense under her hand, though his feet never faltered. The physical reaction told her as much as anything he could have said, but he nodded, glancing away. "I did."

She shoved aside the urge to cast blame. It didn't matter if she thought Lozarr or Arama should have told her. What mattered was looking forward. "I don't know what to do. I thought I had some idea of what to expect, but now I am thrown akilter again."

They skipped and turned in silence, then his voice came, low. "Does it distress you?"

Her mouth dropped open. "Do you suppose it distressed Aevver?" she demanded. She matched the volume of his voice, though; too many people were near who should not overhear.

Lozarr frowned. "It won't--" He broke off and shook his head. "I pray you, hear him out, princess."

"Of course I'll hear him out." She smiled to hide her fury. How dare someone, even Vistaren's dear friend, think she would back out of their agreement without so much as waiting for an explanation? "I would have heard him out at once, if he hadn't been dancing with Orya when I came back."

"A ball is a difficult place to have a serious conversation," Lozarr agreed. "We counselled him to wait, but he couldn't stand the thought of lying to you, even by omission."

And just as quick as that, Azmei's fury dissolved. Poor Vistaren. He simply couldn't win with her, could he? If he lied to her, she would be angry about that. If he told her the truth, she would be hurt and angry and not understand. She sighed and lowered her head, staring at the rich scarlet silk of Lozarr's sash.

"I know it must be confusing for you," he murmured. "But Vistaren does truly care for you, princess. It was a relief to him when he thought you understood the situation you were coming into. And when he realized you did not, that your choice of Rona and Fann was a coincidence..." Lozarr's arms tightened around her, and despite herself, Azmei felt comforted. How could Arama have resisted him for so long? He was steadying and kind as well as handsome.

"I liked the stories," she whispered. She swallowed, trying to force down the vulnerability that was trying to grip her again. "And I liked Aevver."

"No doubt." She could hear the smile in Lozarr's voice. "I can see something of her in you, if I may be so bold."

"You love Vistaren very much, don't you?" She looked up as she asked it, just in time to see regret flicker across Lozarr's face.

"Not enough," he said. It confused her for a moment, and then she realized that her betrothed must have felt a very different kind of love for him. "But I do love him, as my liege lord and my friend. And I believe in the marriage you and he might make, if you will let yourselves."

"It won't change...that...about him," she said, wishing he would contradict her and knowing he wouldn't.

"No." His gray eyes were steady on hers. "But there is much to be said for the love of friendship and companionship, even if it cannot be passion." His cheeks flushed as he said it, as if he realized suddenly that he was talking about sex to his future queen.

If I am truly to be that, Azmei thought. But she didn't feel quite so bleak about it now.

The music ended. With regret, Azmei stepped out of his hold and curtsied as he bowed. She could not use the excuse of dancing to get Arama's council, but dancing with Lozarr had been almost as good.

"I thank you for honoring me with a dance, Princess Azmei," he murmured. His lips brushed against her fingers, and then another Ranarri councilman was asking for a dance. Suppressing a sigh, Azmei allowed the flow of courtesy to take her where it would.

Vistaren approached her again, finally, after that dance ended. She gazed up at him solemnly, her stomach churning at the anxious expression on his face. She was the one who had put that expression there. She took his hands in hers and smiled at him, hoping to reassure him. She wasn't certain if it worked.

Before the music began, a swelling murmur caught Azmei's attention. She looked over to where Orya stood, one hand on Lozarr's arm, her face white and beaded with sweat. He was bending near, speaking to her. Orya's eyes were closed. She shook her head. Movement made Azmei look to her right: Arama was approaching through the crowd, displeasure clear on her face. Did she think Orya was making a play for Lozarr's affection?

"What's wrong?" Vistaren asked.

"Orya. She doesn't look well." Indeed, she was leaning on Lozarr's arm as the general helped her from the dance floor.

"Lo will take care of her. He's good at that."

"I imagine so," she agreed, though her attention was focused on the way Orya clung to him. Arama was frowning. "I hope she isn't ill."

"Probably just overheated. I believe she's danced as many dances as you have, and talking nonstop as she did so." Vistaren spoke wryly. "I like your friend, but she doesn't exactly let one get a word in edgewise, does she?"

Azmei snorted. "She does rather wear on you after a while. I like her, but we only really became friends on the voyage here. She came to Ranarr to sell fabrics. My dress is made from her wares."

"It's a very nice dress. Did I tell you that earlier?"

She glanced sharply at him. "You don't have to do that."

Vistaren recoiled. "I wasn't--I didn't say it because I thought I had to." He pinched his lower lip between his thumb and forefinger. "I like the cloth. It looks pretty on you."

"I'm sorry." She sighed. "Thank you." When she looked over, Lozarr and Orya were leaving the ballroom. Arama was slipping between guests, following them out. "I suppose Arama will help Lo take care of her," she observed.

That made him laugh, thankfully. "Thank you for talking to her. You managed to do what Lo and I have neither one been able to do." To Azmei's questioning glance, he added, "Make her see sense."

Azmei shrugged. "I only spoke the truth. Any woman would have to be mad to turn down such devotion freely offered."

"Ah." He glanced away. "We should probably--That is--I imagine you, ah, have questions..."

"I do. I'm not sure what they are, but I *would* like some answers." She looked up at him. "I'm very confused."

His lips twisted bitterly. "You aren't the only one."

"I really could use some fresh air. We could go out on the terrace and look at the ocean," she suggested. "The sea breeze would be a relief."

He nodded and turned to lead the way. He kept one of her hands gripped in his own, and Azmei couldn't deny that she liked the feeling, though she understood now that it meant nothing to him. *Stop feeling sorry for yourself,* she scolded. *What would Aevver do in this situation?* For that matter, what *had* Aevver done? Had she known about Rona and Fann? Had she been a part of their relationship? Perhaps she had been the one to see the truth of their love before even they understood it.

Lost in her imagination, Azmei didn't hear the fanfare until Vistaren stopped walking. "Damn," he muttered, and turned, a smile pasted across his face. "They're going to make speeches at us."

Azmei looked at him in bewilderment.

"It would be rude for us to slip out while they're talking about how monumental our marriage shall be," he explained.

"Oh." She looked over her shoulder to where a Ranarri Diplomat was climbing the steps to the dais. "Damn."

Vistaren chuckled and tugged her around to stand beside him. His arm draped possessively around her shoulders. Azmei let herself lean into it. They would make a lovely picture, she thought, even if it was all a lie.

Orya had not expected the pirate captain to follow when General Algot escorted her to her chambers. Who was protecting the prince if his two bodyguards were following her? She wondered if they had somehow discovered her identity. Perhaps they were responsible for the shadow she had sensed but never been able to spot or shake. She had wasted her attention on Thorne when she should have been looking more closely at the prince's entourage.

But the general, after seeing her to her door, only waited long enough to discuss the situation with Wenda. He issued orders to Wenda with the calm assurance of someone whose orders are always followed. "Take care of her," he said. "She grew overheated and tired in the ball. She should rest. Give her plenty of water to drink."

Wenda had played her part well, curtsying and agreeing to every order he issued. Once the door was closed behind him, Orya staggered to her room, where she kept her stash of poisons and antidotes. She swallowed the sunder and gulped down an entire glass of water to make it work faster. She had timed her swoon to happen just before the speeches began. It had two advantages: she didn't have to sit through interminable praises of Azmei and Vistaren, and she knew where the two of them would be for at least the next half hour, perhaps longer.

Her hands were still shaking as Wenda helped her undress. She hadn't needed the special alterations to the dress after all, but she would rather have them and not need them, than need them and not have them.

No, she was being dishonest even with herself. She could have used the poison dart to kill Azmei, with no one the wiser until she was well away. She could even have poisoned Eustra's dress. Orya didn't *want* to kill Azmei. She had been making excuses to keep from doing so. But no more. It was Yarro who would pay the price, after all, if Orya defied the patriarch.

"Are you sure you are well enough to go through with this?" Wenda asked. She was standing behind Orya, unlacing her stays, or else Orya would have slapped her. How *dare* she question Orya yet again?

"I am fine," Orya snapped. "Cease speaking and help me."

There was tense silence between them as Wenda helped her out of her dress. As soon as Orya was free, she tugged on a pair of black breeches and a black blouse. A binding vest with pockets and dagger sheaths went over the blouse, and black boots laced up to her knees. To complete the outfit, Orya had a black hood with a half-mask sewn in. It would leave her vision unobstructed while covering her hair and all of her face except her eyes. No one would be able to identify her, and the vest and breeches would make her appear a slender boy rather than a woman.

She drank another glass of water. It would make her need the privies, but she had long practice at outwaiting her body, and she needed the sunder to wash out the last of the redleaf's effects.

"Orya," Wenda said. A hand closed on her shoulder. "You don't have to do this. I know you care for Princess Azmei. There are other ways."

She whirled and struck Wenda in the face. Her cousin staggered, caught her weight on her bad foot, cried out, and fell.

"There are no other options!" Orya hissed. "Curse you for a traitor! The patriarch will hear of this." And if she were particularly fortunate, he would reward her with extra time against her service.

Wenda sobbed. "I'm sorry. I'm sorry."

Orya tried to ignore the twinge of guilt. Perhaps Wenda was right. If she were careful, she could send word to her friends and have them smuggle Yarro to her here in Ranarr. She wouldn't have to do this.

But it was too late. Her course was set.

She stormed out of their rooms, ignoring the way Wenda's sobs sounded like mocking laughter.

The speeches finally ended, but then the music started up again, and Azmei and Vistaren were expected to lead the dancing for the first set. They didn't speak as they danced. Azmei could think of nothing to talk about that didn't involve asking why he would wish to marry her if he loved men. She didn't know why Vistaren was silent.

She saw when Lozarr returned to the ballroom, but she didn't break her silence to point it out to Vistaren.

Lozarr looked perturbed. Arama hadn't come back with him. Had they argued again?

Vistaren's voice broke into her thoughts. "Could we go somewhere more private and talk?"

She looked up at him, abandoning her speculation. "We should," she agreed. "As long as you're sure it will occasion no talk."

He gave her a crooked smile. "I imagine it will occasion some talk, but nothing of the sort we don't want." He touched her chin gently with one forefinger. "The gossip will have us madly in love and reluctant to wait until our wedding day for more than a single kiss. We will never be truly alone, so no one will be able to allege we have behaved with impropriety, but we can manage enough privacy to talk without anyone overhearing."

She felt her cheeks burning even though she knew he didn't want her. Maybe it was because he didn't want her. "Yes, let's go outside."

Without waiting for him, she turned and headed for the tall double doors that stood open to the night. When they were out of the crush of people, she slowed and raised her eyes to the sky. She could see stars scattered across the sky like handfuls of diamonds. She took a breath and let it out slowly.

"This way," Vistaren said, touching her elbow. "There are alcoves over there that will let us talk without leaving public view."

As they made their way to an empty alcove, Azmei felt her shoulders tightening. She didn't want to talk about this, didn't want to be rejected by him, even though she knew they must. Why couldn't this have been simple?

They stood in silence for a time. Torches burned in sconces at either side of the alcove they had chosen, but inside the alcove, the light was dim enough that she couldn't see his expression. She could still see the stars, though, and she leaned against the balcony wall, staring up at them. It must be lovely to be a star. They were so beautiful and distant. And what did the stars know of love? They neither loved nor wished to be loved. How wonderful.

Vistaren sighed. "I'm sorry I wasn't open with you from the beginning. I wished to tell you sooner. I always intended to tell you before we were married."

"It's what you meant when you said you would have no secrets between us when we wed," Azmei remembered.

"Yes. And then I began reading your translation, and even with my broken Tamnese, I realized you weren't certain about the relationship between Rona and Fann. I began to wonder if you'd chosen them because you'd heard the rumors about me." He brushed a hand over his hair. "I haven't made much secret of it at home. I've always known I would probably have to marry for heirs, since I am my parents' only child. It was always possible you'd heard."

Azmei jerked her shoulders. Orya hadn't known about him, since she'd made remarks about Vistaren possibly having bastards. Had Destar known? But he would have said something, wouldn't he? He'd said Vistaren wasn't very war-like, but that had nothing to do with who the prince loved.

"I didn't mean to deceive you, Azmei." Vistaren gripped her shoulders, his fingers too tight. "You must believe me. I like you. I respect you. I know I lied to you once, but I wouldn't do it again. Especially not about something so important."

She forced herself to meet his eyes. "I lied to you first. I shouldn't have been angry about it at all."

He pursed his lips. "Will you at least give me a chance? Not call everything off right away? We can make this work, and I believe it will be for the betterment of both our kingdoms."

"Make it work the way Rona and Aevver did?" she burst out. "And what happens to me when you meet your Fann? Or is that just how you do it in Amethir? Marry the woman for show and heirs but love your man in secret?"

She forced herself to stop talking. Her voice was too raw. He would be able to tell how much he had hurt her, how much she had wanted to love him. How much she had wanted him to love her.

"No!" He stared at her, brows drawn together, mouth open. "I would never do that to you! I've made you a vow. I would never, *never* be unfaithful to the vow I made."

"No?" She stepped close to him, pressing her body against his. It was seductive and improper, and it would have no effect on him whatever. "And what can you give me? Can you give me children? Can you give me any kind of love at all, when you are not made to love a woman?"

Vistaren swallowed. "I..."

She tilted her face up, cheeks burning. It wasn't kind. "Will you even try to please me?" she whispered. She stood on her toes until their lips were all but touching. "How can you, when you don't even want to kiss me, Vistaren?"

He looked miserable, but he bent his head and pressed his lips against hers. His hands gripped her upper arms, holding her where she was, as he opened his mouth against hers and brushed their tongues together. She felt warmth stealing through her body. She jerked away.

"You don't even like it," she whispered, breathing hard. And she *had* liked it, more than she wanted to. She didn't want to end up like Lozarr, desperately loving someone who would never give her what she longed for. How could Vistaren ask it of her?

Tears filled her eyes and she lowered her head. Vistaren's arms went around her hesitantly. They were comforting, even as she wished they wouldn't be. She went rigid in his arms, but he didn't let her go. She mustn't cry, she told herself. She must be strong, like Aevver. She must act in a way that would make her father and brother proud.

The thought of her brother made her suck in a shaky breath. She had said she wished to serve him, hadn't she? All those weeks ago, standing on the ship. *It is time to allow me to protect you,* she had said. And he had sworn to her that she didn't have to do it, that she could come home if she wished. But how could she go back on her word?

"Oh, Azmei, I wish I could make it easier for you," Vistaren whispered. "I wish I could make it easier for both of us."

Azmei let a single sob escape. "So do I." She put her arms around him and hugged him tightly. "I do care for you, Vistaren. I hate the thought of tying you to me and making you unhappy. You'll hate me for it someday."

"I won't," he protested.

She pulled away and straightened, looking at him and feeling the ocean breeze dry her wet cheeks. "You won't want to. You'll try not to, I know that at least." She managed a small smile. "And I shall try to be content if you can give me children for us to raise together."

She saw the relief hit him. It went through him like a shiver, and then his expression opened up. "You won't call it off?" he asked. "You won't dissolve the treaty?"

"How can I? If you are willing to sacrifice your own chance at romance for your kingdom, how can I do less for mine?" Azmei took a deep breath and found that smiling wasn't quite as hard as it had been. "And both of our countries shall be stronger together. Perhaps we shall yet manage to end this horrible war."

They might never be lovers in truth, but she knew she could come to love him. The happiness it gave her to see such joy on his face told her that. She smiled up at him and he smiled down at her. There would be more questions to ask, and doubtless they would face difficulties unique to their situation, but she was suddenly confident they would weather those difficulties together.

She never saw the knife.

She saw Vistaren recoil, face dissolving into horror. She felt him jerk her towards him. She stumbled forwards, balance gone. A sharp punch to her side took her breath away.

Then she was falling. Vistaren was shouting, but his voice seemed rather far off.

The stone floor of the veranda was suddenly very near and then her chin smacked against it. The impact stunned her. She stared at bright spangles of light in her eyes. She dragged in a breath that seemed to rasp against her lungs. Then she heard someone swear and realized it was her.

Azmei's hands and feet were so cold she couldn't feel them. But whoever had attacked her would hurt Vistaren. He was a gentle man. Did he even know how to fight? She had never thought to ask. She heard scuffing feet. Someone

grunted and swore. She couldn't leave her be-
trothed--her *friend*--to fight alone.

She staggered to her feet. It felt like all the sirens in the
ocean were devouring her stomach, but she managed to
stand. A shadowy figure grappled with Vistaren. The
attacker blended into the night; Azmei had to blink and
squint to see him. Vistaren, gentle or not, was holding
his own against the attacker, perhaps through sheer size
difference, since the attacker looked much slighter than
Vistaren.

Azmei felt absurdly grateful to the attacker for turn-
ing his back on her. Some part of her mind suggested
it ought to frighten her for some reason--did he think
her so badly hurt she was no threat?--but Azmei was
just glad he couldn't see her fingers fumbling with her
hairstyle to draw the dagger she wore there. Her fin-
gers were so cold they kept slipping, but on her third
attempt, Azmei managed to draw the dagger.

She envisioned herself dashing across the small alcove
to disable the attacker. Her body lurched obediently
forward when she told it to, but instead of a graceful
swoop, Azmei crashed into the attacker from behind.
The flare of agony in her back drove a scream from
her lips, but the impact also made her attacker grunt.
A blade clattered against the stone floor and Azmei
realized she had stabbed the attacker in the elbow.

With the attacker disarmed, at least momentarily,
Vistaren landed a solid punch to the attacker's nose.
There was an audible crunch. The cry their attacker
gave was high pitched. A young boy? Azmei reeled and
stumbled backwards in an attempt to keep her balance.

"Azmei!" Vistaren had grabbed the boy, who was trying to turn his to face his stubbornly not-dead victim. Azmei grinned fiercely into the masked face despite the sticky wetness that plastered the back of her dress to her skin.

"You're a terrible assassin," she told the boy. He was flailing his shoulders and wriggling with little real effect. Vistaren hooked his arms under the boy's and locked his hands together at the boy's neck. Azmei stumbled forward, lifting a hand towards the mask. He tossed his head from side to side, trying with little success to break away.

Vistaren's face twisted in a snarl and he jerked one arm. A sickening sound made the boy cry out and go limp. As soon as he quit struggling, Azmei tugged off his mask.

A cascade of dark curls tumbled free around the bloodied face of Orya Perslyn.

Azmei gasped and fell back a step. Orya's eyes were wet, but the defiance in them told Azmei the tears were only from the pain of her dislocated shoulder and broken nose.

"And a false friend," Vistaren growled. He was out of breath, but he stood steady as a rock. Gods, how easily she could love him if it would do any good! To her horror, Azmei felt tears spill over her own cheeks. Why had Orya betrayed her?

Orya hung her head, but she immediately sucked in a breath and looked up again, straightening as much as she could within Vistaren's restraint. Her dark eyes met Azmei's. Azmei wondered what Orya saw there. She took a deep breath that made her whimper as Vistaren's grip tightened.

"It was nothing personal," she said. "You're a princess setting up the peace. You had to be stopped."

"Why? For whom?" Vistaren's voice almost unrecognizable. Azmei felt grateful he wasn't angry at her. She couldn't quite remember why he was so angry at Orya. Her lips and eyelids felt numb.

"Contract." Orya's gaze was fixed on Azmei's. Could she see how tired and hurt Azmei was? "I don't know who," she continued. "It isn't something I needed to know to get the job done." Her lashes lowered. Azmei thought she saw tears clinging to them. Maybe that was her own lashes.

"Az!" Vistaren was shouting at her. Azmei forced her eyes open and took a breath.

"I thought you were ill," she told her friend. "You left with Lozarr."

"Gods, Lo!" Vistaren paled, and Azmei remembered her realization earlier. He loved Lozarr, didn't he? Or he had, and since Lo couldn't love him back the way he wanted... Azmei swayed and put a hand to her lips. She felt so very odd.

Orya let out a noise that was half laugh and half sob. "Lozarr's fine. He came back to the ball. She won't be, though."

For a moment Azmei thought Orya meant she had harmed Arama. Then she saw Orya nod at her. Oh. Azmei was the *she* Orya meant. "Poison?" she mumbled.

Orya looked oddly stricken for a woman who had tried--successfully, it seemed--to kill her. "It was because of my brother," she blurted. "He isn't like the others. I didn't want him to--"

She broke off, her eyes widening. "Huu..."

Azmei looked down and saw a crossbow bolt lodged to the fletching in Orya's chest. Vistaren was shouting for Azmei to get down. He dragged Orya down with him and then seemed to realize she was dead. He let go of her and crawled towards Azmei.

There was a lot of shouting now, but it was hard to hear through the roaring in her ears. She was dying. What a stupid, pointless way to die, she thought in annoyance. Ambushed by a friend.

She was lying on warm, wet stone, her face only inches from Orya's. And Orya wasn't quite dead after all. Her chest was heaving and shuddering, her eyes so wide Azmei saw the whites around her pupils. Orya was trying to form words with bloodied lips. Azmei couldn't hear her, but she could read at least one word.

Yarro.

Azmei closed her eyes. She didn't want to watch Orya die. They had been friends, however false Orya proved to be.

Oh, Gods, Razem would never forgive her for this. Someone was tapping her cheeks, but her eyelids were just so heavy.

"Azmei. *Az!*"

She couldn't. With a sigh, Azmei let go.

CHAPTER THIRTY-SEVEN

DEATH WAS LIKE AN ocean. It rocked her, soothing with the swells and creaking. Azmei kept her eyes closed. Did the dead have eyes? She was content to be rocked by death. Perhaps the afterlife was an eternal sea voyage.

Gradually, though, she realized there were other noises besides the slap of water and the creaking of boards. There was a voice, calm, emotionless, but someone penetrating her fog of death. She wanted to swat it away like a mosquito, but her limbs would not obey her. Or perhaps she didn't have limbs. She was probably a disembodied spirit, floating directionless on the seas of eternity.

"I know you hear me. I saw your eyelids flutter." The voice seemed amused. "The peacehealer said you would wake today. It's why they brought me to you. Time is short. There has been a great deal of confusion in the days since your death."

Oh, good. Confirmation of her death meant she could perhaps rest forever.

"No, little one, wake. Wake." That was a different voice, one that boomed and whispered all at once. Azmei whimpered without meaning to. The mosquito voice broke off while the booming one laughed.

"Az!" That urgent call was Vistaren. She smiled. Her betrothed, whom she loved, Or...

No, not love.

"*Wake*," commanded the whisper.

Or not only love. Friendship. Respect. Companionship.

"Az, please. Try. For me." Vistaren pleaded. "For our kingdoms."

"*WAKE*," whispered the thunder.

Azmei woke.

The first thing she realized, with a flash of stupid disappointment, was that death had seemed like an ocean because she was on a ship. She sighed and opened her mouth.

"Glack," she managed, which sounded nothing like the 'Good evening,' she had intended.

With a wordless exclamation, Vistaren pressed a glass to her lips. She drank greedily until the amused voice that had first roused her said, "Enough."

Vistaren looked over at a shadowy corner of the cabin. When he looked back at her, a rueful smile on his face, she saw he had a spectacularly purple bruise around one eye.

"I'm fine," he said. "We captured the second assassin before she got away. She had a lame foot, if you can believe it. Though--"

"Enough." The voice cut him off. "I came as you requested, but my time is not cheap. Let me speak with the princess alone."

To her shock, Vistaren nodded. He squeezed her hand and kissed her cheek. Then he withdrew. Who was this man, to speak so to princes and be obeyed?

"You may call me Tanvel," the man said. "Prince Vistaren went to great lengths to find me, though he may not have succeeded, had Captain Thorne not taken pity on him." The man called Tanvel shifted in place but did not come out of the shadows.

"Who are you?" Azmei rasped.

"An interested party." His voice was clipped. "Your Captain Thorne came to me the moment your ship docked. He feared for your safety and believed his skill and resources might not be enough to protect you." The voice warmed with amusement. "He demonstrated great wisdom in coming to me. My code would not allow me to accept his contract to protect you if I had already accepted one to end your life. From the moment I took his coin, he could be confident the biggest threat was not working against him."

Azmei allowed herself a slow blink and had to force her eyes open again. Where were Thorne and Guira? Was Orya truly dead? She seemed to remember watching her friend die. What had Vistaren meant about a second assassin?

"Listen carefully!" Tanvel's voice sharpened. "You have a difficult decision to make in a very short time."

Azmei cleared her throat and croaked, "I am listening."

"I do not know who took out the contract on your life," Tanvel said. His voice was low and tense. "The hired killers were Perslyn, from your own kingdom, but they have no true allegiance. The second one killed the first to silence her. She was captured, and let slip that if you lived to marry Vistaren, there would be an all-out assault on the Kreyden District. I believe your brother went to the Kreyden front when you left Tamnen?" Azmei must have paled, because he said, "Exactly. We thought it best to consult you before announcing you had lived." He sighed. "They did not attempt to frame Vistaren, which is odd in itself. That is what I would have done, were I tasked with destroying any hope of peace between your two countries."

Azmei mulled this over. Who would benefit from her death but not Vistaren's? Someone from Amethir? But that made no sense: he'd already told her he needed an heir.

"--are not paying attention!" Tanvel's voice cracked across the cabin.

"I'm sorry! You woke me from my rest and you are telling me all these things I can't remember!" It hurt to talk so much. "Where is Guira? Where is my handmaid?"

"Your handmaid is dead."

The words were a blow that made her recoil as if from a slap. The movement spiked agony through her lower back.

"She sacrificed her life for yours, trying to stop the second assassin. Do her the courtesy of behaving as though that matters."

"Sirens take you," Azmei choked out. "I loved Guira."

There was a bare instant of silence from the dark corner. "Then honor her by living."

"Who *are* you?" she demanded.

"I am a Diplomat. That is all you need know."

She barked out a laugh. "I have met Diplomats. They are nothing like you."

"Of course they are. They answer to the Diplomatic Council and are schooled to be inhuman creatures of logic." There was a glint of white as if he had smiled, though she couldn't tell through the shadows. "I am a Shadow Diplomat, schooled to be an inhuman creature of death. I answer to no one but the Shadow Council and my god."

"Your god?" she burst out. "What god would allow his followers to become assassins?"

"The god of peace." He chuckled. "There is no peace so complete or permanent as that of death, little princess."

But Guira, whispered an anguished part of her mind. She took a careful breath, feeling herself tremble.

"You said I had a decision to make," she recalled.

"You do indeed. At the moment, there are very few who know that Princess Azmei still lives. Your handmaid was killed. Captain Thorne was injured in the fight. He will recover, but he need not know his efforts to save you were successful. Captain Dzornaea and General Algot know you live, as you are currently guarded on their ship, where no one would think to look for a Tamnese princess. Your betrothed, you have seen. No one else knows. We have let it be believed you died." He tilted his head. "It seemed wise. To send one assassin is determination, to send two, fervor. The gods know how many more assassins your obsessed enemy might send against you. There is a storm brewing on the horizon, little princess, and no stormwitch born can avert this maelstrom."

Azmei closed her eyes and took a fortifying breath. "So I am to decide whether to remain dead or to make a miraculous return, I surmise," she said. "But to what end, if I am dead?"

"It need not be forever," Tanvel said. "You will recover in safety under the care of the peacehealer. You will hide until I am able to learn who laid the price on your head." His teeth flashed briefly. "Prince Vistaren is paying me well. I will discover and neutralize the threat."

Why would Vistaren pay him? Azmei wondered. And how long would it take for him to 'neutralize' the threat? "I thought you said you answer to the Shadow Council," she said. "Why would you work for Vistaren?"

Her eyes must be adjusting to the darkness. She thought she could see an approving gleam in his eyes. "The Shadow Council is the ruling body of my order. We are dedicated to preserving peace--or bringing peace, by force if necessary. We only step in when our daylight brothers and sisters fail." His teeth flashed again, and this time she was certain that he had smiled. "I think you will agree that someone trying to kill you is a failure of the peace process."

Azmei narrowed her eyes. "By that reasoning, your very existence is a failure of the peace process."

He laughed. "I knew you were beautiful, but no one told me of your cleverness. My order is a very old one, princess. You cannot expect me to distill it into a sentence of explanation."

She sighed. Her back gave a nasty twinge that reminded her how much healing she had to do. She didn't even know how badly she was injured, but if she had been asleep for days since the attack, she imagined it had been a very near thing. "Very well," she said at last. "You're right--I cannot allow the war in the Kreyden District to escalate, not with Razem commanding there. I will remain dead, at least as

Princess Azmei. But I will *not* remain hidden with nothing to occupy me. I wish to learn about your religion of peace."

He arched an eyebrow. "I thought you did not approve."

"Did I ever say that?" She coughed and felt her back seize up. "I look forward to learning," she grunted. She had to pant instead of breathing deeply. She squeezed her eyes shut, trying not to show how badly it hurt.

She heard the barest whisper of air moving past her eyes. A hand rested briefly on her forehead. "Then I look forward to teaching," Tanvel breathed.

When she opened her eyes again, he was gone.

Vistaren was unhappy when he arrived for their next visit. By then Azmei had met the peacehealer--yet another perplexing institution of this complicated religion of peace, but by far her current favorite, since the man was able to ease her pain and explain her injuries--and dozed off for a time.

When she woke again, breathing without pain in time to the rise and fall of the sea swells, it was because Vistaren had tapped on the door and was peering into the cabin.

"Come in," she said. "I am sorry I cannot rise to greet you."

"Don't be ridiculous," he said. There was a downcast look to his face, but his voice was affectionate. Azmei wondered if it was their shared survival of the assassins' attack that made him comfortable with her, or if it was merely that she knew his secret now.

"The peacehealer says you'll have a long recovery."

She nodded. Orya's knife had cut muscles as well as piercing a kidney, which she had nearly lost. Without the peacehealer, she gathered, she would not have lived. She knew there was no such advanced healing in Tamnen. She wondered if it were a skill one could learn, or if it were a gift of their peace god.

"Will you return to Amethir with us? We're staying long enough for me to be outfitted in mourning clothes." He twisted his lips in a grimace. "I've made certain none of the tailors bought Perslyn fabric."

Azmei sighed. "She said something about her brother. I--"

"I don't care." Vistaren's gaze was hard. She remembered how deliberately he had dislocated Orya's shoulder and found herself glad they were not enemies. He was a gentle man, and peaceable enough, but she suspected his temper, once roused, was implacable.

Azmei touched his hand. "Don't be angry. What's past is past."

His expression relaxed as he looked down at her. "I'm so sorry about Guira," he said. "She seemed like a wonderful woman."

His words threatened the cool shell of denial she had built around herself. She closed her eyes. "She raised me after my mother died. Have I ever told you about my mother?"

Vistaren shook his head. "Tell me now."

He held her hand as she talked about her mother's illness and death, which led naturally into the way Guira had stepped in, not as a replacement for her mother, but to serve her as she had served her mother. She told him about the many times Guira had nagged her to set aside her books and work on embroidery or calligraphy or some other more feminine art. At some point her words became tears and Vistaren stroked her hair as she wept for Guira. Eventually, Azmei slept.

"I can't do anything for her." Vistaren was pacing again. He knew it was driving Lo and Arama mad, but he couldn't seem to help himself. He hated that there was nothing he could do to ease Azmei's pain and grief. He hated how damned powerless he felt.

"You've given her time," Arama said. She was sitting cross-legged in the window-seat. They were all dressed in black, trying to keep up the pretense that Azmei had not survived Orya's attack.

He hated that that had been her decision. He wanted to think that he could protect her by marrying her, but Master Tanvel had made a convincing argument, and as much as Vistaren hated it, he had to concede it was probably correct.

"Time to do what?" Lo murmured.

Arama shot him a look that Vistaren couldn't quite interpret. He still wasn't certain exactly what had gone on between the two of them during their stay here. Not that it was his business, but he couldn't help wondering what had finally brought Arama to her sense about letting Lo love her.

"Maybe just time to get her feet back under her," she said finally. "As long as she pretends to be dead, she protects her father and brother. Once she decides she is alive again, that's a decision she can't take back." She looked at Vistaren. "You're giving her the time she needs to be certain. And if you're serious about waiting, you're giving yourself time, as well."

"Not like that," Vistaren muttered, blushing. He hadn't agreed to postpone their wedding so he would be free to foster dalliances with stableboys or handsome guardsmen. It didn't seem right or respectful, when they hadn't had a chance to discuss what it meant that he couldn't love her the way she deserved. And it didn't seem necessary to discuss it now. He could visit her on the *Dawn Star*, of course, and try to make her understand. But it didn't seem to matter as much in the light of her near death.

We'll figure it out when she comes back, he told himself, and didn't allow himself to hear the little voice that whispered, *If she comes back.*

"We might have to talk your father out of going to war with Strid for destroying the treaty," Lo said. "I don't know his majesty's mind on this, but Amethir would be well within her rights to take offense at Azmei's assassination."

"We don't know who sent Orya," Vistaren said. "It might not have been the Strid."

"Who else would it be?"

Vistaren shrugged. He didn't have an answer, but he didn't think his father would go to war over something so uncertain. Not open war, at least. He had no doubt his father would encourage Arama to take as many Strid prizes as possible. The Tamnese ships had been off-limits for a year now, ever since the first treaty proposal left Maron.

"You shouldn't part without a full understanding between you," Lo said.

"I won't," Vistaren promised. "We both deserve that."

Arama smiled brightly at him. "Yes," she agreed. "You both deserve that."

CHAPTER THIRTY-EIGHT

AZMEI SPENT ANOTHER WEEK on the *Dawn Star*. As soon as she was able to sit propped up, Arama took a pair of scissors to Azmei's hair, trimming it close to her head. She saved the hair, promising to have it woven into a wig for when Azmei no longer had to hide. Azmei didn't tell her how free her cropped hair made her feel.

Vistaren, Arama, and Lozarr spent what free time they could keeping her company. Vistaren was finishing his negotiations with the tax protesters, but he visited Azmei every evening. They went through the translated book of hero tales together, with Vistaren pointing out where he thought she had not quite grasped the intricacies of Rona and Fann's relationship. He gave her a copy of *The Four Daughters of the Storm*, though she didn't read it right away. She wanted to save it for when she had nothing left of Amethir but the book. While she was with Vistaren and his friends, she wished only to enjoy their company.

On the tenth day after Princess Azmei's assassination, Shadow Diplomat Tanvel returned to the *Dawn Star* to collect his new apprentice. He was wrapped in black robes, a cowl shrouding his face. When his gaze landed on Azmei, his eyes narrowed. For a moment she feared he was angry, then she realized he was smiling behind the cowl.

"I see you are determined to leave Azmei behind you," he said. "You will need a new name, if you are to come with me."

Azmei gave as much of a bow as she could manage. She had already given this a great deal of consideration. "I am Aevver Balearic," she said in Amethirian. "And I am pleased to become your apprentice."

Tanvel flickered a glance from her to Vistaren, who stood behind her, one hand on her shoulder. "Prince Vistaren? I have your permission?"

She heard Vistaren snort. "It's Az--Aevver's permission you should be concerned with," he said. "But yes, you have it. As well as the promised gold."

Tanvel shrugged. "In giving me this treasure of yours, I believe you have given me something more precious than gold."

Azmei took a shaky breath. She had already left behind the home she had always known. It shouldn't be so frightening to give up the far more nebulous home she had thought she was going to. She was merely trading one unknown for another. Yet at least the first time she abandoned her identity, she had known there would always be a country to return to, where she could be Razem's little sister and a princess in her own right. Now there was nothing to look forward to, until Tanvel could learn who had tried to kill her and why.

Vistaren's hand tightened on her shoulder. "You don't have to do this," he whispered.

Azmei swallowed and straightened, looking over her shoulder at him. He nodded. He had known what she would choose. They both had.

Arama kissed both Azmei's cheeks. She gripped hands with her and said, "If you are ever in need and can get word to the *Dawn Star*, know that I will come. Not just for Vistaren's sake, but for my own as well."

Lozarr enfolded her gently in his arms. "You will be a queen to make any kingdom proud when you return to us," he murmured in her ear.

Vistaren tried to kiss her lips, then made a face and kissed her forehead instead. "I will honor our betrothal, Az--Aevver. As I swore to you on the veranda, so I remain. I will marry none other, and I will take no lover. I swear it."

She swallowed against a lump in her throat. "You shouldn't," she whispered, but he pressed a finger to her lips.

"Read *The Four Daughters of the Storm*," he said. "And you'll understand why I should." He smiled, and Azmei thought he looked older than he had only two months ago when they met. She wondered if she would ever have mistaken him for a servant in the prince's entourage if he had looked like this on that day in the courtyard.

She smiled back at him. "I'm taking it with me." The book was tucked into her bag alongside the stationery set that had saved her life. She had only two sets of clothing in her bag, along with the comb she had purchased for Guira, her sea dragon bone pen, and Vistaren's gifts.

And nestled in her heart, she had a name: Yarro Perslyn. Should she ever have the resources, she would find Orya's brother and bring him to her. Until then, she would keep Orya's secret.

Once the sun had slipped beneath the waves, Shadow Diplomat Tanvel and his new apprentice took their leave of the Amethirians and vanished into the darkness.

S TEPHANIE A. CAIN WRITES epic and urban fantasy. She lives in Indiana, where she works at a small liberal arts college and is writing the next book in the Storms in Amethir series. She enjoys hiking, reading, birdwatching, and general geekery. She has three cats, which she is well aware puts her firmly in crazy cat lady territory, and owns way more dice and painted miniatures than she needs.

Connect with her online:
Website: StephanieCainOnline.com
Facebook: StephanieCainFiction
Email: stephanie@stephaniecainonline.com

Also by Stephanie A. Cain

Sow the Wind
Fire Soul

Storms in Amethir
A Song of Storm and Shadow
Stormseer
The Weather War
Shroudling
Witchery's End (forthcoming)

Storms in Amethir Holiday Novellas
The Midwinter Royal

Circle City Magic (urban fantasy)
Shades of Circle City
Circle City Psychic

With Other Authors
Equus (Rhonda Parrish's Magical Menageries #5)
E is for Evil
F is for Fairy
G is for Ghost

If you would like to receive updates on new fiction, please join my monthly email newsletter list. I give newsletter subscribers first look at everything I do!

9 781944 774134